LEAVE ME BREATHLESS

CARRIE ELKS

LEAVE ME BREATHLESS by Carrie Elks

Copyright © 2022 by Carrie Elks

140223

All rights reserved.

Edited by Rose David

Proofread by Proofreading by Mich

Cover Designed by The Pretty Little Design Company

This book is a work of fiction. The characters, events, and places portrayed in this book are products of the author's imagination. Any similarity to persons living or dead is purely coincidental.

CHAPTER 1

She was an hour early, thanks to the empty highway that led her from Washington D.C. to West Virginia. Or maybe she'd allowed herself too much time. Nicole Rice pulled her Mazda M3 into a parking lot of the Winterville town square, and exhaled heavily.

So this was Winterville. The little town in the West Virginian mountains founded by actress, Candy Winter, and maintained now by her grandchildren – one of whom was her brother's best friend, Gabe Winter.

Nicole's brother, Matt, had been best friends with Gabe for years, ever since they'd both come onto the snowboarding scene. They'd been roommates during training and competitions, and – if the rumors were true – wingmen during their legendary nights out with the ladies.

Whipping out her cellphone, she quickly typed the message she'd promised her brother she'd send.

I MADE IT SAFELY. – N

. . .

IT WAS LESS than ten seconds before her phone started to ring.

She smiled, because Matt was one of her favorite people. Sure, he was five years older than her, but he still managed to tread the thin line between over protectiveness and friend.

"Hey," she said, accepting the call. "What time is it there?" It was three o'clock here in Winterville, and the town was bustling.

"I have no idea." His voice became muffled, as though he had his hand over the mouthpiece. "Wait... what time is it, honey? I mean, quelle heure est-il?" Right now he was training in the French Alps, and clearly making the most of his time in the region. "Huit heures? It's eight. At night," he added. "So you made it okay? You doing all right?" His voice softened. He'd been calling her daily since last week's horrible discovery.

"I'm fine. The drive was good, and I got to listen to an audiobook I've been dying to hear."

"Romance?" Matt asked, amused.

"Of course. What else?" Her whole family thought her romance book addiction was hilarious. But she also was the only one of them who opened more than one fiction book a year.

"That's good that you can still read them. After everything..."

"Yeah, I know." Her throat thickened. "But I still believe in love. Just need to repair my picker." Because she'd sure picked the wrong man. No, make that the *wrong men*. It was as though she'd become a beacon for emotionally stunted guys.

"Are you sure you want to do this? Shouldn't Luke be the

one leaving town? You did nothing wrong, yet you're paying the price."

"We both know why Luke can't leave town," she pointed out. "And anyway, the change will do me good. Winterville is beautiful. I never realized how lovely it was. You've been here before, right?"

"A few times with Gabe. Speaking of Winter, are you at his house?"

"No, I'm an hour early. I figured I'd take a walk around the town, acquaint myself. I have a few leaflets to leave in the shops, too, if they'll let me." If all went to plan, she'd be in Winterville until Christmas. And though she had enough money saved to see her through, it felt like a good time to use her Yoga qualifications and set up a business offering one on one training.

Her next stop was finding a studio to run classes while she was here, though she had no idea where there'd be a location suitable in Winterville.

"Call him. He'll leave work early. He's a good guy."

"I'm sure he is." She'd met Gabe Winter a couple of times – when she was barely more than a kid. Matt rarely came home and until recently she'd always had classes or work when he was competing.

It had been Matt's idea that she stay with Gabe for a while. It was one of the reasons she had enough money to manage this. Because she'd offered to pay rent, but Matt was adamant that Gabe wouldn't accept a penny.

"I really appreciate you arranging this for me," she told him.

"I wish I could be there." He sighed. "Or that you'd agree to fly here and be with me."

"I can't leave the country right now. You know that."

"*I* did."

A smile curled at her lips. "Maybe you're further along than I am. Mom and Dad felt better when they knew I'd only be a drive away. I didn't want them to make a fuss."

Her parents were scientists. Her dad was a professor at the Lincoln University in Washington D.C., and for as long as she could remember he spent more time in the lab than he did at home with his family. Her mom wasn't much better – as a research scientist for one of the big pharmaceutical companies, she was always at work or at conferences around the world.

Right now, her dad was even more preoccupied than usual. His research was hitting a key milestone that he had to complete to secure more funding. He and his assistant had pretty much set up camp at the university.

His assistant being her ex. Luke Nicholson. And by ex, she meant very recent ex – last week in fact.

If her dad found out what Luke had done to her he'd be apoplectic, especially since Luke was his second in command. And she knew how that much stress could impact his health. Better to pretend she needed a break from Luke than to tell the truth right now.

That she'd walked in on her boyfriend and his assistant in her bedroom.

Matt had been the first person she'd called as she stumbled out of there and ran to the nearest coffee shop. He'd urged her to tell their parents, but she'd refused. Luke was the only person who could take the workload from her father. If her dad fired him, he'd be swamped and he was already constantly stressed out. She hated the thought of him having to cope with her personal life on top of his workload.

No, this was much better. "I really appreciate you arranging for me to come here to stay," she told her brother.

"Yeah, well Gabe's the closest thing I have to a brother. He's the only guy I trust you with."

Nicole burst out laughing. "I'm not exactly here for a hook up." She'd learned from her mistakes.

"I know that. But guys look at you, you know that, too. It's the old Rice charm." His voice was warm. "You've either got it or you haven't, and you and I've got it, kid." He cleared his throat. "Anyway, I owed you one."

"You didn't owe me anything."

"You were the only one who stood up for me when I dropped out of college. You were thirteen years old, and you stood there and shouted at our parents to give me a break. I haven't forgotten that."

"Well look at you now. You proved them wrong." She was so damn proud of her brother. He'd won medals, traveled the world, and was clearly living his best life. Like their parents – and their sister – he'd planned to become a scientist, though he'd dropped out during his freshman year to pursue his snowboarding career. His plan was to return to his studies once he was too old to compete.

That would make four scientists in the family.

And her. The non-scientist.

"You will, too, sweetheart."

Her chest felt full. "Thank you. I should go, this call must be costing you a fortune. And it sounds like you have company."

"Okay. But call me any time, and say hi to Gabe from me."

"I will."

Ending the call with a smile on her face, Nicole grabbed her purse and climbed out of her shiny red Mazda. It looked tiny parked next to so many trucks and four wheel drive vehicles. People in the mountains obviously loved their big cars.

She spent the next half hour walking around town, popping into shops, introducing herself, and asking to leave leaflets about her one-on-one Yoga sessions. Once she'd exhausted all the commerce that Winterville had to offer, she walked into the coffee shop – aptly called the Cold Fingers Café – and inhaled the warm aroma of caffeine.

Damn, that smelled good.

As well as a romance novel addiction, she'd picked up a coffee addiction over the years. She'd tried decaf – all too aware of the effects of caffeine on the body – but it didn't work as well.

It was her one vice. Okay, maybe not her only one, but still.

"Can I help you?" the woman behind the counter asked. Her dark hair was pulled back, revealing a cheerful face. Her smile was bright enough to light up the whole coffee shop.

Nicole found herself smiling back. "Can I have an Americano? Black." She looked over at the glass cabinet full of pastries, and as if on cue her stomach started to rumble. "And a Danish, please."

"Coming up."

"Hey, you're new." A man – around her age or maybe a little older, leaned on the counter next to her.

"How can you tell?" she asked.

"Because I haven't seen you around here before." He shrugged. "I'm Kyle Walker. Of Walker Woods." He paused, as though she was supposed to respond. When she didn't, he lifted a brow. "We're important around here. One of the biggest employers in the mountains."

She gave him a polite smile. "Oh, of course. Walker Woods, right."

"And you are?"

"Um, Nicole." She offered her hand. He took it, but instead of shaking it, he put his palm against the back of her hand and turned it over.

"Soft," he murmured. "You married?"

"Kyle Walker, stop hitting on my customers." The woman behind the counter shook her head. "You know better than that."

"Sorry, Dolores. Gotta get in quick, you know?"

Dolores shook her head. "Don't make me call your mama. Because you know I will."

"C'mon now. There's no need to do that," Kyle mumbled. The twenty-something, muscled man looked terrified at the thought of his mom being called. "I'm just being friendly."

"Sure you are."

Dolores passed Nicole her pastry. "Go take a seat, honey, and I'll bring over your coffee." She raised a brow. "Kyle was just leaving."

"Ah, I got some time." Kyle shrugged.

"Your daddy will be waiting on you," Dolores pointed out. "Now shoo. Before I call him, too."

Shaking his head, Kyle leaned forward, until his lips were brushing Nicole's cheek. "How long are you in town?"

She shrugged. "A while." He was a good looking guy, and smelled pretty nice. But none of her buttons felt pushed. Maybe Luke had ruined them forever. Or maybe her radar was getting better.

"In that case, I'll see you around. Don't go shacking up with anybody else until I see you again. I have dibs."

"What is this? Kindergarten?" Dolores pointed at the door. "Now go."

"See ya later, Nicole." Kyle winked. "And if you need me, just call Walker Woods. They'll patch you right through."

He turned and sauntered out of the café, and the smile she'd been biting down won through, tugging her lips up. Sure, she wasn't interested, and he had a little too much swagger for her, but it was nice to be noticed by a guy, especially after Luke had been noticing somebody else.

Taking the pastry from Dolores, and passing her a few bills for payment, she turned to walk to a table, the smile still on her face.

And bumped into a chest so hard she almost ricocheted off of it. The breath knocked out of her, and she looked up, ready to apologize, but then she saw a pair of dark blue, angry eyes, and the words died in her throat.

GABE HAD BEEN SITTING in the Cold Fingers Café with a flat white, catching up on his emails, when he'd seen the woman walk in. Of course he'd looked, who wouldn't? She was dark haired and curvy – and wasn't from around here. Everybody else had looked, too.

And then Kyle Walker had made his move.

Gabe had known Kyle since they were kids. Though the Walkers lived in Marshall's Gap, the next town over from Winterville, the local area was small enough for them to know all the kids in the vicinity. The Walker brothers had always had a strange rivalry with Gabe and his two brothers – North and Kris. Whenever they came into contact – which thankfully wasn't often – the Walker brothers were clearly jealous of Gabe and his brothers' successes.

Unfortunately, he'd been coming into contact with the Walkers more often as of recent. Since retiring from snowboarding, Gabe had teamed up with some friends to buy a whole lot of land just east of Winterville to create a ski resort. Walker Woods was one of the companies they'd contracted to clear the trees needed for building the resort and slopes. Luckily, most of his interactions had been with Kyle's dad.

When Kyle had walked up to the pretty woman, Gabe had lowered his head to his laptop, not wanting to get involved. It looked like the woman could give as good as she got, anyway.

It was only when he heard Kyle say her name that his head lifted. Nicole. That was too much of a coincidence. Gabe pushed the screen of his laptop down and stood, his jaw ticking as Kyle ambled out of the café, before he strode over to where Nicole was with her pastry.

And that's when she walked right into him.

He reached out to steady her, his fingers biting into her skin as she lifted her head, her wide doe-like eyes meeting his. A shot of warmth rushed through him, itching him from the inside out. Damn, if he didn't feel himself stir.

He released her like she was on fire, stepping back to give himself some space. He'd promised Matt he'd take care of his little sister, and dammit, he was going to do just that.

"Nicole?"

"Gabe?" She blinked, thick lashes sweeping down. She had a line of freckles across the bridge of her nose. How long ago was it that he'd last seen her? He'd imagined her to be a kid like the last time he'd seen her. And distraught, if Matt's description was anything to go by.

Not a strikingly beautiful woman with the most expressive eyes he'd ever seen.

Get ahold of yourself, Winter. She's absolutely off limits.

"Yeah, I'm Gabe." He felt better now that there was some

air between them. He reached out his hand and she shook it. "I was expecting you later. You got here fast."

"I made good time on the interstate." She gave him a soft smile. "I thought I'd hang out here until it was time for us to meet at your place."

"I can take you there now, if you like. You got your car here?" His gaze flickered over her shoulder.

"Oh no, it's fine. I don't want to disturb you. Matt said you were extremely busy with your new resort. I can drink my coffee and meet you at the agreed time."

"It's fine," Gabe said gruffly. He noticed a pile of flyers sticking out of her purse. "You flyposting the town already?"

"What?" Her brow creased, then she followed his gaze and laughed. "Oh no, these are to advertise my Yoga sessions. I figured I might as well do some work while I'm here."

"You want to leave some on the counter, honey?" Dolores asked, obviously listening in to their conversation.

"Could I?" Nicole grinned and it lit up her face. "That would be fantastic, thank you."

Dolores took a pile, then looked at the print. "I might try one of these sessions myself."

"You should," Nicole said. Damn, she was chirpier than he'd imagined. Was she always like this? "I'm also hoping to run some group classes, if I can find the right space."

"Ooh, I like the sound of that." Dolores nodded, then ran her finger along her jaw. "Hey, what about the Winterville Inn? They have an old studio there. Don't they, Gabe?"

Gabe nodded. "Yeah, I think so."

"You should call Alaska," Dolores said to Nicole. "She'll be happy to help. She runs the Inn for the family." She winked. "And Gabe will put a good word in for you. Alaska's his cousin."

Nicole looked at him with cool eyes. He had no idea what she was thinking.

"I couldn't ask you to do that," she said softly. "I'll call myself."

Her eyes met his again, and he felt a strange protectiveness wash over him. "I'll message Alaska now." Before Nicole could protest, he tapped out a message to his cousin. Within a minute, she'd replied.

"You're all set," he told her. "She'll meet with you tomorrow. I'll give you her details and you can arrange the time between you two."

Nicole blinked. "It's that easy?" she asked, sounding perplexed.

"Why should it be hard?"

"I don't know. I've been looking for studio space in D.C. for months. There's nothing at all. Then I arrive here and within five minutes you've found me somewhere."

Dolores chuckled. "Welcome to Winterville. Everybody knows everybody and we try to help each other out."

Nicole's lips parted, her voice soft. "Thank you," she said to Gabe. "I'm going to have to repay you big time."

Embarrassment washed over him. Had he overstepped? But Dolores was right, he did know everybody around here. Things were simple most of the time.

And she was Matt's sister. Which meant she was practically part of the family already.

He cleared his throat. "Listen, I'm going to grab my laptop and head home. You finish your coffee and meet me there when you're ready, okay?"

"Are you sure?" Her brows knitted. "I can come now."

He nodded. "No rush." Because he needed to get over the fact that Matt Rice's baby sister wasn't a damn baby anymore. "I'll see you when you're ready."

CHAPTER 2

Gabe's house was a sprawling ranch home at the far end of a Christmas Tree Farm. As he'd opened the door for her, he'd told her that his older brother, North, ran the farm, and that he'd bought this land from him to build somewhere permanent to live.

Inside the home wasn't what Nicole was expecting at all. She'd imagined that he be as untidy as her brother, and had no time or desire to make somewhere look homely and inviting, but East Winter Ranch was beautiful. The hallway was expansive, lined with warm wood along the floors and a grey stone up the walls, which met the vaulted roof with beams that looked so thick they could withstand a million tons.

There were other touches that made the hallway feel welcoming. Jewel-colored patterned rugs scattered on the floors, woolen throws on cream overstuffed chairs added color and comfort to the wood-and-stone interior, and there were paintings and photographs decorating the walls.

And at the end of the hall was a cabinet full of trophies.

Nicole walked over, taking them all in. At the center was the biggest of them all – a shining gold medal.

"My girl cousins made me put the trophy cabinet here," he mumbled.

She looked at him over her shoulder. There was a strange expression on his face. Like he'd been caught watching her or something. "So you should. You've achieved a lot to be proud of."

"Yeah, well that's history now. I'll show you where your bedroom is. There's a guest suite at the far end of the ranch. So, you have your own bathroom attached to the bedroom. We share a kitchen, and the living space, but I'm not around that often. The housekeeper comes tomorrow, and if you leave a list for her she'll get your groceries."

"I can do my own shopping," Nicole said. "If you like I can cook for you."

Gabe blinked. "It's fine. I'm not home that much. I come and go at weird hours, and I eat at the Inn a lot."

"Oh. Okay." A wave of disappointment washed over her. This was a huge house to be all alone in.

He rubbed the back of his neck with his palm, shifting his feet. "I mean, ah, maybe we can share meals a couple of times a week or something."

"Was I that obvious?"

A smile ghosted his lips. "Kinda."

"Sorry." She wrinkled her nose. "I'm not used to being alone."

"You'll find it almost impossible to be alone in Winterville. Everybody wants to know your business." He cleared his throat. "Speaking of which... Kyle Walker. It's best if you stay away from him."

"He seemed harmless. And I don't know what Matt told

you about why I'm here, but I'm not exactly looking for a guy right now."

"He told me you caught your boyfriend…"

"In bed with his grad student." Her face flushed. She hated that anybody knew. But at least it was only Gabe and Matt right now – oh, and Luke, of course.

Gabe shifted his feet. "I'm sorry that you had to deal with that."

She gave him a tight smile. "It's fine." No it wasn't, but it would be. She'd get there. "But you don't have to worry about Kyle Walker and me."

"That's good. I promised Matt I'd take care of you."

Their eyes met again, and for a moment she imagined being taken care of, and it felt so damn good. A blush stole over her cheeks.

"I won't cause you any problems," she said softly.

"It's not you I'm worried about. It's Kyle. Keep away from him, okay?"

"Agreed."

He nodded, satisfied with her answer, then inclined his head toward the rest of the ranch. "Come on, I'll show you to your room."

THE EVENING HAD BEEN MUTED. Gabe had spent most of it in his office, which he'd pointed out on the tour. It was next to the kitchen, and as well as a huge oak desk covered in computer equipment, it also had what looked like the comfiest leather sofa and a big TV screen fixed to the wall.

It also had a lock on the door. And from the way he'd barely let her step inside it gave the vibe that it was off limits. Which was fine, because his living room with black leather sectional sofas and another TV screen so big it felt like she was at the movies, was more than enough for her.

She watched six back-to-back episodes of *Below Deck* before she finally felt tiredness overcome her. Grabbing her empty glass, she made her way to the kitchen and put it in the dishwasher. Everything in here was pristine, just like the rest of the house. Gabe clearly liked things in order.

"I'm heading to bed," she called out as she walked back into the hallway.

"Okay, goodnight." His voice echoed out of the office. He didn't bother to walk out and maybe that was a good thing. She didn't want to be annoying.

But she also didn't want to feel invisible either.

As she walked down the hallway toward the guest suite, another wave of fatigue washed over her. The optimism she'd felt earlier, that maybe this time away would make everything better, had disappeared.

It didn't take her long to unpack her bags, or to shower and brush her teeth before getting into a pair of short pajamas. Luke had always joked that she was a human furnace. Luke. Ugh. She sat down on the huge bed, and closed her eyes, remembering the last time she'd seen him. Had it only been last week? It felt like a lifetime.

He'd called her about an hour after she'd walked in on him and his grad student. And as the platitudes had spilled out, she'd realized that she didn't want this. Didn't want to hear his excuses, or his promises.

She just wanted to get away.

That's when she'd called Matt and they'd hatched this plan of her staying in Winterville. It had felt like a safe haven compared to home. Sure, she'd had to go through the excruciating experience of lying to her parents and saying she needed time to think about her relationship with Luke, without them knowing that he'd been cheating on her.

But now that she was here, wasn't she supposed to feel better? Instead, she just felt lonely, and that was a horrible place to be.

A hot tear ran down her cheek, and she didn't bother to wipe it away. It was already being followed by more. Maybe a good cry was what she needed. She'd been dry eyed since the day she'd found out. And more than most, she knew that crying was cathartic.

She'd cry, then sleep and tomorrow would be another day. She'd find her optimism again – hopefully at the bottom of a huge cup of coffee. And if all else failed, she'd read a romance novel and let herself get carried away by a hot book boyfriend who would never ever cheat on the heroine.

But for now, she let herself be sad.

She was crying. Gabe could hear her as he walked down the hallway, intending to wish her a good night properly. He'd been in the middle of a call when she'd called out that she was going to bed, and he felt bad that he hadn't even opened the door to her.

But Cam Hartson was a difficult man to track down, and as one of the key investors in Gabe's ski resort, he needed his go ahead to make some decisions on the build. Cam was an ex-football player turned stay at home dad, and trying to talk to him during the day was like calling a kindergarten. It almost always ended in tears. So he'd taken to calling him when Cam's kids were in bed. Which usually meant ten at night.

Another sob echoed through Nicole's closed door, and he froze. He really wasn't good with tears. Maybe he should call one of his cousins – they'd know what to do.

Yeah, and they'd also laugh at you, because you're being a dick.

Sighing, he softly rapped his knuckles on the door. He'd promised Matt he'd keep an eye on her, and that's what he was doing.

When she didn't respond, he knocked again.

More silence made him hesitate. Should he walk away and leave her alone, or go in and check on her?

With three girl cousins – not to mention all of his female snowboarding friends – he wasn't completely green when it came to women and their dating miseries. He also wasn't great at finding the right words to make things better either.

Sighing, he tapped one more time, then pushed the handle and inched the door open. He'd just check that she was okay for Matt's sake. Then he'd leave her to it and head to bed. But his mouth went dry when he saw her lying face down on the queen sized bed, a pair of wireless headphones in her ears. She didn't stir, though he could hear her ragged breathing.

She was wearing a pair of silk shortie pajamas. One of the straps had fallen down her shoulder, revealing her shoulder blade, her skin luminescent in the lamplight. Her legs were stretched out behind her, long and slender like a colt's. He could see a few freckles peppering her pale skin.

Not stopping to think twice, he pulled the door shut softly, hoping she hadn't heard him come in. He frowned, because the image of her body splayed out on the bed had stayed with him, burrowed into his mind.

Exhaling sharply, he walked back to his bedroom and

headed straight for the shower. Turning it on, he shucked off his clothes and stepped beneath the spray.

What the hell was he doing, looking at his best friend's baby sister?

The baby sister who'd just been cheated on. Who'd come here to feel safe. He squeezed his eyes shut because this was not what he'd planned.

He'd thought she'd be the same kid he'd met all those years ago. With limbs too gangly for her body, hair tied back in a braid, and a thick as hell retainer that looked like it belonged in Fort Knox.

He felt protective toward *that* Nicole. But this one? He felt anything but protective.

He was as bad as Kyle Walker. A jerk. She pushed buttons he didn't know he had. And he didn't like it, because he was never, *ever* going to go there.

She was verboten. You didn't touch your friends' sisters. Everybody knew that.

Shaking his head at himself, he turned the faucet to cold. Maybe that would help get the image of her out of his brain.

SHE'D HEARD her door click during a break in narration. Opening her eyes, she pulled off her headphones and saw that the door was closed. Frowning, she padded across the deep pile rug and put her ear to the door. She could hear breathing outside. Had Gabe been in here? She had no idea, her eyes had been closed as she was listening to the hero describe how much he wanted the heroine.

Her heart bumped against her ribcage, the rhythm fast.

Why hadn't he said anything? Was it because he didn't want to disturb her, or had he heard her crying?

She swallowed hard, because she was so damn desperate for companionship. Steeling herself, she finally opened the door, only to find the hallway empty.

Oh. Maybe it hadn't been Gabe after all. It could have been her imagination, or a breeze making its way through the ranch. Strange houses always brought strange quirks. Water pipes that creaked, roofs that rattled, maybe doors that mysteriously clicked?

Shaking her head at herself, she stepped back into her bedroom, and switched her audio book off, making sure to skip back a couple of minutes. Then she climbed beneath the covers and pulled them tightly over herself.

She already felt better. A good cry had done her some good.

CHAPTER 3

The following morning Nicole was having a minor crisis of confidence. What the heck should she wear for her meeting at the Winterville Inn? Some kind of business-friendly skirt and blouse to make it look like she meant business? Or a pair of yoga pants and a sweatshirt to make it look like she actually knew yoga?

Alaska had been as sweet as Dolores and Gabe had promised in her email back to Nicole, which was full of enthusiasm about setting up classes in the Inn's basement. She'd suggested they meet right away to discuss it, because, as she'd put it, the room needed a fair amount of work before it would be ready for classes.

In the end, Nicole chose a pair of dark pants and a cute silk camisole, grabbing a pink tailored cardigan to go over top, since it was getting colder outside.

Slipping her feet into her favorite ballet style shoes, she walked into the kitchen, and did a double take when she saw Gabe sitting at the breakfast bar.

He was staring into space, his large hands wrapped around a coffee cup, three tiny lines formed on his brow. But that wasn't what caught her eye. It was the white shirt he was wearing, unbuttoned at the neck to reveal a hint of chest hair, the cotton tight across his broad shoulders, following the line of his chest to his waist.

The dark navy pants he wore were tight against his muscled thighs as he sat on a stool. She swallowed hard, because *damn*, she wasn't used to guys this big. Luke wasn't overly muscled and only stood at five-foot-nine – not much taller than she was.

Hence her collection of ballet shoes.

"You look fancy," she said, because she wanted to warn him that she was coming in the room.

He looked up, his eyes heavy lidded, as though he was still half in his thoughts. "Hey." A half smile pulled at his lips. "Yeah, I have a thing at work. They want me to record some marketing videos." Standing, he brushed the non-existent wrinkles from his pants. "You want a coffee?"

"I got it." She'd already acquainted herself with his cupboards, and walked to the one in the corner to grab a mug. "You need a top up?"

"Nah, I'm good."

When she turned, she noticed his gaze had lowered. Surely he wasn't looking at her ass?

Although she had to admit it looked particularly splendid in these pants. They were high waisted and had a thick waistband, making her hips look curvier than they were. Walking over to the coffee machine, she put the mug under the spout and pressed a capsule into the holder.

"How's the construction going?" she asked him. Her brother had told her about Gabe's all-consuming project. Creating a ski resort a few miles away from Winterville.

"It's good. We're on the third stage. Hoping by this time next year we'll be accepting our first guests."

"Who's we?" she asked, pouring cream into her freshly brewed coffee. "Your co-workers?"

He leaned his head to the side. "Yeah, I work with my... I don't know. He's kind of like my brother-in-law, but married to my cousin. What does that make him?"

Nicole lifted a brow. "Cousin-in-law?"

"Yeah. Well he's that. He married my cousin Holly last year. She helps run the town."

"You have a big family," she noted, lifting her cup to her lips.

"Mostly cousins, but yeah. There are six of us, plus spouses. We're close, you know?" The corner of his lip quirked. "You have a pretty big family, too, don't you?"

"Well you know Matt." She smiled, and his expression softened. "And there's Kara. And they're both like our parents. I guess I'm the odd one out."

"In what way?"

She ran her tongue along her bottom lip. "Our parents are scientists. My dad works in molecular biology and my mom works for a pharmaceutical company. Kara's a doctor and I guess once Matt retires from snowboarding he'll go into something similar."

"What about you? Did you never want to be a scientist, too?"

She smiled. "I'm terrible at science. Always have been. My mom used to joke that she brought home the wrong baby from the hospital."

He lifted a brow. "That sounds kind of mean."

"It's fine. It's her attempt at a joke." And she'd gotten used to being the odd one out.

"What time are you heading to the Inn?" he asked, as though he knew she wanted to change the subject.

"At eleven." She looked down at her camisole and black

pants. "Do you think this looks okay? I wasn't sure what to wear."

He scanned her up and down, then looked away. "You look fine. Good."

Well okay then. "I wondered if I should go in a yoga outfit. Just to show that I'm really an instructor."

Gabe immediately grinned. "If that was the case, I'd be going to work in my snowboarding clothes every day."

She couldn't help but laugh. And for a moment their eyes met and she felt a strange jolt.

"Alaska wouldn't notice if you were wearing a tutu." His eyes flickered over her again. "She's all about the person within. She's good people."

There was a softness to his voice that wasn't there when he talked about his other cousins. She liked it. It reminded her of how Matt talked with her.

Gabe finished his coffee and stood, rolling his neck as though he had knots in his shoulders. "I'm heading out. I'll probably be home late tonight. You okay to take care of yourself?"

"Sure." She tried to hide the brief flash of dismay that went through her. "I'll be fine."

"Okay then. Good luck at the Inn."

"Good luck with your filming."

He lifted a brow and cleared his throat. "Thanks. I'm going to need it."

THE WINTERVILLE INN WAS A WIDE, sprawling building with a tiled roof that overhung the brick walls. Nicole parked her car in the almost full lot and climbed out, grabbing her purse and the file she had with her credentials inside. She couldn't help but smile as she walked into the lobby. They really did take the motto of 'Christmas All Year Round' to heart here. The sweet smell of smoke came from a huge inglenook fireplace, and the room was tastefully decorated with garlands and wreaths and a huge fir tree in the far corner.

It only took Alaska a few minutes to arrive after Nicole gave her name at the desk. The young woman walked toward her with a big grin, her hand outstretched.

"I'm Alaska. You must be Nicole."

There was something so genuine in her smile that it made Nicole's chest feel full. She'd met a few people in her life that she'd clicked with immediately, and she had a feeling that Alaska would be one of them.

Which made it even more important that she impress her.

"Let's go talk in the conference room," Alaska said. "It's a little more private. I know you've only been in town for a day, but I'm sure you already know that gossip is everybody's pastime of choice."

"I kind of got that impression." Nicole smiled as the two of them walked toward the door to the left of the reception desk. "I visited the coffee shop yesterday and everybody had an opinion there."

Alaska smiled. "Including Kyle Walker," she said, her voice teasing.

"You heard about that?" Nicole winced.

"As I said, it's a small town with big mouths." Alaska opened the door to the conference room. "Would you like a drink?"

"A water would be great."

"Done." Alaska poured two glasses from a jug that had

been set up on the table. "Take a seat. Tell me about yourself. How long have you been a yoga instructor?"

"For about eighteen months, but I've been practicing for a lot longer. I started going to classes when I was in college and had been finding my course load stressful. A friend suggested I try yoga to relieve some of the anxiety. And after that first class I was hooked."

"Where did you go to college?"

"Emerson. You probably won't have heard of it. It's a small arts school in Maryland." Nicole took a deep breath. Did she need to tell Alaska that she'd flunked the first year? "It wasn't a great fit. So I spent a couple of years abroad being an au pair. And then I came home and started working for a PR firm." One her mom had links to. And that had been a bad fit, too.

She'd been the bane of her parents' existence back then. They couldn't understand why she couldn't commit to one area of study like they had. Why she didn't want to change the world one molecule at a time.

She'd spent so much time as a kid twisting and turning, trying to fit her square peg into the round hole they wanted to place her in. And every time she let them down it felt painful. When she'd met Luke, it had felt like she was part of the family again. Plus her dad absolutely loved the guy.

For once she'd exceeded their expectations.

"And for the past year and a half you've been teaching classes at the local Y?"

"That's right." They'd been extremely understanding when she'd told them she had to leave. There were no shortage of instructors ready to take over her slots in D.C. Plus, her plan had always been to save enough money to start her own studio. "They've given me a leave of absence while I'm here. But I'd like to keep working in the meantime." She needed to. Sure, Gabe had given her a place to stay, but she still needed to be able to support herself.

"Will you be going back to D.C. eventually?" Alaska asked her.

"Yes." Nicole nodded. "But if there's enough interest in my classes, I'd be happy to find a replacement to keep running them whenever I leave."

Alaska nodded slowly. "That sounds good. We haven't run any kind of classes here before. We have a small gym that some of our guests use, but really we're a leisure hotel, so most of our guests are relaxing or visiting the town. I have to be honest and tell you I'm not sure how much of a demand there will be, at least from hotel guests, but if you're okay with that, then we can talk next steps."

"I'm absolutely fine with that," Nicole told her. "I have a few ideas of how to drum up interest."

"That's good. Would you like to take a look at the room I have in mind for you?"

"Yes, please."

"Follow me."

Alaska led her out of the conference room and down some stairs toward the basement, pointing out the gym which could be seen through a glass wall. It was surprisingly light down here, thanks to the sloping nature of the land that the Inn was built on, with windows on one side of the building allowing the morning sun in.

"I need to tell you that this room hasn't been used in years," Alaska said. "My grandmother originally built it so she could practice her dance routines in peace. She died a few years ago but stopped using it a while before that."

"I'm so sorry." Nicole gave her a sad smile.

"It's okay. When I got Gabe's message this was the first

room I thought of. She'd love that it would be getting used again."

Taking a deep breath, she turned to face Alaska. "You don't have to help me just because Gabe asked," she told her. "I'd understand if it wasn't a good fit."

Alaska's eyes widened. "But I want to help. And if Gabe vouches for you, that's good enough for me." She pushed down on the door handle. "Anyway, I love the idea of offering yoga classes. But this room is going to take a bit of work."

When Alaska opened the door, Nicole could see what she meant. The bones of the room were good. It had a high quality hardwood floor that you could tell had the right amount of give only by walking on it, even though it was covered in a thick layer of dust. One wall had windows overlooking the mountains at the back of the Inn, but they were covered in half-broken blinds that needed to come down.

The mirrored wall looked pretty much intact, although some of the dark spots covering the surfaces looked like they'd be impossible to get out. A little thrill flashed through her. It had always been her ambition to own her own studio, but with real estate prices in D.C., and the fact that there was so much competition, she'd put it on the backburner.

But this could definitely work. At least for the next few months while she tried to get her life back on track.

"I love it," she whispered, taking it all in.

"You do?" Alaska sounded surprised.

"Yeah. It's perfect." Nicole caught her eye. "How much are you thinking of charging for rent?" She prayed it wasn't too high. Not when she had no idea if she'd be able to recoup the money with actual paying attendees.

"I kind of have a proposal for that." Alaska shifted her

feet. "I don't have the time to get this room ready. So if you took that on, you can have the use of it for free."

Nicole blinked. "Free?" Was she serious? This kind of space would cost a fortune in D.C. "I can't do that."

Alaska wrinkled her nose. "I know it's kind of a mess. I guess we could help you get it ready somehow…"

"No, no. I meant I can't take it for free. Even if I do all the cleaning and painting – which I'm willing to do – I'd still be taking advantage of you."

"Oh no. You'd be doing us a favor. This room has been empty for too long. It'd make me happy to see it being used again. Plus it's kind of a trial – if enough people are interested, we could look at running more classes, for different stuff." Alaska grinned. "It's a win-win."

"Are you sure?"

"*Positive*. Is it a deal?"

Nicole nodded. "Hell yeah." She shook Alaska's outstretched hand before she could change her mind.

"When do you want to start on getting this room ready?"

Nicole looked around the studio again. She couldn't remember the last time she felt this excited. Maybe it was when Matt was competing in the Winter Olympics. "Is now too soon?"

CHAPTER 4

It had been over a week since Nicole had moved in, and thankfully the days had passed in a blur. The marketing videos that were supposed to take two days had extended to three – thanks to his mess ups with remembering his lines – and then he'd had to travel to the other side of the state for meetings with investors. Gabe was glad for the break – he was still getting used to having Nicole in his house. It wasn't just the fact that there was another body to fill the space that had always been his. It was her.

The sweet smell of her shampoo when she walked out of her bedroom in the morning, her wet hair pulled back and braided. The sound of her bare feet padding around on his hardwood floors. The low husk of her voice when she asked him questions about the stove or the alarm system.

But he could deal with those things. Sure she was attractive, but his brain knew she was off limits to him. He owed Matt that, at least. The thing that really got to him was her soft crying when she thought he was in bed. He'd stand outside her room and listen and fight with himself over whether he should knock on her door and offer solace or walk away.

But really, what kind of solace could he give? He had never been in a long-term relationship. His relationships barely lasted for more than a few months. He had no idea how it felt to lose the person you thought you'd spend the rest of your life with.

He felt helpless and out of his depth when it came to relationships. So instead he made sure she was comfortable during waking hours, making jokes just to see her laugh. And when she walked bleary eyed and disheveled into the kitchen every morning, he'd wordlessly make her coffee and hand it to her.

Just to see her smile.

He was back in the office today, along with Josh who ran the business side while Gabe ran the design and construction of the resort. The office was the first thing they'd built, knowing they needed somewhere they could bring investors to and show their vision. It had an open area for their thirty-strong office team, plus extra desks for those they brought on when needed. Plus break out rooms and a grand conference room that was full of marketing photographs with mock ups of how the resort would eventually look.

It was a multi-million dollar project. They needed to be able to show investors that it was worth their while.

Josh's desk was covered in photographs of his wife, Holly – Gabe's cousin – and their daughter, Candace. She was two months old, and cute as a damn button. She also seemed to be ruling Josh's world, so much that he had to call his wife multiple times a day to check if Candace had smiled, or burped, or filled her damn diaper.

"I see the Walkers are clearing trees today," Josh said, as he walked in from yet another phone call to his wife.

"Yep." It still rankled Gabe that Walker Woods was the best logging company around. He'd do anything to give the contract to somebody else. Well, anything except jeopardize the resort.

"I still don't get why you and North dislike them so much." Josh walked over and held his phone out to Gabe. There was a picture of Candace laying on her tummy. "How cute is that? She's trying to crawl, I swear."

"Do kids crawl that early?"

"No, but my kid is different."

Gabe stifled a laugh, because Josh was serious. "And for what it's worth, we hate the Walker brothers because they're assholes. They made a play for Holly once, so you should hate them, too."

"When?" Josh frowned.

"About thirteen years ago."

Josh shook his head. "Damn, man. I thought you meant recently."

"And they tried to buy North's farm off him, just because they wanted all those trees."

"Okay..."

"Plus Kyle's a dick. They're all dicks. Enough said."

Josh gave him an amused look. "Whatever you say."

Gabe stood, because he was in a bad mood now. He needed to walk it off. "I'm going to check on their work."

"You sure you're in the right mindset to do that?" Josh asked him.

"We pay their wages. I can do whatever I like."

It would have taken him almost half an hour to walk to where the Walkers were clearing what would become the green ski slope, so instead Gabe climbed on his ATV and started the engine. It wouldn't be too long before he'd need to switch to the snowmobile, but for now there was no snow up here. The engine purred as he pulled a helmet on, firmly placing his thick leather boots on the running boards before leaning forward to curl his palms around the handles.

He'd been riding ATVs and snowmobiles since he was a kid, and knew all the trails like the back of his hand. One of the bonuses of growing up in a small town – Gabe and his brothers had been allowed to do the kinds of things urban kids never could. Ski and snowboard alone, hike the trails without an adult, camp in the wilderness – though he didn't do much of that anymore. At least not alone.

There was nothing like the feel of air rushing past you as you dodged the trees. Of kicking up dirt and dust as you turned corners. Or leaning forward to keep your balance as you hurtled down slopes. He loved skating on the edge of danger, of knowing that if he lost control just a little bit, things could get bad.

It was the same feeling he used to get when he competed in snowboarding. An edgy sensation that made him feel truly alive.

As he approached what would become the green slope, the sound of saws and shouting filled the air. Wood dust and shavings were all over the ground, so he stopped the ATV and walked the rest of the way.

The first person he saw was Tyler, Kyle's younger brother. He gave Gabe a curt, I-know-you're-the-boss-but-I-still-hate-you kind of nod.

"Kyle around?" Gabe asked him.

"He's over there." Tyler nodded at one of the logging trucks they'd managed to get onto site.

Gabe walked over to where Kyle was shouting at one of his employees. The older man was shaking his head and pointing at something.

"Is there a problem?" Gabe asked.

Kyle's lazy gaze slid over him. "You shouldn't be up here without protection."

"I have steel toed boots."

"You need ear protection. And a helmet. You know that."

"I tell you what, if I get fined for not wearing protective gear, I'll pay it, okay?" It rankled him, having Kyle tell him what he should be doing, even if he was right. "How's the clearance going?"

"It's fine. A few hiccups, but nothing you need to worry about." Kyle turned to talk to his employee again, but Gabe reached for his shoulder.

"There's something else we need to discuss."

Kyle frowned. "There is?"

"Nicole Rice. Leave her alone. She's not interested."

Kyle grinned. "I heard she's shacking up at your place. She yours now?"

"She's not mine. She's a friend. That's it." Not even a friend. Not really. "But it's my job to protect her, and that starts with you. Leave her alone."

"The last time I saw her she looked like a grown woman." Kyle's eyes narrowed, though he was still smiling. "A really grown woman, if you know what I mean. Womanly in all the right damn places. So I assume she has her own mind, too, and if she wants me to back off, she'll tell me herself."

"You already called her?" Gabe frowned. It was exactly the kind of thing Kyle would do.

"No. But now that I know it'll piss you off I will." Kyle ran his hand over his jaw. "I could make her feel real good, you know?"

Gabe's jaw tightened. He leaned closer to Kyle, his voice low. "Keep away from her. That's not a request, that's an order. Touch one hair on her head and you'll regret it."

Kyle didn't flinch or step back. There was amusement in his eyes as Gabe glared at him. "What's it got to do with you anyway? She ain't one of your cousins."

"She's a friend's sister. And it's my job to look after her."

"Sure it is." Kyle winked. "Have fun doing that."

This was pointless. He was wasting his words and entertaining Kyle Walker at the same time. Taking a deep breath, Gabe narrowed his eyes.

"Just keep away. That's all."

"What you gonna do if I don't, big man? End our contract?"

"No. I'll end you."

"I'd like to see you try." Kyle finally stepped back, though he was still smirking, goddamn it. "I need to get on with my work now. Bye bye, boss."

Gabe gritted his teeth. He'd come out here to make himself feel better, but instead he felt worse than ever.

And his fist was itching to connect with Kyle's annoying grin.

Nicole woke early on her first day of class. A mixture of excitement and nerves made for a strange cocktail in her stomach as she climbed out of bed and padded across the thick carpeted floor. A loud bang made her stop halfway across the room. Followed by another, then more coming in a steady rhythm. Was there somebody at the door? Grabbing her robe, she quickly tied the sash and walked into the hallway.

The sun had only just come up, and the light had a strange quality to it. Yellow and soft, like you could almost touch it. When she got to the front door, a glance through the peephole told her there was nobody there.

Then the banging started again. It was coming from Gabe's office. Were there burglars? A shot of alarm rushed through her, and she carefully tiptoed down the hallway to the door next to the kitchen, her panic rising when she saw the door was ajar.

Her hand was shaking as she pushed at it. Maybe she should wake Gabe – but then whoever was in here could get away. No, she was a big girl, she could do this. Bracing her shoulders, she stepped inside.

Bang!

There was another door, this one leading from the far end of Gabe's expansive office to a small gym. In the center was a punching bag, swinging from the force of his blows. He was wearing a pair of gym shorts and nothing else, and the breath caught in the back of her throat.

There was a sheen of sweat on his skin, and it high-lighted the tautness of his muscles, and the sheer strength of his shoulders. He was the epitome of pure power that rippled and tightened as he punched the bag again and again.

Each time his fist made contact with the bag he gave a soft grunt that made her bones feel like jelly. She opened her mouth to say something, to alert him to her presence, but no words came out. She'd seen her share of bare backs, but not one had looked like this.

Skin glistening with sweat. Knotted muscles contracting and releasing as he swung his arm back then launched it forward.

He rolled his neck, as though to ease the stress, then punched once more. A second later he turned, his eyes glassy as they connected with hers, as though he was some-where far, far away, and she wasn't invited.

"Nicole?" Even her name came out like a grunt. She felt like a peeping tom.

"I heard a noise. I thought someone had broken in."

He blinked, his lashes long and thick. "So you came to confront me?"

"I..." She needed to stop looking at him. She couldn't think straight. "I thought I could scare them away."

The corner of his lip quirked. He reached for a towel that was hanging on the rail, looping it around his neck. Using the end, he wiped the sweat from his face. She could smell the sheer masculinity of him, and it wasn't helping. Not one bit.

"How much do you weigh?" he asked, his gaze sweeping her body. For the first time she realized she was almost as naked as him. Her long legs were bare from the top of her thighs down. And part of her robe had slipped, exposing her bare shoulder. She hastily lifted it to cover herself.

"That's a rude question," she pointed out.

He bit down a smile. "One hundred? One-ten?"

"One thirty-five, actually. I have a lot of muscle."

"I'm almost two twenty. You'd have no chance against me. Next time you think we're being robbed, call nine-one-one, or even better, come find me."

"I just did," she pointed out, annoyed at his inference. She could stand up for herself. She didn't need a man.

Not even one as fine as him.

He rolled his neck again, making it click. It was weirdly sensual. He was a man who knew the power of his own body. "I promised your brother I'd take care of you. That doesn't include you fighting burglars."

"There's only one person fighting in here. That's you."

"Well, now I'm going to shower." He stalked toward her, his expression a mix of annoyance and amusement. "Try not to fight any criminals while I'm gone, Batman."

"Batman?" She arched an eyebrow.

"I figured Batgirl would land me in trouble."

"How about 'Thank you for wanting to protect my house, Nicole?'," she said, putting her hands on her hips. "If I *had* been a burglar, you just saved all my computer equipment."

He stopped right next to her. So close she could feel the heat radiating from his skin. His hair was pushed back from his face, revealing a broad brow, straight as a die nose, and those piercing eyes that seemed to see everything.

But hopefully not her thoughts.

"Thank you, Nicole," he murmured, dipping his head so their gazes connected. "I'd be terrified without you here."

She swallowed, because his closeness was making her body react in a way it hadn't for a long, long time. Maybe ever. There was this tantalizing feeling that all he'd have to do was push her against the wall and take her, and she'd be his.

She'd always believed relationships should be equal on every level. Not only financially, or emotionally, or in taking turns emptying the damn dishwasher. But sexually, too. Her love life with Luke had been okay, though over the last year it had become rare.

She had a feeling that sex with Gabe was a completely different story. He'd be the dominant one, the one who called the shots. She hated that the thought made her feel so warm.

They were still staring at each other, electricity pulsing in the air between them. His eyes were hooded, narrow, and she could see herself reflected in the darkness of his dilated pupils.

"You should go shower," she said huskily.

"Yeah. I should."

His eyes dipped to her lips. They were parted where she was trying to get enough breath. The pulse in her neck matched the speed of her heartbeat. He leaned closer, and for a second she thought he was going to kiss her.

"It's a good thing I'm not a burglar," he murmured, reaching out to tuck a lock of hair behind her ear. "Because with the way you're looking at me right now, the computer isn't the only thing I'd steal."

Her heart hammered against her chest. "Yeah, that's a good thing."

"Go back to bed, Batman. You have a class this morning." He stepped back, and she immediately felt the cool air wrap around her.

He was ending this, because she couldn't, and she hated that. Hated the way that one look from him was all it took to make her legs feel weaker than they'd ever been.

"Go take a shower, Robin," she replied, still stinging from his almost-rejection. "You smell."

CHAPTER 5

*Y*ou smell.

Had she really said that to her brother's best friend?

Oh yeah, you said it. And you meant it, because you had to have the last word. And also, you're like five years old.

He'd laughed when she'd told him to take a shower, then shaken his head and stalked out of his gym. She'd let a minute pass before she followed him out, needing the distance to center herself.

And then she'd showered and headed out to the Inn, after making a quick stop at the Cold Fingers Café for her morning coffee.

It had taken a week of hard work, but everything in the studio was pristine. The walls were painted a soft white, the mirrors clean and perfectly shiny, and Alaska had sent over a team to sand and refinish the hardwood floor, refusing to take any money from Nicole, because she said it was an investment for the Inn.

She'd also found some beautiful plants in one of the local shops, which added a sense of peace to the room. In the corner she'd set up an equipment rack, and filled it with the mats and blocks she'd ordered. She hadn't bought anything other than that – for now the classes she'd teach would be basic. But maybe one day, when she had more money and a permanent studio, she'd be able to invest in more. The thought warmed her. She'd never be intellectual like her family, but there were other ways to accomplish things in life.

They'd tested out the stereo system that had been added to the room about six or seven years ago. Thankfully it had been state of the art when it had been installed, and it had stood the test of time. Nicole had created a fifty-five minute playlist to cover the class length, and planned to play it low, so people could hear her voice.

That's if anybody came, of course. Dolores said that a few of her customers had sounded interested when they took her leaflets, and Alaska had mentioned that she had a few friends who might come.

But every fitness and yoga instructor knew that intentions were never quite met with actions. She'd skipped classes herself when she was just a trainee.

"Hey," Alaska said, pushing the door to the studio open with a smile. She stepped inside. "I wasn't expecting you to be here so early."

"I couldn't sleep. I thought I'd go through my routine one more time before class starts." Nicole smiled at her, because they'd become good friends in the past week since she'd started renovating this room.

"Well I'm glad you're here, because we have a slight problem."

"What kind of problem?" Nicole's stomach did a flip. *Was this over before it began?*

"I had a lot of hotel guests call reception last night

asking about the class. Too many to fit in here." Alaska wrinkled her nose. "So I kind of suggested that you'd run a second class after the first." She put her hands up, as though to protect herself. "Please don't kill me."

Nicole blinked. "Why would I kill you? That's great news."

"It is?" A smile spread over Alaska's face. "Thank God. I thought you might need a break after the first one."

"It's wonderful. If the people want yoga, they'll get yoga."

"So then you won't mind that I asked our IT guy to make you a booking system? I thought it would be easier if it's attached to our website. That way you'll have an idea of how many people are coming, and if it's full, you can add more classes for the day."

Nicole's eyes stung. "That's so kind of you."

"It's good business." Alaska shrugged. "We like happy customers. Plus the more people we get through these doors, the more money we make. It's a win-win."

Nicole took her hand and squeezed it. "I appreciate it. Thank you."

When it was almost time for her first class to begin, the nerves really began to hit. She went over her introduction in her head about five times, checked that she had enough mats and blocks, and did a dummy run of the stereo system and the little microphone she'd have attached to her headset. They all worked, but she was still as angsty as all heck.

Checking her watch, she saw she had five minutes to go. Might as well go see if anybody had actually turned up. She opened the studio door and stepped into the hallway, and the loud sound of chatter immediately echoed in her ears.

Her mouth dropped open. There was a line of at least thirty people. Some of them she recognized – Alaska was there, wearing the cutest little shorts and tank top, along with two other women she introduced as her sister, Everley, and cousin, Holly – who was responsible for running the town. Dolores was there, too, wearing a leotard that looked like it belonged to the Jane Fonda era. She was surrounded by women who were talking so fast Nicole couldn't make out what they were saying. Whatever it was, it sounded like gossip.

And then her eyes met piercing blue. Gabe was there, wearing gym shorts and a tank, and next to him was a dark haired man she assumed was his brother, North.

Her heart did a little flip, because they'd all come to support her. People she hadn't known a couple of weeks earlier. Some she still didn't know. Yet here they were, dressed in their finest workout gear, ready to put themselves through an hour of hell to give her some encouragement.

Apart from Matt, her family had never been interested in her love of yoga. Sure, they'd tried to show some enthusiasm, but the topic always turned quickly to how her dad's latest experiments were going, or a breakthrough her mom had in her research.

Seeing all these people made her feel warm, yet wistful.

"Um, hi." She smiled at them all, avoiding looking at Gabe because she still hadn't quite recovered from their morning encounter. "Please come in. Take a mat and roll it out. You'll need a couple of blocks each, too. And if you can take your socks and shoes off, you'll be so much more comfortable. Once you're all ready, I'll start."

"Please tell me this won't hurt," Dolores said, catching her hand as she walked into the studio. "The last time I exercised Ronald Reagan was in the White House."

Nicole squeezed her hand. "You'll be fine. This is a beginners' class, and I'll show you lots of modifications if you can't hit the right poses. Do you have any injuries or medical problems I should know about?"

"Nope. I'm healthy as an ox. And about as heavy as one."

Nicole shook her head. "You look fabulous to me."

It took five minutes for everybody to get ready, laying their mats out and taking off their shoes. When it looked like they'd all turned back to gossiping again, she turned on her microphone and faced the class.

"Is everybody ready?" she called out, and the talking quietened. Thirty pairs of eyes were trained on hers. She was thankful that Gabe and his brother were on the far end of the front row, so she didn't have to see him watching her.

That won't help when you have to adjust his poses.

Getting the best out of a yoga class was all about hitting the right poses, and aligning your body with your breathing. Sometimes that meant she'd have to adjust their poses manually, pressing them down or up, getting close enough to them that your bodies were almost one.

The thought of doing that to Gabe was both terrifying and tantalizing. But she was a professional, she wouldn't let him pose wrong. Not on her watch.

She started by taking them through some basic poses. The mountain, plank, downward facing dog. A few of the participants needed some extra help, but most of them held the right shape perfectly.

Including Gabe, thank goodness.

When she demonstrated moving from downward facing dog to child's pose, she could see him watching her intently. There was something very sensual about yoga. It was about knowing your body and how to use it. Being at one with Earth and nature. Tapping into your chakra – the inner energy everybody possessed, and being in control of the breath that gives you life.

Once they'd mastered the basic poses, she took them through the sun salutation sequence, demonstrating first so they could see the right way to pose. She began in prana-masana, the prayer pose, then inhaled before arching backward, curving her body until her feet remained on the floor and her body and chest were facing the ceiling, forming herself into an 'r' shape in hasta uttanasana. She spoke softly, telling the class the modifications they could make.

When she ended the salutation in another prayer pose, she smiled at the class and asked if they were ready. From the corner of her eye she could feel Gabe staring at her, and it made her heart skip a beat. What was going on here? She was supposed to be mad at him after this morning's encounter in his office.

Near the end of the class, she noticed that Gabe's core was slightly misaligned. Until that point he'd gotten every pose down perfectly, not that she'd expected anything less from an elite athlete.

"Your back is a little too arched," she murmured, as he held a lunge. She put one hand on his stomach, the other on his spine, encouraging him to straighten. It felt like her palm was touching a steel sheet. His stomach was so hard it made her breath catch. She felt it contract as he engaged his core, straightening his back.

When she looked up there was a half-smile on his face. "Sorry, Batman," he murmured.

"Batman?" his brother asked. "Why Batman?"

"Because she fights off all the criminals in Winterville." Gabe winked at her, and she shook her head.

He wasn't going to let this go, was he?

Dolores fell to the ground with a huff on the other side of the room. Grateful for the distraction, Nicole walked over and scooted down next to her. "You okay?"

"Just old. And tired. Can you do a chair based class? Preferably about ten minutes long?"

"If there's enough demand, I'll do it." Nicole grinned at her. "We have about five minutes left until savasana. You can either take a breather until then or do the modifications. Just listen to your body, okay?"

"What's savasana?" Dolores asked, looking suspicious.

"You'll like it. I dim the lights, put on soft music, and you get to lay down and relax. Connect with your mind. It's just as important as your body in yoga."

"I like the sound of that. Can you do a whole class of that?"

Nicole laughed. "I think that might be a step too far."

A few minutes later, she watched as the whole class lay in corpse pose, soft music filling the air.

She always loved this part of a class. Knowing that her clients would leave the room energized but also rested. That the power they'd put into their muscles was returning to the center of themselves. Somehow she found her eyes turning to Gabe once more.

He had the most amazing body. She'd known it when she saw him in the gym this morning, but then she'd only been able to appreciate him from behind. Now she had the chance to take in his strong, muscled shoulders, his broad chest, and slim hips, leading down to powerful thighs.

A shiver wracked down her spine and she had to pull her eyes away, reminding herself that she was his *goddamned teacher.*

The music was coming to an end. She pushed herself to standing and softly walked over to the lights.

"Take your time to sit up. There's no rush. If you feel dizzy, lay back down and I'll come over and help." She walked back to her own mat, and sat down, putting her hands together in prayer. "I'd like to end the class wishing you all peace. Namaste."

"Should we wish you Namaste, too?" Dolores asked.

Nicole smiled. "I'd love that."

All of them placed their palms together, and called out, "Namaste." There were smiles on their faces, and it made her stomach do a strange, yet sweet twist.

A few of them came forward to talk to her as others put their equipment away, and slid their socks and shoes on. She was explaining the difference between beginner and intermediate lessons to one lady when Gabe walked over, tipping his head to the side as he listened.

"I'll probably run a couple of intermediate classes a week if there's demand for it, and maybe an advanced, too."

The woman nodded, pleased, and walked back to join her friends, leaving her alone with Gabe.

"What did you think?" she asked him, aware of how desperately she wanted his approval.

"I think you kicked my ass. You can do things with your body I only dream of."

The double meaning of his words made her cheeks warm.

"You were good," she told him. "Have you done yoga before?"

"Only a couple of times. I did pilates when I had a back injury years ago. That kicked my ass, too."

She grinned. "Well any time you need a one-on-one lesson, you have your own live in instructor on call."

His eyes dipped to her lips, then lifted again. "That's probably not a good idea."

Her smile faded. She hadn't meant it as anything other than a friendly offer, but he'd obviously taken it the wrong way.

Two rebuffs in one day, that was a record, even for her.

"Probably not," she said, trying to keep the hurt from her expression.

"I'll, ah, be working most of the afternoon. But I'll be home for dinner if you want to share takeout or something," he said, as if he wanted to soothe the wound.

"Take out sounds good. Thank you." She kept her voice even, because she didn't want him to know how desperate she was for company. *Any company.*

But especially his.

"I'll see you later."

"Yeah, you will."

She watched as he left the room, then turned her attention to a couple who wanted to ask her about her one-on-one sessions.

Since this morning, there was a weirdness between her and Gabe, and she couldn't quite shake it off. But the bigger question was, did he feel it too?

CHAPTER 6

When Gabe walked into his ranch house early that evening, the first thing that hit him was the mouth-watering smell of food. Something warm and cheesy that made his stomach do a little flip. It reminded him of being a kid and coming home after a day skiing down the mountains, to find that his mom had been baking up a storm.

But he wasn't used to it in this house. Sure, he could cook for himself, but most of the time he either ate out or grabbed something on his way home from work. The smell made his house feel different.

More homely.

Nicole was standing by the stove, her back to him, a fresh pair of yoga pants clinging to her curved hips. She was swaying from side to side, singing as she stirred the pot in front of her. He cleared his throat, but she didn't notice, so he walked over and lifted one of her headphones up.

She jumped about half a mile. "Oh my God, Gabe, who's a damn ninja now?" She looked down at the pale gray tank she was wearing, which was now splattered with cheese sauce.

"Did it burn you?" he asked her, frowning.

"No. It missed my skin." She smiled at him and grabbed a dishcloth and dabbed at her top. "I'll go change once I've layered up the dish."

"I did call out. You didn't hear me. You were, ah, dancing."

"I thought you'd be home later. I was going to surprise you with dinner." She put the cloth down. "Is that okay? If you'd rather have takeout I can freeze the lasagna."

"That lasagna's going nowhere except in my stomach." He lifted a brow at her. He was already salivating and it wasn't even in the oven yet. "I can't remember the last time I had a home cooked meal."

A smile pulled at her lips, and it reminded him of just how damn pretty she was. "Matt called earlier. Said to say hi. And to thank you for taking care of me." She winked at him. "I didn't tell him that I'm mostly the one taking care of you."

He lifted a brow, pleased that things were normal again after the strange atmosphere in his office that morning. "Is that right?"

"Yep. I scared away the imaginary burglar earlier, after all."

He nodded slowly. "Yeah, that's true. I'm a lot safer from all kinds of pretend criminals now that you're around."

"They don't call me Batman for nothing."

He smiled, walking over to the refrigerator. "We should open a bottle of wine to celebrate your first day of classes. Is Sauvignon Blanc okay?"

"That would be lovely."

Her phone started to buzz. Over her shoulder he could

see that it was an unknown number. Shrugging, she accepted the call, wedging her phone between her ear and shoulder so she could continue to stir the sauce.

"Hello, Nicole Rice speaking." She grabbed a pinch of pepper and added it to the pan. She paused for a second, and Gabe pulled a bottle from the refrigerator as she spoke into the phone. "Oh, hi Kyle."

He froze for a moment, tipping his head so he could listen in. What the hell did Walker want?

"Um, yeah, that's right. When were you thinking?" she asked. Gabe slammed the wine bottle on the counter, and pulled out two glasses, watching her from the corner of his eye.

She looked over at him, her eyes widening when she saw the expression on his face.

"Tomorrow morning would be fine. Do you have a room with enough space? We need around ten feet by ten, at least."

Gabe twisted the bottle lid, yanking it off and throwing it on the counter.

"Of course I'll go easy on you. Yoga is perfect for loosening tight muscles. I'll see you tomorrow at ten. Can you text me your address?"

Gabe poured the wine, sloshing some over the side of the glasses. His jaw was tight, anger coiling around his stomach because he knew Kyle was doing this just to get to him.

And it was working.

"Okay then, thanks Kyle. Have a good evening." Nicole hung up and put her phone on the counter, then turned off the sauce. "That's the tenth private client I've had book today. I guess word is getting around."

"You're not going."

She blinked, turning to look at Gabe. "What?"

"I don't want you going to Kyle's house. He lives alone. It's not appropriate."

"You're kidding, right?" She started to smile, as though they'd both join in some laughter, but when she saw he was serious her amusement melted away.

"He's only after one thing. And we both know it's not yoga."

She blinked. "We know nothing of the sort. Unless you think I was so bad today that the only way I can get clients is if they want to have sex with me."

Something inside him tightened when she said the word sex. He tried to push it away. "I didn't say that." Why was this coming out so wrong? He just wanted to stop Kyle from getting his dirty hands on her.

"But you implied it. What if Kyle really wants to learn yoga? He told me his mom was at the class today and recommended me to him. She thinks I can help with some aches he's getting in his back."

"I really don't think that's the ache he needs help with."

Her eyes caught his and she was silent for a moment, as though she was weighing his words. "I guess I'll find out tomorrow."

"I'm asking you as a friend. Don't go teach him. Please."

She looked torn. "It's my job, Gabe. I need to earn money. I need clients. I can't turn them down because you don't like the look of them."

"I get that." He really did. But Kyle Walker, dammit...

She slid the pan to the side of the stove then turned to look at him with those wide Bambi eyes. He knew exactly what Kyle Walker saw in her.

A mixture of innocence and sex appeal that made him want to protect her in one moment, and push her against the wall with his hips in the next. But he wouldn't do any pushing, he wasn't Kyle. He was her brother's best friend.

He'd made a promise.

They were still staring at each other. He could feel his jaw tic rhythmically, as she swallowed hard and let out a soft sigh.

Jesus, those lips. Those pretty, swollen lips. What he wanted to do to them.

"I need to go shower," he muttered, because this tension was so damn overwhelming. He wanted to get out of here before he made an idiot of himself.

"Story of our lives," she muttered.

"What?"

"We argue, you shower. It's the second time today."

Yeah, it was. And damn if that didn't make him feel like an asshole. "I'm sorry. It won't happen a third time." He meant it. He was supposed to be taking care of her, not making things worse for her.

"You know I'm still going tomorrow, right?" There was a determination in her voice.

"Yeah." He nodded. "So am I."

"What?"

"I'll take you to Kyle's tomorrow. If he sees me, he won't try anything stupid."

She pressed her lips together, her eyes seeking his. The glassiness had gone and she looked like she wasn't sure whether or not to laugh.

"You're crazy, you know that?" she asked him.

"Yeah, I know." But he was still taking her to Kyle's.

~

SHE HADN'T REALIZED how lonely she'd been until tonight. There was a warmth in her core as Gabe ate a third serving of her vegetable lasagna, shaking his head as he pushed his plate away, rubbing his stomach and giving a contented sigh.

"Best damn lasagna I've eaten. Vegetable or otherwise."

He'd looked like a wounded puppy when she'd first told him there was no meat in the dish, but as soon as he'd taken a bite and let out a low, growly moan, she knew he'd gotten over it. This was her signature dish – the one she'd learned to cook at eighteen and brought out whenever she wanted to impress somebody.

Did she want to impress Gabe? Yeah, it felt like she did.

"It's nice to cook for somebody other than me," she said, taking a sip of wine. It was crisp and delicious. "There's no point in making a lasagna for one."

"Well you can cook for me any time." He winked.

"When you're home."

The smile slipped from his lips. "I'm sorry I haven't been around much. I'm used to living by myself. Matt would probably laugh if he found out I've become a workaholic."

"It's okay," she said softly. "You're not my babysitter. And now I have classes to run and clients to see so it will be easier. Plus, Alaska suggested a girls' night soon, so that's something to look forward to."

"Yeah, well I'll try to get home earlier sometimes. Maybe cook you something."

"I'd like that. I'm still getting used to being alone, you know?"

He tipped his head to the side. "How long were you with your ex?"

"Almost two years." She looked down at her plate.

"That's a long time to be with someone. I'm sorry he hurt you."

Looking up, she gave him an embarrassed smile. "Ugh, it's like a soap opera. Who walks in on them like that? I always thought they'd hear the damn door at least."

The corner of his lip quirked. "He's an idiot. Losing somebody like you."

Something deep inside of her warmed. "That's not what he thinks. Maybe he's right. She was his student. They probably have more in common than we did."

"He works with your dad, right?"

Nicole nodded. Matt must have filled him in. "My dad's a professor at Lincoln University. Luke works full time with him on his research projects."

"What does your dad think about him cheating on you?"

She looked him straight in the eye. "He doesn't know."

"What?" Gabe frowned. "Why the hell not?"

"Because he's in the middle of an important piece of research and he needs Luke to get it done."

Gabe folded his arms across his chest. "If they don't know what happened, why do they think you're here?"

"I told them I was having second thoughts about our relationship and needed some time away to think about things." Her eyes wouldn't meet his. She knew how lame it was. But they'd accepted it without question, because they were too busy to see the holes in her story.

"And they bought that?"

She took another sip of wine. "I have a reputation for being a little bit, I don't know, flighty, I guess. They think I'll come around and go back when I'm ready."

Gabe narrowed his eyes. "So he's getting away with it?"

"Luke?"

"Yeah."

"I guess." Yes, that sucked.

"Don't you want him to pay for what he's done?" Gabe

was looking at her as though she was crazy. "He cheated on you."

"But it won't only be him who pays. It'll be my family."

Gabe wrinkled his nose. "That's shit."

"Yeah, it is. But on the plus side, I get to spend time here in your beautiful house. And drink your lovely wine." She lifted her glass as though to toast him. "And anyway, I hate arguments. And confrontation. This way things can calm down and when I go back home and announce I'm definitely breaking off our relationship they'll be ready for it."

"Will you tell them about his cheating when you go back?"

She shrugged. "I have no idea."

"I don't get how you're so chilled about this. The guy forced you out of your home town."

"Would it be better if I was angry? Throwing things all over his car and slashing his tires?"

Gabe chuckled. "Probably."

"That's not my way. I'm zen. That's why I like yoga, I guess. Plus I believe in Karma. It'll get him one way or another."

"You're way too naïve for your own good," Gabe said, shaking his head. "You know when you said you didn't need my protecting?"

"Yeah?"

"Well you were wrong."

CHAPTER 7

"Okay, so the session lasts an hour. Are you really going to wait here for me, or do you want to pick me up afterward?" They were parked in Kyle's driveway, and Gabe was tapping at the wheel of his black Mercedes G Class. She'd thought he'd have second thoughts about driving her this morning, but when she'd gotten up and ready for her private session with Kyle, Gabe had been waiting for her in the kitchen.

He was wearing a pair of jeans so soft they must have been washed a thousand times, and a black Henley that clung to every muscle he possessed. He looked like a cross between Christian Grey and a bodyguard. It made her smile inside. This was stupid, but his protectiveness was also kind of endearing.

"Actually, I'm coming in with you," he said, releasing his seatbelt and pulling at the door.

"No, you're not."

"Are we really doing this again?" He cocked an eyebrow at her. "Because yes I am."

She shook her head and exited the car, walking to the

door of Kyle's house. It was more compact than Gabe's, but with the same view of the mountains, just a few miles further away. Sighing, she pressed the doorbell, all too aware of Gabe's presence inches behind her.

"Hey sweethear—" The word caught on Kyle's tongue as he saw Gabe standing on the step below hers. He blinked, then stepped back. "Come on in," he said, regaining his equilibrium. "Don't worry, daddy. She'll be back with you in an hour."

"I'll come in and watch," Gabe said, his voice low and ominous.

"I don't remember inviting you." Kyle smiled at him. "But feel free to wait on the stoop like a creep."

Nicole winced. "I asked him to come," she lied, because she didn't need the tension. "I want to show him what I do in a private session."

Gabe gave a grunt behind her but said nothing.

Kyle looked over her shoulder with narrowed eyes, as though he was weighing his options. "Okay," he finally said. "But you can sit in the corner and say nothing."

"Sure," Gabe said, his voice even. "Works for me."

Kyle had followed her instructions, pushing his furniture to the side so they had enough room in his living area to lay out their mats. Gabe followed them in, grabbing a chair from Kyle's small dining table and carrying it to the corner of the room, sitting down on it and folding his arms across his chest.

He definitely looked like a bodyguard. Nicole was somewhere between amused and horrified.

"Okay. So let's start by sitting cross legged on the mats," Nicole suggested, ignoring the way Gabe was staring at them. "You can talk me through the aches you have in your back and any other medical issues."

"I get twinges here," Kyle said, as he sat next to her. He took her hand and placed it on his right shoulder blade.

"No touching," Gabe said.

Kyle started to laugh. "This is a yoga session, not a lap dancing club."

Nicole blinked because that's exactly what this felt like. As though they were in the private room and Gabe was making sure that Kyle looked but didn't touch.

It was going to be a long hour.

"I need to touch him," she said, shooting a warning look at Gabe.

"And we agreed you wouldn't say anything," Kyle said, grinning because he knew he was riling Gabe up. "Right?"

Nicole brought her attention back to her client. She was going to have to give him this one for free, because there was no way she could charge him for putting up with Gabe. "Okay, I'm going to start by showing you a few poses. Then we'll run through them together and put them into a sequence. Any time you feel a twinge in your back, tell me."

Kyle nodded. "I have a question."

"Okay, shoot."

"If you touch me, does that mean I can touch you?"

She caught a glimpse of Gabe's thunderous expression. "Only if I ask you to."

Kyle winked. "Well, ask me anytime."

She connected her phone to Kyle's stereo and started up her music, then showed him some poses. He picked them up quickly, only wincing once when he tried to bend his back over his hips, and she made a mental note to skip that pose when they got into the sun salutation. She adjusted his legs a couple of times, and tried to show him how to breathe into the flow, but mostly he was doing great.

They were about forty minutes into the session when he

turned his head toward hers as they were in downward facing dog.

"Nicole?"

"Yeah?"

"You want to go out with me sometime?"

She sensed, rather than saw, Gabe lean forward. She could hear him clear his throat though.

"I don't date clients." She shot him a smile.

"What if this was our only session? I wouldn't be your client then."

"I'm sure there's a line of women a mile long who'd kill to have a date with you," she said softly.

"Yeah, but I don't want to date them. I want to take *you* out."

There was a noise like the scraping of the chair. She looked up, her gaze clashing with Gabe's. He looked mutinous. She shook her head at him.

"Let's not rile Gabe up any more, shall we?" she said to Kyle, pushing herself up to standing, and Kyle followed. "We're going to move into savasana next. It's the rest post. We need to be serene, not talking about dates."

"Rest pose?"

"We lay down on our backs and close our eyes."

"Together?" Kyle lifted a brow. "Nice."

"Shut up and lie down," Gabe grumbled.

"Did you hear something?" Kyle asked her. "Because I distinctly remember him agreeing not to talk."

"It's fine." She shot Gabe a warning look. "Lay down, please. Relax your body and mind. I'm going to close the drapes."

"You know what I think?" Kyle said, as he lay down on the mat.

"What?" Nicole asked, closing the curtains and dimming his lights.

"I think Gabe wants you for himself. That's why he's doing this lap dance bouncer act. He can't stand the thought of another guy touching you."

Gabe's eyes narrowed. "One more word, Walker. Just one more."

"I can't hear you," Kyle sang. Nicole took a deep breath. Ten more minutes and this would be over.

It couldn't happen fast enough.

"I don't get it. Why does it matter if she teaches Kyle Walker yoga?" North asked, passing an axe to Gabe. "And can you help cut some logs while you're here? I need to replenish my stack. It feels like winter's finally coming in."

As soon as he'd dropped Nicole back at the house, Gabe had headed over to North's place. He'd told Nicole some lie about needing to do something for his brother, but the truth was he was kicking himself for being such a dick to her at Kyle's place.

"You know why it matters. Kyle's a dick. All the Walkers are. You feel the same about them, I know you do. Remember when you and Riley Walker went at it over that girl from Marshall's Gap?"

North raised a brow, his own axe in his hand. "That was about fifteen years ago. We were kids. The Walkers are okay, man. A little full of themselves, but hey." He grinned. "Who isn't?"

Raising the axe, North brought it down sharply, splitting the trunk he'd placed in front of him.

"I promised Matt I'd take care of her. And that includes not letting assholes like Kyle get in her pants."

North started to laugh. "So what are you gonna do, put her in a chastity belt? I don't get it. Matt asked you to give her a roof over her head and you've done that. She's a grown woman, surely the rest is up to her."

"She's been hurt. I figure I'll help her not get hurt again."

North lifted a brow. "Where's this all come from? You don't get intense about anything." He swung again. "Except this, I guess."

Gabe took the axe North had given him and lined it up with the log in front of him. Maybe this was what he needed, something to wear him out. Take away the aggression he felt whenever Kyle Walker's name was mentioned.

North was right. He rarely got riled. He liked being the cool headed brother. North was the protective one, Gabe was the one who made people laugh. That's how it was supposed to be.

He swung the axe down and the log crunched, splitting into two. He lifted it again, splitting the log into smaller and smaller pieces until North yelled at him to stop.

"I need logs for the fire, not matches," he said pointedly. "Jesus, man, you're in a state."

"I'm just pissed, that's all. And you of all people should understand. Look what you did when you found out about Josh and Holly."

North lifted a brow. "Yeah, I was protective of her because she's our cousin."

"And I'm doing the same with Nicole."

"Sure you are." North snorted.

Okay, so now he was pissing Gabe off. "What's that supposed to mean?"

North put his axe on the ground and turned to face Gabe. "I'm just trying to point out something obvious. You didn't give a shit about Holly and Josh, and she's our cousin. So why are you getting all overprotective over somebody you hardly know?"

"Yeah, well Josh isn't Kyle Walker, is he? He was in love with Holly. He still is. He wasn't after her for only one thing."

"Mmhmm."

Gabe inhaled sharply. "You're really annoying me right now."

North laughed. "Good. You should be annoyed. There's something going on with you that I can't put my finger on. You're... I don't know... edgy, I guess. It's so unlike you and I don't know what to say."

"I'm not asking you to say anything. I'm just telling you I'm pissed with Kyle Walker."

"Noted." North pressed his lips together and nodded, then lifted his axe again. For a moment they were both silent, the only noise the splitting of wood and the grunts of their breath as they repeatedly brought their axes down against the logs.

A minute later, North stopped and looked up again. "You know what I think?"

"What?" Gabe was really regretting coming here. He thought he'd be able to unload on his brother and feel better. He hadn't expected him to be so damn reasonable. This was the man who hit Josh Gerber for having a pair of their cousin's panties in his pocket for chrissakes. He was supposed to understand Gabe's fury.

Not be all damn reasonable about Kyle Walker.

"I think you're attracted to her."

Gabe frowned. "To Nicole?"

"Yeah. It's the only way to explain this caveman thing

you have going on. You didn't have it with Holly and Josh because she's our cousin. You didn't have it when Dylan and Everley got back together either," North said, referring to Alaska's older sister, who ran the theater in Winterville. "So it can't be a brotherly feeling. Which means it has to be something else."

Gabe gritted his teeth. "I'm not attracted to Nicole."

"You sure about that?" North asked.

"Positive."

"Well that's good. Because if you think *I* was pissed about Holly and Josh, imagine how Matt would feel if you made a play for his sister. The guy knows all your skeletons." North shook his head. "And there are a lot."

"I've had a healthy sex life. Doesn't mean I'm an asshole."

North shrugged. "I know that, and you know that, but Matt? He was your wingman when you were snowboarding. The guy's seen women come and go when you're around. I imagine he wouldn't want his sister to be anywhere near you if he thought you were a threat. So it's a good thing you're not attracted to her, right?"

Gabe frowned. "Right." And he wasn't. Not one bit.

Didn't mean he wasn't still pissed with himself, though.

CHAPTER 8

"Hey Nicole!"

Nicole turned to see Alaska waving at her as she walked up the stairs from the basement. Since Sunday, she'd barely seen Gabe. She wasn't sure whether he was annoyed with her or genuinely busy with work. Either way, it felt awkward. To try to relax she'd taken advantage of the sauna in the gym after her class, followed by a long, cool shower that soothed every muscle.

"Hi." She gave Alaska a genuine smile. "Your sauna is to die for. If I ever build my own place I'm going to get me one of those."

"It's great, isn't it? Grandma loved the idea of a European sauna when she built the Inn. She visited Sweden once, and apparently everybody there would go from the Sauna into the snow and then into a frozen plunge pool."

"Yeah, and they'd also do that naked," Alaska's sister, Everley, added. She was leaning on the counter next to Alaska, looking amused.

"Can you imagine our guests running naked in the

snow?" Alaska gave a shiver. "I think we'll skip the plunge pool option."

"Well maybe they're onto something. My muscles feel so relaxed I could sleep for a hundred hours." Nicole let out a contented sigh.

"That's a shame. I was about to ask you to join us for lunch. We're meeting our cousin Holly. You remember her from your class, right?"

"The brunette who did the sun salutation without a single error?" Nicole grinned. "Yeah, I remember her. Are you sure it's okay to join you? I don't want to intrude on a family meal."

"You're kind of family since you're staying with Gabe," Alaska pointed out. "Plus it's just a casual thing. And we can make some plans for our girls' night out. Holly's desperate for it."

"It really will be casual," Everley agreed. "Especially since Candace will be there."

"Who's Candace?" Nicole asked.

"She's Holly's baby. Two months old and cute as a button. Unless you deny her anything and then she turns into Satan's child." Everley was beaming. "She takes after her auntie."

Alaska nodded, her face serious. "Unfortunately for us."

"Shut up." Everley laughed. "You love me really."

Nicole followed them to the dining room, loving how easily the sisters teased each other. It made her feel wistful. She'd never had that kind of relationship with Kara. She'd always been too busy. And by the time Nicole was a teenager, Kara was at college, busting her ass to get into medical school.

The aroma of baked bread filled the air as they walked over to the table where Holly was already sitting. Baby

Candace was in a car seat and was sleeping peacefully, or at least she was until Everley and Alaska started to coo over her.

And then she let out the most almighty wail.

"If I didn't love you two so much, I'd probably kill you right now," Holly muttered, picking Candace up and cradling her against her chest.

"I'll take her," Everley said. "It's my fault she woke up."

"But then I'd be rewarding you for being bad," Holly said, shaking her head.

Everley grinned. "That's the best kind of reward."

The next few minutes were manic, as Everley attempted to rock Candace to sleep, and the waiter came to take their drink orders, and tried to talk through the specials menu between the baby's wails. But then she'd calmed enough for Everley to sit down, though she refused Holly's offer of putting Candace back in her chair.

"It's fine. I'll hold her. This way she won't wake up again."

By the time the waiter brought their drinks over, the table was quiet enough for them to place their food orders. Nicole asked for the tomato soup and grilled cheese, needing a carb injection after a long morning of classes. Everley and Alaska followed suit, while Holly ordered a salad, telling them she had about ten more pounds to lose to get back to her pre-pregnancy weight.

"But you look great. Seriously." Nicole gave her a smile. "I can't believe you could do yoga so easily when Candace is so young."

"I used to do it when I worked as an accountant," Holly told her. "I hadn't realized how much I missed it until I did your class. I'm definitely scheduling in another. Or I might try to persuade Josh to join me in some private sessions."

Everley bit down a smile. "Can you believe we all used to be party animals, and now you're talking about doing yoga with your husband?"

"Speak for yourself, I'm no party animal," Alaska said, wrinkling her nose.

"How about you?" Everley asked Nicole. "Do you like to party?"

"I guess." Nicole tipped her head to the side, thinking. "I haven't partied much in the past few years. Unless you count going to fundraisers with my ex."

"Gabe said you'd recently broken up with somebody." Alaska wrinkled her nose. "I'm sorry."

"Did you live with him?" Everley asked Nicole, her voice full of sympathy.

"Um yeah. But it's over. Completely over."

"Long story?" Alaska asked.

"Just a boring, sad one. I caught him with his grad student. I basically became a cliché."

All three of them let out a sympathetic sigh. "I'm so sorry," Everley said, shaking her head. "What an asshole."

"You want to talk about it?" Alaska asked.

It was weird, but Nicole really did. She told them about her and Luke. How he was her father's right hand man, and that she was concerned about her dad's research. They were so easy to talk to, asking soft questions in the right place, telling her she was doing the right thing.

"And now you have Gabe to look after you," Alaska said.

"Yeah, that's not working out quite as planned either." Nicole filled them in on her visit to Kyle's house for a private session. When she described the banter between Gabe and Kyle they all burst out laughing, the somber atmosphere of moments ago fading away.

"Gabe seriously told Kyle to keep his hands off you?" Alaska shook her head.

"It doesn't surprise me. They've always disliked each other." Everley rolled her eyes. "Remember that time Kyle danced with me at the bar?"

"And North stormed over and pulled you away?" Alaska took a sip of her water.

"Yep." Everley nodded. "And then Gabe gave me a lecture about guys and that they're only after one thing."

"Our boy cousins are so protective," Holly told Nicole.

"I get that impression." Nicole tried not to smile. It made a change from being surrounded by men who couldn't even form an emotional attachment. She'd dated her fair share of idiots who were only after one thing.

Maybe that's why she'd thought Luke was different. Hah. How wrong she'd been.

"It's understandable why they're protective," Alaska said, her voice soft. "Especially after everything Gabe went through." She and Everley exchanged a look that seemed to have something deeper in it.

"What did Gabe go through?" Nicole asked. There was a little pulse in her neck at the thought of him.

"It doesn't matter. It's history. But it made him wary of others. He sowed his oats for a while when he was younger, but then he took up snowboarding and he got so much better. It kind of saved him." Alaska smiled. "Gave him something else to be intense about."

"He doesn't seem that intense," Nicole said, but then she frowned, because yeah, he was pretty intense at Kyle's house. He was intense when she'd thought he was a burglar, too. His eyes dark, his mouth tight. The memory of it sent a thrill through her body.

"He's a lot deeper than most people think," Alaska said.

"He gives off this easy-going persona, and yeah, most of the time he is. But if you hurt his family, he's gonna get pissed."

"And I'm guessing he sees you as family," Everley added. "Since you're his friend's sister."

Those words should have warmed her, but they didn't. She didn't want him to think of her as a little sister.

She wanted him to see her as a woman. Because that's how he made her feel when he looked at her with need in his eyes. Like she was beautiful. Wanted.

Not a reject.

"Enough talking about Gabe," Everley said, clapping her hands together. "Let's talk about our plans for our girls' night out instead."

"Where should we go?" Alaska asked. "It's not exactly a fun night if we come here. Or even to the Tavern. We'll just end up talking to the locals."

"We should go to Marshall's Gap," Everley said, her eyes lighting up. "There's that new bar, what's it called?"

"Wild Sally's." Alaska blew out a mouthful of air. "Did you know they have a mechanical bucking bronco there?"

Holly winced. "I'm not getting on a bucking bronco. There aren't enough Kegel exercises in the world for that."

"I bet Nicole would be great on the bronco," Everley said. "All those muscles and core strength."

"I've never been on one," Nicole admitted. "And I'm not sure I want to start now." But she was smiling anyway, because the thought of getting out and letting loose was making her feel warm. She liked these women. They were welcoming and funny, and she knew they'd all have a good time at Wild Sally's.

It had been a long time since she'd kicked free and had some fun.

"Okay, so the bronco is optional. Cocktails are a requirement." Everley grabbed her phone. "I'll make us a Whatsapp group and we make some concrete plans."

"That's if you're in?" Alaska said gently.

"Yeah." Nicole nodded. "I'm in."

THE HOUSE WAS quiet as Gabe let himself in that evening. It was almost ten o'clock. He'd had a late meeting then taken an investor out to dinner. It was one of those weeks when he'd barely had a moment to himself.

And when he did, he'd spent most of it beating himself up, because he'd been such a damn idiot at Kyle's house on Sunday. There was something about that man that irked him.

And something about Nicole that pushed all his buttons.

At first he thought Nicole must be in bed, it was so quiet, but then he walked into the living room and saw her curled up on the sofa, holding one of those e-readers in her hand, her thick hair covering her face. She was wearing a pair of yoga pants and an oversized hoodie, even though it was warm in here. He'd cranked the thermostat up a couple of days ago when the first cold spell of winter had come in.

She was so engrossed in her book that she hadn't noticed him come in. Behind the veil of hair, he could see her lips were open and slightly moving as she read. There was something so peaceful about it, that it made him feel strange.

Like he didn't want to disturb that ease. But that he wanted to be part of it. Wanted to lay his head in her lap and let her play with his hair as she read.

What the hell, Winter?

This was all North's fault. He'd put things in Gabe's head

that had no business being there. He cleared his throat, puncturing her tranquility. She blinked, as though she'd been a million miles away, then looked up.

"Your bat sensors are off," he murmured. "I could have been a burglar."

"I decided to take the night off. The metropolis of Winterville feels pretty safe without my constant patrols." She looked pleased to see him, and that sent a little thrill through his chest. She switched off her Kindle and put it on the table in front of her, then looked up at him. "How was your day, dear?"

He bit down a laugh. "Long. Boring. How was yours?"

"Actually, I had lunch with your cousins." Her eyes sparkled.

"You did?"

"Yeah. They're lovely."

"Yes they are." He sat down on the sofa, being careful to keep some space between them. This pull he was feeling for her wasn't healthy. "Did you talk about me?"

"Yes?"

This time he laughed at her embarrassed expression. "I was kidding. But it's good to know I'm still providing some entertainment."

"I kind of told them about you and Kyle." She grimaced. "Was that wrong?"

He let out a sigh, because that stuff was still playing on his mind. "No, not wrong. Embarrassing because I was such a dick. But not wrong."

"You weren't a dick. And it was kind of funny watching Kyle react to you. He wasn't exactly putting his all into yoga. I get the feeling he was more interested in getting a reaction from you."

"I think he was more interested in getting a reaction

from *you*," Gabe corrected. "Or in getting *something* from you."

She sighed and tipped her head back on the sofa. "I think you're right. I'm not going to teach him privately again."

"You're not? Because of me?"

She looked him in the eye, running the tip of her tongue along her dry bottom lip. He'd never met a woman who could rock the sports casual look so perfectly, and he'd been around a lot of sports people. He had no idea if it was the yoga, or if it was just her, but she had this perfect combination of softness and spine.

Cashmere over steel. It was enticing.

And off limits.

"I don't want to annoy you, Gabe. You took me in when I needed a friend. I'm really thankful for that. And you're almost certainly right. Kyle's trying to get into my pants. And I don't mix business and pleasure."

The word pleasure reverberated through his ears. "Do you want him in your pants?" His chest felt weirdly tight.

Her gaze connected with his. She looked a mixture of wary and something else. Something he couldn't put his finger on.

And Christ, he wanted to put his finger on her. More than a finger.

Damn his brother.

"I don't think so, no," she finally said, and the buzzing in his ears calmed. "But if I did, that would be okay, because I'm single and he's single and eventually I'll be ready to move on from Luke. Maybe sooner rather than later."

"Of course you will." He nodded. "And you should."

She pulled her lip between her teeth. "And I guess I kind of liked the attention from Kyle, you know? Not that I'd do anything about it, but it's nice to be wanted by somebody. It's been a long time since anybody's made me feel attractive."

His chest felt tight. They were straying into dangerous territory. "You *are* attractive, Nicole. You have to know that."

She looked up at him, her eyes wide. She opened her mouth then closed it again, as though she thought better of what she was going to say.

"What?" Because now he was desperate to know what was making her blush.

"It doesn't matter." Her cheeks were burning now. "You're very sweet. But I don't think I'm that attractive. And Luke definitely didn't think I was."

"Luke's an idiot." His voice was low.

"I should have known something was wrong. He stopped wanting..." She took a deep breath. "You know."

"Sex?"

She nodded. "I guess he was getting his needs met elsewhere. Shame he didn't send me the memo."

There was pain in her voice and he hated that. Hated even more that he had no idea what to say to her.

"I'm sorry, you don't need to hear this." She pulled her sleeves down over her hands and looked away, her eyes shining.

"I want to hear it." He moved a tiny bit closer to her, threading his fingers together, his eyes on her.

Her gaze caught his. "I just feel so stupid," she told him. "I mean our sex life was never going to set the world on fire, but I should have known what was up when he stopped wanting me."

"This wasn't your fault, Nicole. None of it. He was your boyfriend, he owed you loyalty and he didn't give it to you." He looked down at his hands, trying to find the words. If only Alaska was here, or Everley. They'd know what to say.

He felt like he was stumbling in the dark. But he wanted her to feel better. Wanted to see her smile again.

And he couldn't help but think her sad mood was his fault. If he hadn't been such a dick about Kyle, she wouldn't be upset now.

"Do you know what got me the most when I caught them?" she asked him.

"What?"

"The passion he had for her. He never had that for me. Sure, the sex was okay. Good, even, but he never felt that way for me. He never made me feel that wanted. That desired."

"Well he should have. That was his job."

"Maybe that's why I read romances," she said, gesturing toward her Kindle on the table. "The heroes in the books always put the woman first."

"And they should. Because that's what the good guys do." There was a tightness in his jaw that echoed the tightness in his pants. "He should want you to feel beautiful. He should want your pleasure. That's not just in books, that's real."

"Is that what you do?" She looked at him through her thick lashes. The electricity in the air felt so thick he could almost taste it. She was breathing fast, enough for her chest to hitch beneath her hoodie.

"Yeah..." he strung the word out, just to feel it on his tongue. "That's what I do."

Her eyes met his and he couldn't look away. There was electricity in the air, drawing him to her. The thought of giving her pleasure was tantalizing.

"But I would never do that to you," he said, his voice thick. "Because you're Matt's sister."

Her bottom lip trembled, and he could see the dark, pink skin inside her mouth revealed. He wanted to suck it between his own lips, dig his teeth into her. Show her exactly what pleasure could feel like.

"I know," she said softly. "I guess it's a good thing I have my books. And my fantasies."

Yeah, that wasn't helping.

"And I'm going out with your cousins soon. They're taking me to a bar in Marshall's Gap. Maybe I'll find someone there who's as good a guy as you are."

"There are no good guys in Marshall's Gap," he warned.

She smiled. "Maybe I'll find a bad guy then."

He shook his head. "Please don't do that. I'm not sure I'll survive it."

HE'D JUST FINISHED a video conference with the resort's PR company when he noticed his phone screen light up. It had been a few days since his tension-filled discussion with Nicole. For the past couple of nights they hadn't mentioned their conversation, instead he'd watched football on the big screen while she read a book and he'd started to wonder if they really could make this living together thing work.

But his misgivings all came back when he saw the name on his phone screen.

Matt Rice.

They'd messaged a few times since Nicole had arrived – just Matt checking in to make sure his sister was okay – but they hadn't talked. For the first time in a long time, Gabe had found himself grateful for the time difference between them. Sure, he hadn't done anything with Nicole, but he'd thought about it.

And that was bad enough.

"You gonna answer that?" Josh asked, looking up from his desk.

"Yep." Gabe grabbed his phone and swiped to accept the call, then strode out of the office onto the veranda that overlooked the development. It was cold enough for his breath to turn to vapor in the air as he greeted Matt and tried to ignore the twist in his gut that told him he was an asshole of a best friend.

"Hey, sorry I haven't called before now. Training has been fucking terrible." Matt's voice was crackly. "Just wanted to thank you again for all your doing. I spoke with Nicole yesterday, she said how great you are."

"It's what friends do." There was a metallic taste in his mouth.

"How is she really?" Matt asked. "Has Luke contacted her, do you know?"

"Not that I've heard." And good riddance to the boy who didn't know how to give a woman pleasure. "She's doing good. She's started teaching yoga at the Inn. My cousins have kind of taken her under their wing. She seems pretty content, you know?"

"That's good news." Matt sighed. "I'm hoping that I might make it home for a couple of days before Christmas. It's not guaranteed, but if the stars align I'll have a few days between training and my first competition. I was thinking it might be a good time for Nicole to come home to talk with our parents."

"I thought she was staying for a while longer."

"Yeah, I know, but I'm not sure I'll be back anytime soon after that and I don't want her facing them alone. My parents aren't always the best at giving her their full attention, if you know what I mean."

"Then why go back? She can stay here as long as she likes." Gabe looked out at the snow topped mountains. In the distance between, he could see the Walker crew still clearing trees.

"Ah, you're a good friend. The only one I'd trust with her. I'm grateful to you, man." Matt's voice was warm. "But even you have your limits. She has to come home eventually."

"Yeah, I guess she does. But in her own time."

"I know. And nothing's set in stone yet. Don't say anything to her. I don't want her getting her hopes up and then me not being able to make it happen."

"Of course I won't."

"Thanks. I owe you one. No, I owe you more than that. Not sure I can ever repay it since you don't have a sister."

No he didn't. But he did have an asshole Matt would rip if he could read the dirty thoughts Gabe had about Nicole.

Not that he'd ever tell him.

"If North ever gets a girlfriend and splits up with her, you'll be the first person I call." His voice was deadpan.

Matt laughed. "I'd definitely be up for that. You're the best."

CHAPTER 9

"Hey, did you remember that I'm going out tonight?" Nicole looked at Gabe as he grabbed his wallet, stuffing it into the pocket of his dark blue pants. She still hadn't gotten used to exactly how good he looked in a pair of dress pants and a shirt, unbuttoned casually at the collar.

Or in a pair of sweats and a dark t-shirt, as they watched a Netflix series together.

And in a pair of shorts and a tank, as he emerged from his gym in the mornings, his body covered in a sheen of sweat that seemed to radiate pheromones straight to her belly.

Yeah, the man looked good in anything.

Or nothing.

She blinked to get that thought out of her mind. It was a good thing she was going out tonight. She was getting too used to spending her nights with him, even if he was the perfect gentleman. Neither of them had mentioned the loaded conversation they'd had a few nights ago, though the memory of it still lingered.

Now she had the visual of him making sure a woman's pleasure came first, and it was near impossible to push that out of her mind.

She'd always been aware of her body – part of the discipline of yoga was to center your mind and body together, to be aware of the power and strength you possessed with your muscles and bones. But now she was aware of it in a different way. A way that made her realize how needy she was.

Maybe finding somebody to fulfill that need was her next step in getting over Luke. And Gabe had made it abundantly clear that person wasn't going to be him.

She knew that was a good thing, even if it made her feel wistful.

"I'm going out tonight, too. A couple of our investors are in town. I'm taking them out for dinner." Gabe grabbed his suit jacket and shrugged it on, smoothing down the fabric. "So I'll probably be getting home at the same time as you."

"If I come home," she said, a smile pulling at her lips.

He lifted an eyebrow at her. "I thought you weren't planning on antagonizing me anymore."

"I was, but it's kind of fun to see your reaction."

"You like pushing me."

She tipped her head to the side. "Something like that."

Leaning forward, he brushed his lips against her cheek.

"Have a good evening. But not too good. And watch out for the guys in the bar. They're not all good like me."

She smiled. "I'll be too busy on the bucking bronco to notice them."

Gabe narrowed his eyes and looked at her for a minute, then shook his head and grabbed his keys. "Okay, so don't have a good night. Have a sensible one."

"Right back at you." She was still smiling when he

walked out of the door. And he was right, she did enjoy antagonizing him. Because in those moments, she liked what she saw in his eyes.

Glancing at her watch, she realized she was going to be late for her first class if she thought on Gabe any longer and didn't hurry.

"WHAT TIME IS Cam Hartson getting here?" Josh asked when Gabe walked into the office.

"Just after lunch. He's staying over in Marshall's Gap tonight with his wife. Said something about needing to be away from his teenagers." Gabe walked straight to the coffee machine and filled up his cup with the steaming black liquid. He didn't bother to add any cream – he needed the caffeine to go straight to his bloodstream.

Cam Hartson was one of their investors. An ex-NFL player who Gabe had met a few times over the years, mostly at charity golf tournaments. When Gabe had the idea to build a ski resort a few miles away from Winterville, Cam had been one of the first investors he'd approached. For a start, he liked the guy, but he also knew that Cam was looking for something to get involved in after retiring from the game and having a family. He'd jumped at the chance to be a part of Gabe's plans.

"What time are you taking him to dinner?"

"Around eight. I booked that little bistro in Marshall's Gap."

"You know I can't come, right?" Josh shrugged. "The girls are all going out tonight so I'm on babysitting duties."

"It's fine. I've got it." Gabe sat at his desk and fired up his laptop. He had at least a dozen emails that he should have replied to yesterday. "It'll be good to catch up with Cam again. And his wife's good company, too."

"If the girls weren't going out, you could have taken Nicole with you," Josh said, glancing at Gabe from the corner of his eye.

Gabe sighed. Not Josh, too. "That's not going to happen."

Josh gave a little chuckle. "So it's just a coincidence that you're eating out in Marshall's Gap, about a mile away from where the girls will be tonight?"

"I'm just going to where our client is staying."

"Sure." Josh lifted a brow. "And our client happens to be staying in a hotel you booked him into." He leaned forward, an amused smile playing at his lips. "Tell me, why didn't you book him into the Winterville Inn like we do all our investors?"

"Because he wanted something small and romantic. Winterville doesn't have any boutique places like that."

"Cabins are romantic," Josh pointed out, still smiling.

"Are we really discussing this now? Because I have a shit ton of work to do before Cam arrives, and you're supposed to be making sure that everything is ready for our meeting with him this afternoon."

"Andi has already been out to walk the construction area to make sure everything's ready for his tour," Josh said, referring to their PA. "The ATVs are all fueled up, lunch is ordered, and the Walkers know that we have a VIP coming." Josh gave him another sly glance. "You know the Walker gang go out in Marshall's Gap a lot, right? Wouldn't it be interesting if they went to Wild Sally's tonight?"

Gabe ignored the taunt in Josh's voice. He was enjoying his discomfort way too much. "Good for them."

"I was just thinking how great it is that you'll be close by if there are any problems. I'll rest easy at home knowing

Holly will be taken care of." He smirked. "And Nicole too, of course."

"I won't be going anywhere near Wild Sally's. I won't be dancing and I won't be taking care of anybody. I'll be meeting our investor, having a meal, and coming straight home." He met Josh's cynical gaze. "So can we stop talking about this and get on with our work?"

"Sure," Josh said, his voice easy. "Let's do that."

SHE'D FORGOTTEN how much fun it was just getting ready for a night out with friends. Maybe she'd spent too many of the last few years living in yoga pants. No, that wasn't right. She'd been to charity galas with her family and Luke, too. But somehow getting ready for those always seemed to raise her anxiety. She'd worry about wearing the wrong dress or saying the wrong thing.

She shook that thought away, because she wasn't in that place anymore. And that was probably a good thing, because the dress she'd bought from the little boutique at the Inn was completely inappropriate in all the best ways. The black skater style dress clung to her bodice, then flared out where it ended mid-thigh, the sleeves were cut off and ruffled, and the neckline plunging. Her thick hair cascaded over her shoulders, and she'd taken the time to put on smoky makeup, making her eyes look satisfyingly big and wide.

She felt attractive for the first time in forever, and it was a good feeling. With the success of her classes, and the calm she'd found in living here with Gabe, she felt confident and strong.

And she couldn't wait for her night out with the girls.

Not that she had to wait long. She heard the car pull up just before seven. Everley's husband, Dylan, had offered to drive them all over to Marshall's Gap. They'd booked a booth at Wild Sally's, and had agreed that having dinner first would be a good thing, since they were all out of practice at this and probably needed to fill their stomachs.

Everley was sitting in the front next to her husband, and through the gap in the seats Nicole could see Dylan's hand resting lightly on his wife's thigh. It made her chest feel weirdly tight. Everley was telling them about a male dancer at the theater she managed, who'd inadvertently done the splits in a practice, and had to take the week off because he'd sprained *everything*.

When they walked into the bar, Nicole was pleasantly surprised to see how classy it was – bucking bronco apart. The walls were lined with a smoky gray paper, covered with mirrors and low lights that created an intimate atmosphere. The booths were fashioned in black wood, upholstered with gray velvet cushions. The four of them slid into one and ordered their first round of cocktails from the waiter.

"Can you bring some nuts or something, too?" Holly asked. "Otherwise I'm not going to make it through the night."

"We don't have to drink *that* much," Alaska said. "They do virgin cocktails, too."

"It's ladies' night. Virgin anything isn't an option," Holly said, deadpan.

"Absolutely." Everley beamed. "Everybody's drinking and everybody's getting laid tonight."

"I'm not getting laid, thank you." Alaska wrinkled her nose. "I remember when most of the guys here used to fill their diapers."

Everley turned to look at Nicole. "You're our only hope."

Nicole shook her head, amused. "Your cousin would kill me. And anyway, I'm off guys, remember?"

The waiter brought their cocktails over, and she took a sip of her margarita. It tasted dangerously good.

"Why would Gabe kill you?" Everley said, tipping her head to the side. "Did he say that?"

"I figure if he had a fit when I taught Kyle Walker yoga, he'd probably implode if I brought a guy home. He's completely overprotective." And it was maddening.

Everley ran her finger around the rim of her cocktail glass. "You could go back to the guy's place."

"And then he'd go crazy because she didn't come home," Alaska said. Her eyes met Everley's, and there was some kind of weird communication between them again.

"Yeah, I guess. But that doesn't stop us from having a good time tonight, right? And if I happen to send Gabe a few photos of us having a good time, then it's my bad." Everley grinned.

"Please don't do that." Nicole couldn't help but laugh at Everley's expression. She was clearly the naughty one out of the cousins. "I have to live with the guy."

"Josh thinks he has a thing for you," Holly said. All three of them turned to look at her. Nicole's heart did a little loop in her chest.

"Why does he think that?" She tried to keep her breath even.

"Because he's at a restaurant about a mile away from here with an investor right now. And he *never* goes out in Marshall's Gap."

He was here? He hadn't said where he was eating tonight but she'd assumed it would be in Winterville. Her skin started tingling at the thought of him being so close. But she was mad, too, because he could have told her that he'd be in the same town tonight.

What was wrong with him? Why couldn't he have a normal conversation with her. Yes, he was gorgeous and pushed all her buttons, but he drove her crazy, too.

A huge smile pulled at Everley's lips. "He's here? That's too good an opportunity to miss."

Nicole's stomach fluttered. "What do you mean?"

"I mean, we're going to have a good time tonight. A very good time. And we're going to show Gabe the evidence." Everley called the waiter over. "Let's start with another round of cocktails, and some food. Then it's on."

CHAPTER 10

She couldn't remember the last time she was this drunk. Or the last time she'd had this much fun. They ordered more cocktails, then attempted the bucking bronco – and Nicole had been thrown off, her thigh landing heavily on the ground in a way she knew was going to bruise like hell.

Now they were on the dance floor, moving wildly to the beat. Holly was so drunk she kept stumbling, and Alaska had to hold her up a few times. Everley was in the center of their group, her long slim arms up in the air, her lithe dancing attracting all kinds of attention.

Nicole felt good. *Alive.* And it wasn't just the alcohol – though she was all too aware that she'd maybe had a teeny tiny bit too much. It was this group of friends who had welcomed her in like she was one of their own. It was the freedom to be who she wanted to be – not feeling like she was on the outside looking in.

She felt like her true self. Nicole. And she loved it.

Everley leaned in, pressing her lips to Nicole's ear as

they continued to dance. "There are a bunch of guys watching you. They're hot."

"Where?" Nicole looked over her shoulder. Sure enough, her gaze immediately connected with a guy by the bar. He was tall and dark, leaning on the counter, a half-smile pulling at his lips.

"He's not my type," she said to Everley, turning her head back to their group.

"Who is your type?" Everley asked.

Your cousin.

"I don't know. I'll tell you when I see him." A bright light flashed in her eyes, and when the stars disappeared she saw Everley holding her phone, tapping away on the screen.

"What are you doing?"

"Sending another photo to Gabe." Everley smiled.

"Don't do it." Nicole's eyes were wide. She'd thought Everley was joking about sending him the evidence.

"Too late. Anyway, I've already sent a few throughout the night. The one of you on the bronco was very sexy." Everley grinned.

Nicole's mouth was dry. "Did he reply?" Part of her hoped he had. The other part was afraid, because he must think they were crazy.

Everley's smile slipped. "No. Not yet. Maybe he's busy eating." She glanced at her phone. "Wait, there are three dots." Triumphantly, she turned the screen around for Nicole to read. There was a single word there.

Behave.

It sent a thrill through her. One that made her thighs feel tight and her insides like melted chocolate. She could picture him, jaw tight, eyes narrowed.

Could imagine him whispering it in her ear.

"I need to sit down before I fall down," Holly said. Even in the gloom of the dancefloor her lips looked green.

"Me too. Let's go," Alaska agreed. Everley huffed, but joined them, Nicole following behind. As soon as they sat down, the waiter came back over.

"Just bring me water, please," Holly told him. "Lots of it."

"I'll have a soda." Alaska beamed at him.

"And two margaritas," Everley added. "Because some of us can take our alcohol."

"That's not strictly true," Nicole said, hearing a slur in her voice.

"Just one more," Everley promised her. "We'll be good girls after that."

Holly gave a drunken splutter. "I doubt you'll ever be good," she said to her cousin. "Nicole might though. We'll see."

Nicole had barely taken a sip of her cocktail when she felt a familiar pressure in her lower belly. "I need the bathroom," she said, pushing her palms heavily on the table to help herself stand. A rush of dizziness washed over her. What the heck was in that cocktail?

Or maybe it was all the other one's she'd drunk earlier.

"I'd go with you, but my legs have disappeared," Holly told her.

Alaska dipped her head under the table. "They're still there."

"Nope." Holly shook her head. "Definitely gone."

Nicole laughed and weaved her way through the dance floor, clutching her purse close to her body so the swaying arms around her didn't catch it. She breathed a sigh of relief when she made it to the lit corridor that led to the bathrooms. Before she pushed on the door to the ladies', she saw the man she'd exchanged glances with when she was dancing – walking down the hall from the men's bathrooms. A slow smile spread across his lips when he saw her standing there.

"Hey." His eyes raked over her.

"Hi." She hoped he'd make this short. The pressure in her lower belly was getting worse. So was the dizziness.

"I saw you earlier," he said, casually leaning against the wall. "You're a good dancer."

"I think the alcohol has a lot to do with that."

"It always does." He grinned. "You want to dance with me?"

"I need to use the bathroom." She tipped her head toward the door. "Pretty urgently, actually."

He chuckled. "I won't hold you up any longer. But come find me when you're done. People say I'm a pretty good dancer, too."

"Sure," she agreed, not planning on doing anything of the sort, then pushed the bathroom door open and stumbled inside.

Thankfully, there were some free stalls, so she made her way to the one at the far end, locking it shut behind her. A wave of dizziness washed over her, and she had to steady herself against the wall. The urgent pressure in her belly reminded her of why she was there, and a moment later she felt nothing but relief.

Oh, and drunkenness. How had she let herself get this bad?

After she washed her hands and splashed water on her face in an attempt to sober up, she pulled her phone out, wanting to check the time. Gabe's name flashed across the screen with a message.

Hope you're having a good time. Call me when you're leaving. I'm not far from you, happy to give you a ride.

Even with her blurry vision, she could see his message was sent almost an hour ago. She tried to type out a reply, but it kept autocorrecting to words she didn't even know existed. Sighing, she hit the call button instead.

"You okay?" His voice was low. She could hear the murmur of conversation and the clinking of silverware. He must still be at the restaurant.

"I'm good." She paused. "And drunk."

"I hear you've been fighting with a bronco." There was an edge to his voice that sent a shiver down her spine.

"I just called to say I don't need a ride. Dylan's picking us up." She looked at herself in the mirror over the sink. Her hair was a tangle of waves, her smoky makeup was smudged from too much dancing. And her lips were swollen and pink.

"It's no problem. I'll call him and tell him I'm picking you all up."

"No, don't."

"Why not?" His voice deepened.

She caught her reflection again, blinking at herself. She could feel the heat of her blood, a thick pulse drumming at her neck. And all she could think about was Gabe.

She wanted him. That was the truth of it. And he was frustrating as hell because he kept pushing her away. She hated that, too, because this thing between them was so damn exciting and delicious.

And dangerous. He didn't want her. Or at least he was pretending he didn't, and she wasn't sure what was worse. All she knew was that she was sick of being invisible. Especially to him.

"I might not come home tonight," she said softly. "A guy just asked me to dance. I think he's interested."

Even in her drunken haze she knew she was being a

brat. Trying to push his buttons because she was desperate for a response. Like a kid playing with a scab.

"You're coming home tonight, even if I have to carry you out of that damn bar."

Warmth pooled inside her. "What if that's what I want?"

"Be careful." His words reminded her of his message to Everley. *Behave.* Little commands that thrilled the hell out of her. Made her pulse throb and her body ache.

"I'm tired of being careful," she told him. "I'm tired of being good. If you want me to come home, you're going to have to come get me."

She ended the call as he was replying, so she had no idea what he said. Another wave of dizziness washed over her. Maybe that conversation wasn't a good idea. She'd almost certainly regret it in the morning.

If she could remember it, that was. And the odds on that weren't great.

She pulled her purse over her shoulder, and attempted to tame her hair, then gave up because it was so beyond taming it wasn't funny. A mixture of perspiration and the heated atmosphere in the bar had turned it into some kind of eighties bouffant.

She'd go straight to the booth and tell the girls what she'd done, then she'd apologize to Gabe for being such a bitch. It would really help if the room would stop spinning.

Slowly, she made her way out of the bathroom, feeling nothing but relief that nobody was waiting for her there. She kept a hand on the wall to steady herself as she made her way back to the bar. The dance floor had gotten busier, and the thought of pushing through it made her stomach twist. Her throat felt itchy and dry, and she had to admit the thought of going home right now was enticing.

"You came back." The guy from earlier smiled at her, taking her hand in his. "Let's dance."

"I don't think I can." A wave of nausea washed over her. This time it wasn't only from the alcohol but how bratty she was being. Too much liquor was a dangerous, dangerous thing.

"Sure you can. Come here." He pulled her closer. She could smell the sweet notes of his cologne, mixed with the musky aroma of beer on his breath. He slid his arms around her, pulling her close to him. She looked up at him, about to tell him that she was definitely going to be sick all over him if he didn't let go, but then she saw the bar door open, and a tall, suited man walk in.

Her heart lurched right in time with her stomach. For a moment Gabe looked around, his tall, muscled body framed by the streetlight flooding in through the open door. He looked at the booths and frowned, no doubt because he saw his three cousins there without her. Then he grimaced and turned back to the dance floor.

Their eyes connected and it felt like somebody had slapped her on the chest. She could feel the intensity of his gaze on her. Could see the tic of his jaw as he watched her sway against the poor guy who had no idea that she was using him to make Gabe jealous.

A frisson of electricity shot down her spine. He'd come for her. And he was pissed. Her heart was hammering against her chest, but it felt like a victorious kind of hammer.

Because he was here.

Swallowing hard, she lifted her head to whisper in his ear. "My boyfriend's here."

The guy blinked. "What?"

She nodded over his shoulder. "He's kind of strong. And angry. You should probably get out of here."

He stopped dancing, and so did she, but the room was still swaying. "You didn't say you had a boyfriend."

She could see Gabe walking through the crowd of people toward them.

"You didn't ask. But you should go. Now." Her voice was urgent. How the heck had she gotten into this mess?

He didn't need telling twice. Before she could take a breath, he'd let go of her and stalked across the floor, leaving her swaying alone like a sunflower in a summer breeze. The throb of the bass matched the rhythm of her pulse as Gabe came closer, his expression grim as he pushed through the final group of dancers, coming to a stop in front of her.

Even when he was angry he was beautiful. Her soft gaze caught his, and she could see the flint in his eyes. "Get your things. You're coming home with me."

She opened her mouth to answer, then threw up all over his shoes.

CHAPTER 11

Nicole turned out to be a talkative drunk. He wasn't quite sure whether to be amused or appalled by the state she was in. Maybe he was a little of both. Thankfully one emotion he wasn't feeling was turned on.

Because as pretty as she was, drunken women held no appeal.

Didn't mean he didn't want to take care of her, though. Somehow he'd managed to get her over to the booth where his cousins were sitting and given her a bottle of water to drink. Her cheeks were scarlet as she swallowed it down.

"I'm taking Nicole home. Can I give you all a ride, too?" He didn't want to leave his cousins here alone. Holly looked as intoxicated as Nicole was, and Everley wasn't all that far behind. Alaska gave him a gentle smile that tried to tell him he didn't need to worry about her.

But he did anyway.

It turned out Dylan was already on his way. He'd arrived ten minutes later and had swallowed down a laugh at the state of Gabe's shoes – a laugh that had quickly melted away when he saw how inebriated his wife was.

Somehow they'd managed to get all four of them out of the bar, and Dylan had gotten Holly, Everley, and Alaska in his car, leaving Gabe alone with Nicole. It had taken some pushing to get her into the passenger seat of his truck – he was cursing himself for buying something so damn high up. Not trusting her to stay upright, he'd fastened her belt and closed the door, then toed off the shoes she'd ruined and dropped them in a nearby trashcan.

"I'm so sorry. I'm sorry. I'm really sorry," she chanted, as he climbed into the driver's seat wearing only socks. "Your poor pretty shoes."

"They were brogues. They aren't pretty."

"But they were such lovely shoes. So shiny I could see my face in them."

He started the engine and she swallowed hard, tipping her head back.

"Don't vomit in my car," he warned her. "If you need me to stop, say so." It was one thing to lose a pair of hundred dollar shoes. Another to pay for a full detail.

"I'm not going to... I don't think."

Leaning over her, he opened the glove box and found a plastic bag, passing it to her before closing it up. "This is for emergencies. Use it if you need it."

"Emergencies. Got it." She nodded, her expression serious. "But your poor shoes..."

"Let's not talk about the shoes."

"Okay. No shoe talk." Her eyes were glassy as she stared out of the windshield. He brought his gaze away from her and onto the street ahead. It was a ten mile drive back to Winterville. Usually it would take him fifteen minutes, but he didn't want to drive too fast because there were so many bends.

And quick bends meant twisted stomachs, and… yeah.

"Can I open the window?" Nicole asked. Even drunk as a skunk her skin glowed like it was lit from the inside.

"Sure." He pressed the button, opening her window halfway. She turned her face to it and gulped in some air, her shoulders relaxing as she leaned back on the seat.

"Are you angry with me?" she asked him.

"No."

"You sound angry."

A chuckle rumbled deep in his stomach. "I'm not," he told her. "I just want to get you home."

"I didn't do anything with that guy." There was only a hint of slur to her words.

His jaw ticked. "It's not my business."

"I mean, he touched my butt. It was kind of nice, but we didn't go any further."

Gabe tightened his grip on the wheel. "I'm glad to hear it."

"Anyway, he wasn't really a man. He ran as soon as I told him you were my boyfriend."

"What?" Gabe frowned. "Why did you tell him that?"

"It was the quickest way to get him to leave. I was scared you were going to punch him."

They were out on the open road now. There were hardly any houses on this stretch between the two towns, just trees and the mountains beyond, not that he could see them in the dark. "Why did you think I was going to punch him?"

"Because he was touching my butt. Duh."

This time he couldn't help but laugh. This was a whole other side to Nicole he hadn't seen before. She was so much more open with him. Alcohol was her truth serum.

He liked that. Maybe too much.

"Do you think I have a nice butt?" she asked him.

Okay, maybe he didn't like it *that* much. "How much did you drink tonight?"

She started counting on her fingers, frowning when she'd bent six over. "Three cocktails. Maybe nine. I'm not sure."

He chuckled again, shaking his head. She was right about one thing, he had been angry earlier. Well, not angry exactly. Exasperated. It had started with Everley texting him photos of Nicole every five minutes. He'd taken one look at her in that black, flirty dress with her hair like a cloud around her beautiful face and had to try to not get a boner.

In front of his investor and his wife.

Then more photos had followed. Nicole laughing at something Holly had said. Nicole climbing onto the bucking bronco. Nicole riding and whooping with her hand in the air.

Then one of her on the floor when she'd fallen off.

Cam and Mia – his dinner guests – had asked if he had a problem at home, because he was spending so much damn time looking at his phone instead of talking to them. Eventually, he'd explained that he was supposed to be looking after Nicole for his friend, and Cam and Mia had exchanged glances.

"Cam has a sister," Mia had told him. "And he's crazy protective of her. So if you want any advice, he's your man."

Fifteen minutes later he'd sent a message to Nicole saying he'd take her home. And then a while after that she'd called him, her words a taunt he couldn't resist.

If you want me to come home tonight, you're going to have to come get me.

It was like she was born to push his buttons. Every single

damn one of them. And he wanted to pretend that it was only protectiveness that made him say goodbye to Cam and Mia and stalk out of the door into the night air.

But there were no older brother feelings inside him when he thought about her with another guy. Just pure jealousy that scratched and snarled at the pit of his stomach. Sure, he could pretend to Cam and Mia that he was feeling big brotherly toward Nicole.

But he couldn't fool himself.

Her vomiting over his shoes had only added to his bad mood. But then she'd leaned on him as he half-carried her to the booth and apologized so many times he'd lost count.

"I'm so sorry I spoiled your night." She was looking at him with those big doe eyes. A little hazy, but not as unfocused as before. "Your business meeting..."

"Was fine. We got done what we needed to do. I was leaving anyway."

Her face froze. "We need to stop. *Now*."

"You gonna be sick again?" He pulled over to the soft shoulder, thanking God there were no cars behind him. He jumped down from the cab, and ran around to help her down, grimacing as his sock covered feet sunk into the ground. Without bothering to see if she could walk, he hoisted her up and carried her a few feet into the trees.

He wasn't going to take the risk of a car plowing into her while she was throwing up, no matter how unlikely it was. Imagine explaining that to her family.

When her stomach was empty, he passed her a bottle of water and napkin from his car, batting her off when she apologized again. "You feeling any better?" he asked.

"Much." She nodded. "Isn't it weird how that works?"

"Better out than in." He gave her a half smile. "You ready to get back home?"

She looked down at his feet. "Where are your shoes?"

"I threw them in a trash can outside Wild Sally's."

"I would have cleaned them for you."

"No need. I'll get some new ones."

"You could have mine." Her logic was still drunken, even if her words weren't so slurred. She lifted a foot, wiggling her sandal at him.

"No thank you, honey. I'll be just fine as I am."

When he'd gotten her back in the truck, he pulled off his socks and stuffed them in the door compartment. They were too caked with mud to wear anymore.

"You called me honey," Nicole said softly.

He tipped his head to the side. "Yeah?"

"I like it."

Okay then. He restarted the engine and pulled back onto the road, the pedals rough against his feet.

"Gabe?"

"Yeah?"

"Do you think I lack ambition?"

He wanted to laugh again, because her questions were so out there. But there was a vulnerability to her voice that touched him. "Why do you ask?"

"That's what Luke said. That I don't even try to understand what he and my dad are working on. That I should have tried harder."

"Is that the reason he gave for cheating on you?" Gabe gritted his teeth. He'd like to have a chance to talk with that asshole.

"One of many. He also said I didn't take care of him, and that I don't give him enough attention. And that I'm not great in bed."

"The guy who doesn't show you any passion accused you of not being great in bed? Now I've heard it all."

"That didn't hurt as much as the ambition thing. It's a big thing in my family."

"Yeah, I guess it is." He shot a look at her. She was frowning, still staring out of the windshield. "But ambition comes in a lot of different sizes. It doesn't mean winning at everything, or being top in academics. Maybe you're ambitious to make the world a better place. To make people healthy and happy. I can't think of a better ambition than that. And if Luke was fool enough not to see how damn beautiful you are, inside and out, then it's his loss."

"My parents love him."

"Of course they do." He'd heard enough about her parents from Matt to know they had all the wrong values. "But parents can get it wrong, you know?"

"I was okay. It was okay." She was whispering now. "Everybody was happy. It wasn't supposed to end like this."

"Were *you* happy?" he asked her.

Nicole frowned as though it was a trick question. "I..." She let out a long sigh, and for a moment he was worried she was going to be sick again. But she didn't show any other signs. "I finally fit in. For the first time. And that felt good."

He pulled up to his house, the lamp glow illuminating her face. Her brows were still furrowed, as though she was trying to think through his question.

"You know, it shouldn't be this hard to figure out if you were happy," he said quietly.

Her eyes met his. They were shiny. "I just wanted to be loved."

And damn if that didn't get to him. Because she deserved love. So much of it. You only had to talk to her to know she was a good person. She cooked for him. She was kind. She even tried to fight off imaginary burglars in his office.

He knew about loneliness. He'd suffered the worst case

of it once, more years ago than he cared to remember. And most of the time he tried not to remember it. Didn't want to think about the scared little kid he'd been then. He'd grown up, taken up snowboarding, become obsessed by it. Been good at it. And that desire to win had papered over the cracks pretty well.

But they were still there. And hers were, too. Maybe that's why he'd spent so much time avoiding her since she'd arrived.

Because he knew her. And he knew the effect she could have if he let her. He wasn't protecting her, after all. He was protecting himself.

By the time he'd walked around to the passenger side, she was asleep, her head lolling to one side, little grunts escaping from her lips. He left her there and unlocked the house, then went back and unfastened her belt, scooping her into his arms, before carrying her into the hallway, then down to her bedroom. She let out a little moan when he laid her on the bed. He took off her shoes, smiling at the thought that she'd wanted to give them to him, then went to unzip her dress, but thought better of it.

If she woke up naked or in her pajamas, she'd know it was him who'd done that, and he didn't want to embarrass her. Sure, she'd sleep less comfortably in a dress, but he could live with that.

He didn't want to hurt her any more than she'd already been hurt. And from a distance, people might think that was because he wanted to be her savior.

But he was nobody's savior. He couldn't even save himself.

CHAPTER 12

Everything hurt. Her head, her body, even her teeth were throbbing. She groaned and cracked open an eyelid, closing it quickly as the light flooded in. What the hell had happened? Where was she? Her stomach twisted as reality slowly seeped in.

She was in her bedroom. Or rather Gabe's guest room. Whatever you wanted to call it. And her head was pounding like Roadrunner had dropped an ACME ten-ton weight on it.

She sat up, and a wave of dizziness washed over her. Swallowing hard, she opened her eyes again, slowly moving her head to look around the room. She could see her shoes neatly placed by the closet. Her curtains were closed, but sunlight was streaming in through a gap at the top of the rail. And on the table next to her bed was a glass of water, a bottle of painkillers, and a note.

Nicole,

I have to go into work for a meeting. Can you message me

when you wake up so I know you're still alive? Your phone is on the charger on your dresser, and your purse is next to it. Make sure you take some pain meds and drink lots of water. Hydration is important.

Gabe

HE'D SEEN her in this state? She groaned once more, letting her head tip back against the padded headboard. How drunk had she gotten last night? She could remember Dylan picking them up and taking them to Marshall's Gap. And the first few rounds of drinks. And then – oh God – she remembered riding that damn bucking bronco. Her hand instinctively touched her thigh, and she looked down at a dark gray circle on it. Yeah, she remembered falling off the bronco, too.

And then?

Her breath caught. There was that guy who wanted to dance with her. And she'd called Gabe and taunted him.

Oh no. She wanted to die. Or at least disappear for a very long, Jimmy Hoffa amount of time. Because the memory of what she'd done to Gabe's shoes resurfaced.

Screwing her face up, she lifted the glass of water to her lips and sipped it. It was going to be okay. Sure, she'd made a complete and utter idiot out of the guy she was relying on for a place to live.

The same guy who made her feel more alive than she had in years.

But his cousins were just as drunk. She'd been no worse than them.

Yeah, but they're not trying to impress him.

Ugh. She grabbed the bottle of painkillers and took two, chasing them down with a mouthful of water. Her nose wrinkled because it smelled bad in here. Real bad. She needed a shower and to get out of last night's dress, then she'd figure out how the heck to come back from this.

And if she couldn't come back, she'd find a hole to bury herself away in.

THREE HOURS LATER, she walked into the Cold Fingers Café. Her headache was almost gone, and she was feeling fresher, thanks to a shower, followed by a nap and another shower. Dolores took one look at her, and then put a tiny espresso cup under the spout of the coffee machine and pressed the button, then pulled a banana from the fruit tray on the counter, passing them both over to Nicole, having said nothing.

"You heard." Nicole tried not to sigh.

"It's a small town, honey." Dolores' smile was sympathetic. "If it makes you feel any better, Holly looked much worse than you when she came in. And she had her baby with her."

"Ouch." Nicole grimaced. Maybe she didn't have it so bad after all.

"The caffeine and potassium will chase away any hangover," Dolores promised her. "If you're hungry after that, I'll make you a nice sandwich."

"Maybe just a muffin." Nicole blinked, surprised that she was actually hungry. And now she was feeling guilty because her hangover wasn't as bad as it should be.

"A muffin it is. Go sit down. I'll bring it over."

"Can I order a sandwich and coffee for Gabe?" She was determined to make things up to him. Not that a sandwich made up for last night.

"To say sorry about his shoes?"

She winced. "You heard about those, too?"

"Small town." Dolores grinned. "And y'all are the talk of it right now." She saw Nicole's expression and gave her a wink. "It's okay, tomorrow they'll all be talking about something else. That's just how it goes around here. And if it helps, I hear Kyle is pissed that he had to help his momma with something last night and didn't go to Wild Sally's."

That would have been the icing on the cake. Thank the Lord for Kyle's momma.

She was feeling something approaching human after the coffee and the banana. Even better after she ate the muffin. The pounding in her head was muted and the twisting feeling in her stomach had almost gone.

The regrets were still there, though.

It was a beautiful fall day as she drove the coffee and sandwich up to Gabe's office on the side of the mountain. The air was crisp, the sky a deep blue, and the sun's rays made the light snow on the mountain peaks sparkle. She pulled up into the graveled parking lot, filled not only with SUVs and cars, but with industrial vehicles, too. There was no doubt that this was a huge construction site, there was dirt everywhere.

Her ears echoed with the rumble of machines and the higher, almost piercing shriek of saws. The smell of wood and pine was in the air. Nicole grabbed the brown bag that Dolores had given her and made her way into the administration building in front of her.

She gave her name to the security guard, who nodded her through, pointing her in the direction of the directors' offices. There were no frills in here. No carpeted floor or beautiful artwork adorning the walls like in her dad's building in D.C. No designer coffee machine in the reception for visitors, or TV screens on the walls to watch the political news while you waited.

When she got to the main director's office, it was exactly the same. Open plan, with a huge window overlooking the construction zone. It had about fifteen desks in it, though only half were being used. She looked around for Gabe, but there was no sign of him. She stopped at the nearest desk, where a thirty-something woman was typing furiously on her laptop.

"I'm looking for Gabe Winter," Nicole told her. The woman looked up, her brows lifting.

"He's on site." The woman turned and called over her shoulder, "Josh, do you know when Gabe will be back?"

A dark haired man – around Gabe's age – looked up from his laptop. He looked over at Nicole and a smile pulled at his lips. "Hey," he said, standing up and walking over. "You're Nicole." He held out his hand. "I'm Josh. Holly's husband. I've heard a lot about you."

"Oh God, I bet you have. Sorry." She wrinkled her nose.

"If it helps any, you look a hell of a lot better than Holly did this morning."

"Yeah, well you should have seen me a couple of hours ago. Caffeine and sugar saved me." She held up the brown bag. "I brought Gabe some lunch to thank him for last night. Can I leave it here?"

"Let me radio him," Josh said. "He's out on site."

"No, it's fine. I'll just leave it, I can talk to him later." The last thing she wanted to do was make his day harder. She was supposed to be apologizing, not causing him more work.

"Seriously, he'll be pissed if I don't tell him. Hold on." He grabbed a radio from his desk and spoke into it, then smiled at Nicole's bemused expression. "The trees and mountains can cause issues with cellphones. We use the radios because they're easier," he said once he'd finished telling Gabe she was here.

"That makes sense."

The radio buzzed, then Josh held the speaker up to his ear to listen. A moment later he looked at Nicole again. "He wants you to meet him." He glanced at her clothes. She hadn't been in any state to make an effort with how she looked this morning, and was wearing a pair of old jeans and a sweatshirt under her padded jacket. She'd pulled her hair into a ponytail after her shower, and was wearing an old knit cap of Gabe's she'd borrowed as she walked out of the door.

"Do I need to wear protective equipment?" she asked him.

"Nah, what you're wearing is fine. Gabe's just walking one of the slopes, checking it out. They aren't working near there. I'll get someone to drive you up. They'll have a helmet you can wear.

As she was driven toward the mountain to where Gabe would be waiting, Nicole looked around, amazed by the sheer scale of the work needed to turn the mountain into a ski resort. The area at the base was still mostly green, but as she looked up the mountain ahead of her it slowly turned white.

Gabe was waiting for her at the base of a slope. Her heart did a little skip as he turned to face her, a smile pulling at his lips. Like her, he was wearing jeans and a sweatshirt, his feet clad in battered brown engineer boots, and he was wearing aviator sunglasses to keep the solar glare from the snow topped mountains out of his eyes.

As soon as they stopped, he helped her down from the ATV, and she unclipped the helmet and handed it back to the driver, thanking him for bringing her. Gabe smiled when she pulled the cap back on.

"I borrowed it," she told him. "I hope you don't mind. I'm having a bad hair day."

"Not at all. It's good."

She passed him the coffee she'd carefully held on to during her journey up. "It's probably cold by now, so you don't have to drink it."

"Of course I'm gonna drink it," he said, pulling his sunglasses off and placing them in his pocket. His eyes glowed with appreciation. "Thank you."

"It's a peace offering. To say sorry for last night. There's a Rueben in the bag, too, if you're hungry." She held the bag out for him.

"I'm starving." He grinned, opening the bag and looking inside. "You want to take a walk with me? I'm just checking out the slope."

"You sure I'm not disturbing you? I took enough time from you last night."

He glanced at her. "How are you feeling?"

"Better than I should." She followed him up the slope, hearing the rumble of the ATV as it left for the office building. "I'm sorry I was such a damn pain in the ass. I owe you a new pair of shoes."

The slope was wide and gently curving. There was a dusting of snow covering the hard ground at the base, though she could see it got thicker the higher it went.

"It's okay, you offered me yours."

Her brow furrowed. "I did? Why? We don't wear the same size."

Gabe chuckled and took a sip of his coffee. "What do you remember about last night?"

She sighed. Way too much not to be embarrassed, that

was for sure. "I remember calling you. And being a brat." She grimaced. "And then I remember throwing up on your shoes."

"And after that?"

"Not much," she admitted. "Until this morning."

He ran the tip of his finger along his jaw. She could see a shadow of beard growth there. "So you don't remember the ride home?"

She slowly shook her head.

He grinned. "Interesting."

"Oh God, what did I do? Tell me I didn't throw up in your car. I'll have it detailed."

"No, you didn't. Unless you're talking about verbal vomiting. Because there was a lot of that."

Her eyes widened. "What did I say?"

He smirked. "Doesn't matter."

She reached for his arm, her fingers curling around his hard-as-iron bicep. "You can't say that! Did I say something horrible? Was I rude?"

"No, not rude." He pulled his sunglasses back on, and she could see her reflection in the lenses. It looked as horrified as she felt.

What the hell did she say to him that had him smiling like that?

"You can't leave me hanging," she told him. "I can't take it. I'll be wondering all day."

That teasing smile was still pulling at his lips. It had her thinking all kinds of terrible things.

"You were just chatty, that's all," he said, the smile growing wider. "And you asked if I liked your butt."

"I didn't." Her mouth dropped open. "Tell me I didn't?"

"You want me to lie?" He tipped his head to the side.

"I don't know. Yes?"

Gabe started to laugh. "Maybe we should change the subject. I'm not holding it against you. We all say stupid things when we're drunk. I know I do – you can ask your brother if you don't believe me."

His kindness helped. "I won't be saying anything stupid again," she told him. "I'm never letting another cocktail pass my lips."

His gaze dropped to her mouth, then back to her eyes. "You make a cute drunk, if it helps."

A blush stole up her cheeks. "It does. Kinda." Up ahead, the slope turned a corner. "What grade of slope is this?" she asked him.

"Blue. This is the first blue. We'll actually have two when the place is complete. Plus a green, red, and black. And then there's the terrain park for snowboarders we're building on the other side. It's actually more complicated than you'd imagine, trying to get the right level of slope to attract the right kind of people. You need a black run to interest advance skiers and boarders, but most people aren't advanced, so you need to cater to them, too. And the bunny slopes are important, not only because we want to encourage as many people as possible to learn the sport, but because we want to attract families, and having a ski school for kids is the only way to do that." He took a bite of his Rueben, and let out a growl. "Damn, that's good. You want some?"

"I'm not quite at Rueben levels yet," she told him, smiling. "It sounds like there's a lot involved in designing something like this."

"Yeah. It's not just about the right slopes, but about having them sited on the right part of the mountain. And doing it all in as eco-friendly a way as we can. We only use around five percent of the mountain for the slopes, but we still want to preserve as much wildlife and tree coverage as possible. And we also need to plan for when it's up and running, so we need to have the lifts in the right position to get the best throughput possible, and put the resort itself in the right place so that it's easily accessible."

"Is that why the resort will be at the base of the mountain?" she asked him, loving how his face lit up as he talked.

"Yeah. There are already good roads to the base. If we site the parking lots and all the buildings there, we won't have to worry about building roads up the mountain, which is good for the environment and costs."

"When do you think it will all be ready?"

He finished one half of his Rueben, and took another sip of coffee. "We're hoping to open next November."

"Is that possible?"

"It has to be. Our finances aren't unlimited. And this slope is almost ready, and the green one should be finished before the end of the year. I'm hoping we can start testing this one over the winter, that's why I'm walking it now, because once we have a good snow coverage we'll be inviting a select number of advance skiers to test it and give feedback to us. We won't be completely finished by next year but we can at least use what is."

"Will construction stop when it's covered with snow?"

"Not completely. But it will slow down. We have a lot of specialist contractors who are used to working in the conditions, but they can't work in white outs if we get any."

They continued walking, as Gabe pointed out the features they'd incorporated in the slope. "We wanted to make sure there were good pitches and turns. If it's too pristine it gets boring. It needs to be challenging enough without being impossible to navigate."

"I didn't realize so much went into designing a slope,"

she admitted as the gradient increased. It was so good to get some fresh mountain air inside her body. And even better to listen to Gabe get excited over the resort he was responsible for building. "You love it, don't you?"

He smiled again, and it gave her heart a little jolt. "I'm lucky," he admitted. "I wasn't sure I'd find something I loved after I had to retire from boarding. But this had completely consumed me. I'm even luckier, because Josh knows exactly what he's doing business-wise, which gives me a lot of leeway to concentrate on the course design."

"Has Josh done this before?"

"I keep forgetting you don't know about the history with him and Holly." Gabe glanced back down at the buildings. They seemed a long way off, their tiny windows glinting in the sun. "He worked for a real estate business that bought up land to redevelop and sell before he moved here. His company bought Winterville. They'd planned to develop it into a ski resort."

Nicole blinked. "They were going to build something like this over there?"

"Yeah. And we all got together and stopped him. Except somewhere in the mix he and Holly got together."

"I bet *that* was messy."

He laughed. "Something like that. But the good news is that when I had the idea for building this place, he had all the expertise and connections I needed. And I think it gave him a new lease on life, too. He's not needed to run Winterville and he's a guy who likes a challenge. So we work well together. And between us we got the investment we needed – from private investors and some loans."

"How long is it going to take you to pay them off."

"A while. But it's a long term investment. Once we open next year we'll be able to make some better projections."

"I guess it's harder because you'll only be able to earn for part of the year." She was getting a little breathless now, despite her fitness. "How long is the ski season here?"

"End of November to the end of March, if all goes well. But the plan is to make this a year round resort. The ski runs can be used for mountain biking. Plus we have a lake that we can use to attract visitors in the summer. And Josh's suggestion is to eventually build a spa and golf course in the valley."

"I like the sound of a spa." She smiled. "You could have yoga retreats."

His voice was soft. "That's actually a good idea."

They'd reached the part of the mountain where more snow had accumulated. Gabe glanced at her shoes, then back up. "It gets thicker the further up you get," he told her. "Unless you want to ruin your shoes, we should probably stop here."

"They wouldn't be the only shoes I've ruined this week," she said. It felt weird, but she didn't want to leave him. She was enjoying this time with him too much. His enthusiasm for the resort was catching.

She found herself wondering what it would be like to run a yoga retreat here. To have a reason to come back, and see him in the future, once she'd gotten back on her feet. She really wanted to see him again.

"Let's just keep it to one pair," he suggested. "We're trying to be as eco-friendly as possible here. I'll radio down and get somebody to meet you at the bottom of the slope."

"Are you not coming?"

"I have to walk the rest. I want to make sure it's ready. If we get the covering I'm hoping for over the next week, I want us to start testing."

"Will you be the first to try it?"

He grinned. "Of course."

Part of her wanted to take off his glasses, to see if there was a flicker of excitement in his eyes. She knew he was an adrenaline junkie – her brother was the same. You didn't get to compete at world level without having that. And there was something so damn attractive about his excitement.

Not that he needed to be any more attractive. The man took her breath away.

Maybe it was because she was lonely. And somewhere deep inside of her she knew he was out of bounds. She could be attracted to him safe in the knowledge that it would never go anywhere. He'd made that more than clear.

He pressed the button on the radio, and arranged for her to be picked up at the same place that she'd been dropped off.

"Do you feel okay to walk it on your own?" he asked her once he'd got a reply.

"I'm fine. And I don't think I'll get lost. It's pretty hard to go off track here."

He shook his head. "You'd be surprised."

"I guess I'll go then. Let me take that bag from you. No point in traipsing it up to the top."

He lifted his glasses again, and those piercing blue eyes caught hers. "Thank you for lunch. I appreciate it."

"Let me cook you dinner, too."

"You don't need to do that. You paid your penance with lunch."

"I'd like to. I enjoy cooking, and it's boring doing it for one." Then a thought occurred to her. "But if you have other plans, that's okay, too."

"I don't have other plans. Apart from working."

"Does your boss not let you have a night off?" she teased. "You want me to talk to him about that?"

"I wouldn't. He's an asshole."

"I've heard that. But I don't believe it, not for a second."

His radio buzzed and he answered it. The voice on the other end told him the ATV was on its way.

"Dinner would be good," he said, sliding the radio in his belt. "I'll be home by seven."

"Then it'll be ready by seven-thirty." His smile was wider now, and it made her feel glad she'd offered. It would give her something to do this afternoon, and it would make him happy.

A double win.

"You know, if it's the lasagna you made last time, I wouldn't be completely unhappy," he told her.

"And if it's something else?"

He winked. "If it's as good as the lasagna, I'll be okay with that, too."

CHAPTER 13

"Hey yoga girl."

Nicole looked up from the vegetables she'd been checking out in the grocery store. She'd headed over to the big organic market in Marshall's Gap, because the small mom and pop store in Winterville didn't have everything she needed.

Putting down the red poblano pepper she'd been holding, she turned to see Kyle Walker standing behind her, pushing a cart full of beer and chips.

"Hi." She smiled at him. "Planning a party?"

"Me and my brothers are heading down to our folks' cabin for the weekend. Last chance before everything freezes up." He glanced down at the cart. "I'm in charge of food."

"You gonna survive on just chips and beer?"

"The plan is to catch the rest." He shrugged. "I hear you had a few drinks yourself last night."

Of course he did. Was there anybody in a twenty mile radius who hadn't heard about that?

"It's true." She nodded. "But I won't be doing it again."

"I heard you redecorated Gabe's shoes, too." He smirked. "Good going. I wish I'd been there. Next time you'll have to let me know in advance. Or even better, invite me along."

"As I said, there won't be a next time. I'm going to stay in and watch Netflix until I'm sixty."

"That's a shame."

"It is?" She blinked. "Why?"

"Because I was going to ask you to go out with me."

"Oh." She frantically tried to think of something to say to that. "That's very sweet of you."

"Nothing sweet about me." He gave her a cocky grin. "So when should we go?"

She pulled her bottom lip between her teeth, thinking of a way to let him down. "The thing is, I've just been through a bad break up. I'm not looking for anything right now."

"You're still in love with him?"

She nodded, because it was easier than telling him the truth. That she was getting a little bit obsessed by the guy she was living with. "I am."

"Okay." Kyle shrugged. "He's a lucky guy, whoever he is."

"Thank you. I think so, too."

He laughed and grabbed his cart. "I'd better go. We need to leave soon if we want to get to the cabin before dark."

"Have a good weekend."

"Thanks." He winked at her. "You, too."

Gabe ended up leaving the site earlier than he'd planned. Sure, he could lie to himself that it was because he'd finished everything he needed to do, but there was *always*

more to do when you were building a ski resort. The truth of it was, he *wanted* to go home.

He liked walking into the big ranch house knowing he wasn't the only one there. Liked hearing her playing music or seeing her laying on the couch with her e-reader. And today there was the added enticement of the aroma of cooking to greet him when he opened the door. He almost groaned when it hit him. He hadn't had the chance to eat anything since the Rueben she'd brought him almost six hours ago.

When he walked into the kitchen, she gave him the biggest smile, and it made his skin feel like he was touching a live wire.

"I wasn't expecting you home this early," she said. Her hair was pulled back into a high ponytail, and at some point since he'd last seen her she'd put a little makeup on.

She'd changed her clothes, too. She was wearing a pair of black tailored shorts that exposed her long, yoga-toned legs, clinched in at the waist with a thick leather belt, matched with a pale gray silk shirt that she'd tucked in.

Noticing his gaze, she glanced down at her outfit. "I was going to wear pants, but I had the oven and the burners going. It gets hot in here."

"It does," he agreed. "You look good."

"Thank you."

"I'm going to head to the shower. You need me to do anything first?"

"Nope, I got it. You still want dinner at seven-thirty, or shall I have it ready earlier?"

"Whatever works for you."

"I haven't eaten all day so earlier would be good." She gave him a small smile. "I can have it ready in half an hour."

"Then let's do it. I'll open a bottle of wine when I'm dressed."

She grimaced. "I may have to take a raincheck on that."

"Still not feeling great?" He shot her a sympathetic look.

"I'm okay. I just think my body needs a break from the alcohol. But I'm looking forward to eating with you."

He headed down to his bedroom, a little weirded out by how good it felt to have her cooking for him. Especially in those damn shorts. He knew she had good legs – he'd seen them yesterday when she'd been stumbling all over the dancefloor, after all – but somehow the shorts did something more to him.

He switched the temperature in his shower up and tipped his head back, closing his eyes and letting the hot water rush over him. It soothed his skin but did nothing to ease the heavy heat between his thighs. He slid his hand down, fisted himself, and let out a groan.

She was a few walls away. He couldn't do this.

Not even if it'll make you calmer when you're with her?

Yeah, not even then. He'd made a promise and he was going to keep it. And that included fantasies, too. She deserved more than that.

Instead, he reached for his shampoo bottle, washing his hair and rinsing it, the steam filling his oversized shower compartment with a thick fog. Then he cleaned himself and rinsed every last sud out until his skin felt almost squeaky.

When he walked back into the kitchen, he felt more in control. "You know what?" he said, grabbing a beer from the refrigerator. "We should eat in the living room. Put a movie on. Veg out."

"You don't want to eat at the table?" she asked, surprised.

"Nah. Why don't you go put something comfortable on.

You must be exhausted after last night and today." He took a sip of his beer as she pulled a dish from the oven. "I can fill up our plates while you change."

She shrugged. "Okay. I guess yoga pants would be more comfortable."

"And a sweater. It's cold in the living room."

Nicole shot him a strange look. "The fire's on."

"It's still cold. They're forecasting snow this weekend."

"A sweater it is then."

It took her less than five minutes to change. When she walked out, he breathed a little sigh of relief. Sure, she still looked amazing, but at least he wasn't having to stare at her thighs anymore. She'd put on a pair of plain black yoga pants along with a soft gray sweater. With the black sweats and t-shirt he was wearing, they looked like a couple ready to veg out and relax.

"This looks amazing," he said, passing her a plate. She'd made chicken enchiladas, and the aroma of cheese mixed with the spicy enchilada sauce was making his stomach do a little fist bump. There were sides of guacamole and a roasted pepper salad. The whole thing looked like a rainbow on his plate. "I can't remember the last time I ate enchiladas."

"I had a thing about TexMex when I was a kid," she told him, popping a piece of pepper into her mouth. "This was the first dish I learned to cook."

"Well I'm very glad you did." He winked. "Shall we go into the living room? We can choose a movie to watch while we're eating. I'll clean up later."

She gave him a genuine smile. "Sounds good."

He followed her in, carrying his plate and beer. She took a seat in the corner of his sectional, and he sat at the far end, a cushion's width between them. Grabbing the remote, he flicked on the TV and clicked on Netflix, letting it load while he took his first bite of enchilada.

"This is damn delicious," he told her once he'd swallowed it down.

A huge beam pulled at her lips. "I took a gamble on you liking enchiladas. Not everybody likes the spice."

"I pretty much like everything. Too many years having to watch what I eat for competitions. Now I'm making up for it." He took another bite of enchilada, this time adding the guacamole. "Jesus, this is like tasting heaven."

"I have a secret recipe."

"You'll have to share it with me."

"But then it wouldn't be a secret, would it?"

He smiled, because she was grinning too. "Don't you owe me one for ruining my shoes yesterday?"

"Ugh, I thought we'd agreed not to talk about that anymore." She wrinkled her nose.

"You still feeling embarrassed about it?"

She swallowed a mouthful of salad. "Wouldn't you be? The whole town knows. And tomorrow I have to teach three classes and I'm pretty sure they'll all be talking about my night out at Wild Sally's."

"Something else will come along to take their attention away. Charlie Shaw will start smoking again, or Dolores will burn the muffins. You'll be good in a few days." He leaned over to grab his beer. "And if it makes you feel any better, I've made a fool out of myself more times than I can remember when I was competing. I've eaten more snow than I care to think about."

Her eyes were warm and soft. "That doesn't count. Everybody face plants when they're snowboarding on occasion. And anyway, when you're competing there can only be one winner. So it goes with the territory that you're gonna fail sometimes." She leaned forward, her eyes sparkling. "Give me a really embarrassing story and I might feel better. One that hits the heights of being fall down drunk in a bar then vomiting all over your landlord's shoes."

The corner of his lip quirked. "Okay then. When I was fifteen North caught me watching porn."

Nicole's face lit up. "Nooooo."

"Yep. My friend from school stole his dad's DVDs and was selling them for five dollars each."

"Which one did you buy?" she breathed. "Oh this is good. Almost vomit level good. I need to know everything."

"I think it was called *She Likes it Plugged,*" Gabe told her.

"Seriously?" She was trying not to laugh.

He shook his head. "No. I have no idea what it was called. It was like twenty years ago."

Nicole put her plate on the coffee table, then scrambled until her legs were beneath her, and she was sitting on her heels, facing him. "Were you..."

"Jacking off?"

"Yeah..."

He tried not to laugh at her expression. She looked so damn curious about his teenage antics. "I was. We only had a DVD player in the living room, so I had to bide my time. I waited until everybody was out. Or so I thought."

"What time of day was it?"

This time he did start to laugh. "What does that matter?"

"I'm just trying to picture the scene in my head. I need to know if it was day or night."

"I don't know. Early evening?" He scratched his chin, trying to remember. "No, it must have been an afternoon. Friday afternoon. North was playing varsity that year and I thought he'd be at practice for longer than he was. I have no idea where Kris was."

"And your parents?"

"Were probably away. It's a lot with three boys so close in age. Once we were old enough to take care of ourselves they disappeared a lot."

"Okay, so you were watching this... um... *movie*, and you were busy, um—"

"Jacking off," he added helpfully.

Her cheeks pinked up. "Touching yourself. And North comes in. Didn't you hear him come home?"

"I had the volume up *loud*. Turns out these were pirated. The sound quality was shit. And I'd never heard a woman come before. I was interested."

"I bet you were." She leaned closer, her eyes on his. "What did North say?"

"I have no idea. You want me to make something up?"

She started to laugh. "Yes, I do. I need this, Gabe. I need to know I'm not the only idiot around here."

"Okay then." He gave her a solemn look. "He shouted something like 'fuck' or 'no' and I took my hand off my dick and grabbed the remote control. And because I was a horny little asshole, I probably didn't wipe my hand in between."

Her chest was shaking with mirth. "Then what?"

"He took me aside and explained that porn has no basis in reality. That you can't make a woman come just by pistoning your hips. That sex is about treating women like equals, about putting their pleasure first. Then he made me promise to never watch porn again, a promise I've kept to this day."

She was in bits. He loved that he was making her feel better, terrible imitation of his brother's voice and all.

"How old was North at this point?" she asked once she'd calmed enough to speak.

"Seventeen."

She was laughing so much her eyes filled with tears. "He sounds very mature for a seventeen year old."

"Yeah, real mature. So mature he told Kris who then proceeded to tell everybody at school that I'd been caught watching porn with my hand around my dick."

"He told everybody?" she gasped.

"Pretty much. And of course it got back to my parents, who banned me from watching anything on TV for a month."

"Horny teenagers have it so much easier nowadays. All that porn at their fingertips. They only have to open their phones."

"Or harder." He wiggled his eyebrows and she laughed all over again.

"Did you ever get back at Kris?" she asked him.

"I sure did."

"How?" She'd moved closer, her expression rapt.

He shrugged. "That's a story for another day. Let's just say he has his own embarrassing story to match mine."

"Spoilsport."

"I can't give all my secrets away in one night."

"Why not? I want to know them all." Her eyes met his and it made his chest feel tight.

"You really don't. I'll promise you that."

"Okay then, tell me this. Did it really put you off porn for life?" She ran the tip of her tongue along her bottom lip.

Gabe took another mouthful of beer. "I've watched it since. But imaginary North was right, it's not that sexy watching a woman get hammered in a way you know won't make her come."

Nicole blushed again. He kind of liked it.

"How about you?" he asked, wanting to keep that pink stain on her cheeks. "Have you watched porn?"

She blinked, pulling her gaze from his. "Yeah."

Whoa. A pulse of electricity went through him. It took everything he had to stop the blood from rushing between his legs. And no, he wasn't picturing her lying in bed, her lips parted, her hands sliding down her body while she watched a couple do the dirty on her phone screen.

Not him.

"But you're right," she said softly. "Or imaginary North is. It's not the visual that does it for me, it's what happens in my brain."

"Like in the books you read?"

"Sometimes." She finally allowed her gaze to catch his again. "I find it more, I don't know, real, when there's some backstory to the sex."

"You want the hearts and flowers," he murmured.

"I want the connection. And I want it to get to the point where I can't take it unless he kisses her. That's why I like slow burn romances. By the time they get down and wild I'm practically dry humping my pillow."

This time it was Gabe who laughed out loud. "You can be a little dirty, can't you?"

"Sometimes." She grinned. "But don't tell anybody. My reputation is already in tatters."

"What's a slow burn, anyway?" He changed the subject because the thought of her being dirty was a little too enticing.

"It's a romance where the hero and heroine don't get together until way into the story. You know they're attracted to each other, and they have this amazing banter, and maybe a few near misses, but neither of them will admit that they have feelings for each other."

"Like the opposite of porn then."

She grinned. "I guess."

"We should choose something to watch." He grabbed the remote again and began to scroll. "What kind of things do you like? Other than porn."

She laughed again. "I don't know. You choose."

"You may not like what I choose."

"Then I'll just have to put up with it." She grabbed her empty glass and headed to the kitchen, reappearing a minute later. He'd found a 'Movies of the 2000s' category, and was scrolling through it.

"Come on, help me out here," he said, as she walked past him and slumped back on the sofa. "What do you feel like? Horror? Gangster? Something lighter?"

"Not horror. I won't be able to sleep alone."

Noted. "How about this?" he said, landing on *The Bourne Identity*. "You can't go wrong with an action movie."

"Sounds good. I don't think I've seen it."

"What?" He frowned. "Where have you been for the last fifteen years? Have you seen any of the franchise?"

She shook her head. "I don't think so."

"What were you doing when you were a teenager?"

"Not what you were, obviously." She grinned, and it made him laugh. "When did it come out?"

He pulled up the information box. "Two thousand and two."

"That explains it. I was five years old. Probably not the target demographic."

"You were five?" He blinked.

"Yeah. How old were you?"

"Twelve."

"So while you were getting horny and watching action movies, I was starting kindergarten and learning to read."

"When you put it like that, I'm thinking it's probably past your bedtime."

"Seven years doesn't make so much of a difference once you're both adults." She reached across him to take the remote, her soft fingers brushing his. "But it sounds like I need an education on Bourne. Let's watch it."

CHAPTER 14

Nicole lifted her phone to her ear as she opened her car door and threw her equipment bag on the backseat. It was snowing lightly, and she was wearing her thick puffer jacket and warm boots over the top of her workout clothes. Gabe had been right, the snow had finally started here in the mountains, and it made everything look so pretty.

It wasn't as though she hadn't seen snow before. She'd grown up in D.C. where they got plenty of the white stuff every winter, after all. But it was one thing seeing it pushed to the side of city streets, little piles of white covered in dirt, and another to see it whiten the mountain sides and lay on the rooftops of pretty houses.

"Mom?" she said, when the call connected. "Hi."

"Nicole, I saw you called me. Is everything okay?" Her mom sounded harassed as always. She was probably running between meetings or about to head into the lab.

"I called on Tuesday. Just to say hi." She climbed into the driver's seat and turned on the engine, flicking the air to warm.

"Oh. I only saw the missed call now. But you are all right?" her mom asked.

"I'm fine. Just wanted to check in with you guys. See if you're okay."

"We're good. No change here." Her mom covered the mouthpiece and said something that Nicole couldn't hear. "Your dad's research is going well. Did he tell you he's being given an award at a gala next month?"

"I haven't talked to him." She'd left him a message, too. She felt more removed from them than ever. It was hard not to feel like the little girl she'd once been, waiting hours for one of them to pick her up from an after school club because they'd gotten too tangled up at work.

"We're all very proud. When I get more details I'll let you know. You'll be coming, won't you?"

"Um. I'm not sure."

"Luke will be there." Her mom's voice softened. "Maybe you two can talk about things?" she said hopefully. "Sort out this mess between you."

"I don't think I'm ready."

"Oh Nicole." Just two words and she felt like she was being rebuked. And yes, she could tell her mom the truth, but her mom would tell her dad because they told each other everything.

And the mess would be terrible.

This was the problem with having scientists for parents. They thought everything was a logical puzzle to solve. They didn't take into account human emotions or frailties, and they certainly didn't understand Nicole. It was better not to give them any information yet.

"Is Dad's research going okay?"

"Oh yes. He's pretty much camped at the university right now. I've told Luke to make sure he eats every eight hours or so. Hopefully things will calm down soon. After Thanksgiving, maybe." Her mom barked a command at some poor unsuspecting employee. "You're coming home for Thanksgiving, right?"

"I'm not sure."

"I've asked Luke to come," she said hopefully.

So that was it. Nicole couldn't go. "I'm teaching yoga classes, I don't think I can take the time off."

"I hope you and Luke will sort this little spat out between you two soon. It feels messy and I don't like it."

Nicole took a deep breath. "What if it's not a little spat?" she asked, her voice wary.

"What do you mean?"

"What if I don't want to be with Luke anymore?"

"What's this about, honey?" her mom asked, and for a moment it felt like she wasn't alone in the mountains. "Actually, hold that thought. I have a video conference with one of our suppliers. I'll call you later."

Before Nicole could say anything else, her mom hung up. And maybe that was a good thing, because she'd been dangerously close to telling her the truth about Luke. And she couldn't do that, she just couldn't.

But now she felt more alone than ever as she drove back to Gabe's house and parked under the bare, snow dusted branches of the sycamore tree. Gabe's truck was in his usual spot. For once he'd made it back before her, and for some reason it made her feel better.

If he was home she wouldn't have to think about her parents or Luke. Or the fact that they never would understand the choices she made.

Music was blasting throughout the house when she walked through the front door into the warm hallway. Gabe was in the kitchen, dressed in his usual at-home outfit of sweats and t-shirt, this time all gray. He was leaning over the counter, writing something down on what looked like a map. When he heard her he looked up, an infectious grin on his face.

"Hey."

"Hi." She pushed down the memory of her phone call with her mom and smiled, because there was something about this man that always made her feel warm. "What are you doing?"

"I'm making a plan. We'll have enough snow by Saturday to have our first test runs on the green slope."

"That's amazing." She walked over to him, sliding her hands around his waist, her palms pressing against his warm back. He hesitated for a moment, but then he was hugging her back, his thick arms pressed against the top of hers. She could smell the scent of his shower gel – he must have showered when he got home from work – and it made her remember that she hadn't.

She quickly pulled back. "I need to go clean up."

He gave her a strange look that she couldn't quite read. "You ready for more Bourne tonight?"

They'd been making their way through the franchise all week, though they'd had to skip a few nights when he worked late. She loved the way he got so excited when certain scenes were coming up and he'd tell her she had to watch them, his eyes glued to her face as the action unfolded onscreen.

"Sounds good. Shall I make us something to eat?"

"I got it. I've ordered take out from the Inn. I'll go pick it up while you're in the shower."

"Are you sure?"

He blinked. "It's no big deal to pick up food, Nicole. You cook for me enough, let me feed you for a change."

"Let me pay for half at least."

"Nicole..."

"I know that tone."

The corner of his lip quirked. "Good." He looked at her for a moment, and she wondered what he was thinking.

Probably that you look sweaty and disheveled from three private lessons in a row.

"What size are you?"

Okay, she wasn't expecting *that*. She let out a surprised laugh. "What?"

"You ski, right?"

"Yeah?" She nodded. "But I'm not an expert."

"I want you to come try the trail out with us on Saturday. I got some friends coming, and family, of course. I want you there, too. I figure you don't have any ski stuff here."

"You're right, I don't."

"Then I'll get you some. I just need your sizes."

"It's okay, I can get my own." She thought about her ski pants and jacket hanging up in Luke's closet back in D.C. There was no way she was asking him to send them to her. She'd just buy a new set – find something cheap online.

"I'm asking you to do me a favor by trying out the slope. I wouldn't expect you to pay for your own clothes to do it. It's a business expense, I'll put it through the books." He sounded firm. She kind of liked that.

"Okay."

"And anyway, if you're staying here for a while, you'll need ski gear. I hit the trails most weekends when the snow comes in." He tipped his head to the side. "Do you ski cross country?"

"Yeah. But it's hard work."

He laughed. "I figure if anybody can take it, it's you." He

grabbed his keys and his phone. "I'm going to get the food. Go take a shower, Batman, you stink."

She laughed, because she recognized her own words being thrown back at her. She liked the way he teased her. "Thanks. I will."

THE RESORT PARKING lot was clear, the snow pushed into large banks at the side of the blacktop by one of the huge industrial snow plows they had lined up on the far side. There were at least forty cars here, most of them SUVs with racks attached so the owners could easily attach their ski equipment to the top. She climbed out of her car and walked over to the office building, opening the glass door. She'd finished her classes at twelve and showered at the Inn, then driven straight here.

There was no security guard at the brand-new reception desk, so she made her way to the main office where she'd seen Josh when she'd brought Gabe lunch the morning after vomiting on his shoes. That was empty, too, but through the huge windows overlooking the mountain she could see a group of people standing in the snow, and another group closer to the slopes.

She walked outside, pulling her coat tightly around her. The air had turned icy in the past few days, and though she had a winter coat on it didn't seem quite warm enough.

"Nicole!" Holly called out. "You're just in time to watch Gabe board down the slope." She looked cozy in a thick coat and wool hat with a pompom on top, and thick furry boots. She had a pair of binoculars in her hand. Next to her was a stroller where Candace was sleeping peacefully beneath a blanket. With her other hand, Holly rocked the handle to make sure she stayed that way.

"I made it in time? I thought you'd already be in the middle of testing." She'd beaten herself up for not being here to see them start, but work had to come first.

"Gabe spent most of the morning walking his friends down the slopes and taking their suggestions in. You probably know some of them, right?"

"If they're snowboarders, maybe. I met a few when I'd watch Matt compete. But I haven't done that for a while."

"Oh, he's about to start. Want to watch?" Holly offered her the binoculars.

"I couldn't take them from you."

"Ah, I've seen Gabe board a billion times. He's a show off. Take them."

Taking the proffered binoculars, Nicole lifted them to her eyes, blinking as they adjusted to the lenses. The fir trees that had seemed so far away before felt like they were only inches away now. She could see the detail in their fronds and the snow blanketing their branches. She had to move the binoculars a couple of times before she found Gabe, and she smiled as she watched him joking with the guy next to him as he pulled on his helmet and goggles, then clipped his feet into his board.

"These binoculars are good," she murmured.

"Right? Josh bought them when he moved here permanently. He has a thing for looking at birds. Oh, and when you've finished watching Mr. Cocky, he says you have to suit up and I'll get someone to drive you over to the slope. He left strict instructions to get you there as soon as possible." Holly glanced at her from the corner of her eye. "I'm guessing he's forgiven you for throwing up on his shoes."

Nicole laughed. "Thank goodness."

"I knew he would. Gabe's one of the good guys."

"I'm starting to see that."

Gabe pushed himself off, powder spraying in front of him as his board hit the snow. There was something so easy and natural about his stance. He looked almost like he was part of nature, and that the board was part of his body. He was wearing black snowboard pants and what looked like a green pullover coat, his goggles shining in the sun. His hands were by his side, his body crouched enough to keep his balance, as he lazily slid from side to side.

And then he turned, picking up speed as he throttled down the slope. He hit a bump and rose up, then hit the snow again, powder blasting everywhere, and the guy next to them let out a whoop.

Nicole's mouth was dry. "He's good."

"Did you ever see him compete?" Holly asked.

"A few times. In Oslo was the first time, I think."

"Twenty-twelve?" Holly asked. "I was there, too. I'm surprised we didn't meet."

"It was the only time my parents went to watch my brother compete. I think I was fifteen at the time. We couldn't stay long because my dad had to go to some symposium in Geneva. I tried to catch up with Matt when I could, but I've mostly watched him in the U.S."

Gabe reached the bottom of the slope, leaning left to slow down, and come to a graceful stop. Somebody ran over to him – a woman – and threw her arms around his waist. When Gabe took his goggles and helmet off, he was grinning at her.

It felt like she was watching something she shouldn't. And if she was being honest, she didn't want to watch it. Seeing him hug someone else made her feel weirdly jealous.

And that was stupid, because he was allowed to hug who he wanted.

"Oh, that's Ally Waters," Holly said looking through the binoculars after Nicole had passed them back. "Do you know her? She's a boarder, too."

"I don't think so. Is she new?"

"Been around for a few years. She's taken a year off to finish her degree. I didn't know she was coming today."

"She and Gabe look close." She couldn't help it. It hurt, but she wanted to know what was happening.

"They had something a year or two ago, I think. But then Gabe has something with most people." Holly shook her head, smiling. "He attracts women like flies."

Of course he did. He'd done it to her, after all. She was an idiot, because she'd thought she was special. That he'd chased her to Marshall's Gap because he liked her.

But she was just most people. Gabe was nice to her because she was staying in his home.

And she was his best friend's sister.

"I should go get changed," she said to Holly, forcing a smile on her lips. "Where did you say my ski gear is?"

CHAPTER 15

As soon as Gabe saw her climbing off the snowmobile he walked over to her and helped her off. She was wearing the ski suit he'd ordered for her, and damn if that didn't make him feel good. It was white with black stripes down the sides of the arms and legs, cinched in at the waist with a thick belt. She looked like the winter version of Uma Thurman in *Kill Bill* and damn if that didn't do things to him.

"How was work?" he asked her, letting go of her hand. He was all too aware that people were watching. People who knew her brother, and who had loose lips. He didn't want them seeing something that wasn't there.

"Good." She smiled at him, her eyes soft. "I got here in time to see you board down the slope."

"You did?" He smiled because he liked that she'd been watching him. "What did you think?"

"Holly called you Mr. Cocky."

"Holly's jealous because she's not skiing today. And I don't care what she thought, I want to know what *you* think."

She pulled her bottom lip between her teeth. "I thought you were fantastic."

"Good." He winked. "Right answer. Now do you feel ready to try it out? I've had some advance skiers go down earlier, I need intermediate next."

"You want me to go now?" Her eyes widened.

"Yeah, if that's okay. We'll drive you to the top on the snowmobile, Josh and a couple of our guys are up there. Wait for their signal then ski down. We'll be videoing you so we can see if there are any hazards or turns that are too tricky. And when you get to the bottom Josh has a whole spreadsheet of questions he wants you to answer. Just be straight with us, whether it's too hard or too easy. That's all we need from you, okay?"

She swallowed. "Okay."

There was something about the way she said it that touched him. "Are you nervous?"

"It's just you have all these expert skiers and snowboarders. I don't know why you want *my* opinion on it. They know better than me."

He leaned closer, pulling his glove off and pushing a stray lock of hair behind her ear. She swallowed again, her lips slightly parted.

"That's exactly why I want you here," he said softly. "Because you're the type of person we want to come back again and again. Someone who skis for pleasure, not to win every time. Somebody who enjoys the ride." He gave her a half smile. "I seriously want your opinion. I trust you to tell me the truth. All the rest of the people here will tell me what I want to hear. But not you. I know you don't bullshit me."

Their gazes connected, and he found himself cupping her jaw with his palm. She let out the softest of sighs.

"Can I trust you to do that?" he asked her.

She nodded, saying nothing, her pretty eyes still locked on his.

"Okay. Let's do it." He stepped back and beckoned one of their snowmobile drivers over. "Can you take Nicole to the top?"

HER NERVES only got worse when she reached the top of the slope. Josh was waiting for her, a walkie talkie in his hand, and he beckoned her over as she lifted her skis and helmet from the snowmobile.

She wasn't exactly a novice. She'd skied since she was a child. Learned on the bunny slopes of Boulder Ridge, an hour north of Washington D.C., and on the winter vacations her family would take in Europe. But Matt had always been the breakout star of the family. Her skiing was adequate but nothing amazing. Her style was elementary at best.

"Did Gabe tell you that we want you to fill out a questionnaire when you reach the bottom?" Josh asked, as she clipped her skis on.

"Yeah, said I should make a note of anything I think doesn't fit an intermediate skier."

"Great." Josh smiled. "Okay, if you'll make your way to the top, just wait for my call so we can have the cameras running."

"Are you filming from the base?"

"Yeah, but we're also putting a Go Pro on you. That way we can see it from your point of view, too."

"What if I fall?" That was her worst fear. That she'd make an idiot out of herself in front of all these experts.

"That's fine. We'll take a look and see if it's due to the

slope or operator error." He winked. "And if it's really bad one of us will call the medics."

"Operator error meaning me," she said, giving him a wry smile.

"Yeah. It'll happen a million times once we open. People fall when they ski. So relax and try to enjoy it. It's not often you get to try a slope on the first day."

She made it to the top, and pulled on her helmet and the Go Pro camera Josh handed her, then waited for Josh's signal. When he nodded, she took a deep breath and pushed herself off with her poles, feeling the smooth slide of her blades as she began her trek downhill.

She took it easy. Not just because she was afraid of making an idiot out of herself, but because she'd never been one to hammer it down fast. Matt had always done that, even from her earliest memories she could remember watching him with a mixture of awe and fear. She'd been the one who stuck to the bunny slopes for too long. Who had to be practically dragged to the blue slopes by Matt when he insisted she was good enough.

And now she was making regular turns, slowing down her momentum to a speed that didn't feel too scary, glad that her helmet meant nobody could see the anxious expression on her face.

It took her way longer than felt acceptable to reach the bottom of the slope. She turned again, powder kicking up as she slowed to a stop, and she sent a little prayer up to the Gods of skiing, thanking them for keeping her upright all the way.

Gabe walked over. Her hands shook as she took off the Go-Pro and tried to undo the strap to her helmet, missing the clasp twice. He batted them away softly, then unfastened it, pulling the helmet from her head and looping it under his arm.

She shook her hair out and took a deep breath. He was looking right at her, his brows knitted.

She handed him the Go-Pro and looked over her shoulder at the slope. "Did I do okay? I know I was slow, but I'm a bit rusty. I haven't skied for a couple of years."

"You were great." His voice was soft and low. "You're better than you think. It was really good to watch you, I saw a couple of boulders that I might need to move. You avoided them easily, but I'm not sure a less experienced skier would've."

She was still shaking. She curled her hands around the poles to try to hide it. "I need to complete that questionnaire."

"It can wait." He reached out to tip her chin up until she couldn't avoid his eyes. "I just want to know if you're okay. You're shaking. It's worrying me."

"I was nervous as hell," she admitted. "So scared I was going to fall in front of you all."

"It wouldn't have mattered if you did." He shook his head. "Who told you that you have to be perfect?"

"My parents?" It was a joke, but it fell kind of flat.

He shook his head, his eyes narrow. "You ever listen to that song by John Legend? The one about perfect imperfections?"

"Hasn't everybody? It came out when I was sixteen. I swear my friends listened to it constantly."

He smiled. "You should listen to it again. Being perfect isn't interesting. It's not sexy. It's your imperfections that make you the person you are."

She felt a little flutter in her stomach. "Like getting drunk at bars?"

"And being cute as hell on the ride home, yeah."

"I was cute?" She frowned. "You never did tell me what I said. I wish you would."

He mimed zipping his lips. "What happens in Marshall's Gap stays in Marshall's Gap. Anyway, you know what I mean. Stop getting anxious about not doing everything right. Sometimes you gotta be a little bad."

She laughed, and it felt good. "Like you?"

"Maybe." He lifted a brow. "Come on, let's get you some hot chocolate, then you can fill out that questionnaire, okay?" He put his free hand on her shoulder, and she wished her suit wasn't so padded. She wanted to feel his warmth against her skin.

Instead, she forced a smile on her face as she nodded at the people she recognized, and let Gabe introduce her to those that she didn't.

"Matty Rice's baby sister!" one of the guys called out, as Gabe walked over to watch the next skier. "I remember you when you had train tracks on your teeth."

"You're Matt's sister?" another said, giving her a wink. "My commiserations."

"Do you snowboard, too?" Ally asked her, giving her a bright smile.

Please don't let her be nice, as well as pretty, and talented.

Nicole shook her head. "No, we let Matt take all the glory for that."

"That's big brothers for you." Ally grimaced. "I have three. They're all idiots, but I love them anyway."

"And you have us," one of the guys – Ben – said, looping his arm around Ally's neck. "It's like having a hundred big brothers."

"Don't I know it." Ally grinned. "These guys are the bane

of my life. I don't miss them one bit now that I'm taking a break."

"But you'll be back next year," Ben reminded her. "Better than ever, right?"

"That's the plan." She shrugged. "But it won't be the same without Gabe." She looked over at him, her eyes softening, and Nicole's stomach twisted. She was exactly the kind of girl that Gabe should go for. She loved his sport, she was fun, and easy going.

And she hated that thought.

Gabe walked back, running his hand through his hair. "We've got another couple of skiers to go," he told the group. "Then I'll let you idiots have fun with it."

"You're not going to tell us to board down carefully and avoid going off course?" Ally asked, tipping her head.

Gabe chuckled. "Would you listen to me?"

"No."

"Then I won't bother. And you signed the waiver, so that's that."

"There was a waiver?" Nicole asked. "I don't think I signed it."

"Because you're not stupid enough to go off course." Gabe lifted an eyebrow. "Thank God."

"Imagine what Matt would say." Ally raised an eyebrow. "He'd kill you if you let her."

Gabe shot Nicole a glance. "My thoughts exactly."

She didn't like the way that made her feel. Like she was a kid not getting picked for a sports team.

They started talking about the time Matt sprained his wrist – a time she didn't even know about, thanks Matt – and she was only half listening as the ice-cold wind whipped her skin.

She could see exactly what he saw in Ally. She was so happy and vivacious and at ease in a group of men. Not many women could infiltrate a gang like that, but she did it with ease.

"You okay?" Gabe asked her, bringing her out of her thoughts.

"I'm a little cold. I might head back to the office and join Holly." Nicole glanced behind her. "Can you spare a driver? Otherwise I'll walk."

"If you hang around a while longer I can drive you."

She blinked. "No, it's fine. You're busy, I can take care of myself."

He looked at her carefully then nodded. "Okay."

She said goodbye to Gabe's friends, and Ally gave her a hug.

"Are you coming out with us tonight?" Ally asked.

"Tonight?"

"We're gonna hit the Tavern. Gabe's coming, and all the guys. You should join us, it'll be fun."

Her smile wavered. Gabe hadn't mentioned it. "I can't," she lied. "I have other plans."

"You ready?" Gabe asked, tapping her on the shoulder. He was holding the plastic cord that started the snowmobile in his hand.

"Didn't you find somebody to drive me?"

"I can do it. Josh has control at the top and we have plenty at the bottom. We're almost at the end of the trials anyway." He inclined his head at the snowmobile. "Come on."

It was a smaller version than the one that had brought her here, and he told her he'd bring the skis she'd used back separately. They put their helmets on, and Gabe climbed onto the front, and she slipped on behind him, looking for something to hold on to that didn't include the man ahead of her. She found the handgrips and curled her fingers around them, trying to keep as much space as she could between them.

He started the engine with one hand, keeping his other on the handlebar, then pushed the throttle with his thumb, and the machine lurched forward. Her body gave a jolt, enough to force her fingers from the handgrip.

"Shit!" For a moment she thought she was going to fall, then she grasped at the fabric of his coat and steadied herself. Gabe slowed the speed, and turned around.

"You okay?"

"Just lost my grip," she shouted back. He reached behind him and grabbed her hands, pulling them around his waist.

There was enough padding between them for her not to feel anything but the rough waterproof fabric of his coat against her face as she rested against his back. But it still felt too intimate. Like she was hugging him, and he was letting her. She was a mess of emotions and she had no idea what to do with them all.

She had no idea when she started falling for him. Was it when he'd come to the bar to rescue her? When he'd told her his most embarrassing experience? Maybe it was everything, all tiny pieces of a puzzle that had slotted together to make her feel like she could breathe for the first time in years.

And she knew he didn't feel the same way. Why would he? He was giving her a place to stay as a favor to her brother, nothing more. Sure, he was kind and funny and, yeah, maybe there was an ounce of attraction between them. But he'd never go there, he'd made that clear.

Holding onto him, breathing him in, knowing that in a few moments she'd have to let go felt like some kind of sweet agony. She closed her eyes, pressing her helmet against his back, and inhaled softly, feeling little pin pricks of tears stinging at her eyes.

She couldn't do this anymore. Her mom was right, she should go home. Face her demons and go back to the life that she was supposed to live.

Not this fantasy world where she was falling for her brother's best friend, in some kind of savior worship. Because he wasn't supposed to save her.

She had to save herself.

When they reached the office building, everybody had moved inside. Standing around in the cold had probably gotten to be too much. She released her hold on Gabe and unfastened her helmet, climbing off and handing it to him. He took it and stowed it behind him, then unfastened his own, his blue eyes catching hers as he ruffled his hair into some semblance of normality.

"Are you okay?" he asked, his voice uncertain.

She swallowed. "Yeah. Why?"

"You were quiet all the way back." He gave her a half smile. "That's not like you."

She glanced down at her boots. "I'm just tired. It's been a long day. I'll probably head home now... I mean back to your house."

"It's home," he said softly. "For now."

She took a deep breath. "Okay, I'll head home."

He looked at her for a moment, as though he was trying to work her out. "A few of us are going out tonight. Just to the tavern. You want to come?"

For some reason she didn't want to tell him that Ally had already asked her. "That's very sweet of you, but I think I'll stay home. I need an early night."

His brows knitted. "You sure?"

"I'm sure."

"Okay then."

She lifted her hand in goodbye and turned around, then a second later turned back. "Gabe?"

"Yeah?"

"If you, ah, wanted to bring anybody home tonight. That's fine with me."

He blinked. "What?" He sounded almost angry. She took a deep breath to center herself.

"If there's a girl you meet tonight and you want to, you know, get to know her better. Ally or somebody." She couldn't meet his eye. "I don't mind. It's your house, you have needs and I'll probably be asleep."

"I'm not bringing somebody home to fuck while you're there." He frowned, shaking his head. "What the hell?"

"Would you do it if I was a guy friend staying?" she asked. It was like playing with a scab, it hurt but she needed that pain. "If I was Matt?"

"What does that matter?"

"We're friends, right? If either of us, I don't know, has an urge or something. It's okay."

"So this is about you?" His eyes narrowed. "You want to bring a guy back? Who is it, Kyle?"

"Kyle has his own place."

His jaw tightened. "You didn't answer my question."

"It was just hypothetical," she told him. "We're grownups, we're both single, we can do what we want. And if you meet somebody you like, then go for it."

"I'm not bringing a girl back tonight." His voice was gruff.

Good.

"Okay then." She backed up. And then she had to keep at it, only to make the pain worse. "You can stay out, too. If that's easier."

"Where the hell has this all come from?" His blue eyes pierced the distance between them.

"It's just…" She shook her head. "I don't know. Maybe we should have had this conversation when I moved in."

"You'd just caught your ex cheating. I'd assumed you wouldn't be jumping on the next available guy." His voice was icy. "Maybe I'd assumed wrong."

He'd taken it all wrong. She meant him, not her. She opened her mouth to explain but his radio buzzed. He listened, his lips pressed into a tight line, then gave a gruff, "I'll be there in five." He turned to her, the frown still pulling at his brow. "I have to go, we'll talk about this later."

"Sure." Except she planned on being asleep when he got back. And when he went out again. And tomorrow she'd take a long hard look at herself. It was time to grow up, to face the problems she'd run away from.

Because she couldn't keep feeling like this.

CHAPTER 16

An hour messing around on the mountain with his friends wasn't enough for him to shake off this weird mood the conversation with Nicole had put him in. He was pissed with her, pissed with his reaction, and he couldn't work out why it had put him in such a foul mood.

When the sun started to go down behind the mountains, he'd called them down, much to the annoyance of his friends.

"Come on, one more run."

"It'll be dark by the time you get up there. Insurance doesn't cover it. Sorry." Gabe shrugged.

"It's okay, we need to go clean up anyway." Ally smiled at him. "What time are we all meeting?"

"Seven?" Ben suggested. "We'll need to eat though."

"I'll book a table." Ally smiled. "Just need to take a headcount."

"You coming back to the Inn with us?" Ben asked. "We can get a head start on the drinking."

"Nah. I need to finish here, then I'll head home and shower. I'll meet you at the tavern when I'm done."

"You eating with us?" Ally asked.

"Not sure. If I'm not there in time, go ahead without me."

It took another hour to close everything down and make sure all their equipment was back at base. He'd sent Josh home to join his wife – Holly and the baby had left earlier – along with the rest of the team, promising he'd lock up and they'd talk about the results on Monday.

By the time he climbed into his truck he was exhausted, and in desperate need of a shower. He'd taken his ski gear off and left it hanging in the wet room, and pulled on the sweats and t-shirt he'd worn in this morning.

When he got back to his place he saw Nicole's car in the driveway, and that feeling of annoyance washed over him again. Had she been trying to get him to agree to a new arrangement? Did she want to start bringing guys home? The thought of bumping into some stranger in the morning, knowing exactly what they'd been doing the night before, made him want to punch something.

No, that wasn't going to happen. He'd have to make it clear to her. Nobody was bringing anybody home, and nobody was staying out all night with somebody else.

His body was full of tension when he opened the front door, his eyes blinking as they adjusted to the gloom of the hallway. He flipped the light on and closed the door behind him, frowning when he saw that the living room was empty. She wasn't in the kitchen either, so he headed to her bedroom, tapping lightly on the door.

"Nicole?"

There was no reply. He touched her door handle then froze. He couldn't just walk in there. Not after that first time. Instead he knocked again, a little louder this time.

"Nic? You okay?"

"Hey." He hardly heard her voice through the door. "I'm okay."

"Can I come in?" he asked.

"Sure."

He pressed down on the handle and pushed the door open. She was curled up on her bed, wearing a pair of yoga pants and a black sweatshirt. Her hair was pulled back into a messy bun, and her face was resting on her clasped hands.

"Sorry, I fell asleep." She stretched her arms out like a cat. "What time is it?"

"Almost seven. You had something to eat yet?"

"Wasn't hungry." She sat up, then frowned as her stomach gurgled. "I guess I am now. I'll make something in a while."

"You could still come out and eat with us."

She smoothed a stray hair from her face. "Naw, it's okay. I had a headache when I got home, and I don't want it to come back. There's food in the refrigerator, I'll be good."

"You sure you won't get bored?"

"There's always Netflix."

He narrowed his eyes. "Don't watch any Bourne without me."

She started to laugh. "I thought about it, then decided it wouldn't be fair."

"Good." His expression softened. "If I said something that upset you earlier, I'm sorry."

"You don't need to be sorry. I didn't make myself clear. It was a stupid conversation anyway."

"Yeah it was. Nobody's bringing anybody home."

Her eyes met his, but she said nothing.

"Right?" he prompted.

"Well since you're the only one going out, I think that's up to you."

"Nic…"

"I was serious earlier. Holly said you and Ally used to have a thing. She seems nice. If you want to bring her home, that's fine. It's your house."

He didn't know why he was so pissed with that suggestion, but he was. "This is bullshit."

Her eyes met his. "What's bullshit?"

"You. Talking about my sex life. Like you have this damn fixation about it."

She blushed. "I don't."

"Then why do you keep pushing me? All this talk of bringing home women or staying out or whatever other suggestion you've had."

"I just don't want to be a cockblock."

He raked his hand through his hair. "You're not a cockblock, Nic. And you know what? If I want to look at a pretty woman, all I have to do is turn around and there you are. Every goddamn time."

Her mouth dropped open.

"What?" he said, annoyed by her surprise. "You don't think you're pretty?"

"I…" She frowned. "I…"

"Come here." He reached his hand out and she took it, looking bewildered, as she let him pull her off the bed. He was still furious, and he had no idea why. So he took it out on her, pulling her over to the mirrored doors on her closet, turning her around so she was staring at herself.

He was right behind her, so close he could feel the hitch of her breath.

"Look at yourself."

She looked at him over her shoulder instead. "Why are you so angry?"

"Because you have this idea that I'm some kind of

manwhore who can't go a day without sex. But you know what? I've had you in my house for weeks and I haven't so much as touched you. And look at you, you're exactly my fucking type. Curvy in all the right places. Beautiful as hell. If you think I can't go a night without controlling myself near a woman, then you're crazy, because I've been doing it every damn night since you got here."

She turned back to the mirror. "Gabe..."

"No, don't say anything. I'm already pissed with myself. I shouldn't have said that." He released her shoulders, and she took a deep breath, her body rigid in front of him.

She was looking at his reflection in the mirror, her brows furrowed as though she had no idea what to say. Nor did he. He'd done it again, let himself lose it with her. And now he regretted it.

So much.

"I need to go out now," he said, his voice thick.

"Yeah."

"Don't let anybody make you feel less than you are, Nic. Not even me."

She nodded.

"I'm sorry." He stepped back, shaking his head. "Fuck it, I need to get out of here."

"Have a good night." Her voice was soft. She was still watching him, her eyes full of questions. Ones he wasn't sure he had the answers to.

Space. That's what he needed. Some time away from her. Because living with her was messing with his head.

And he was one step away from making a move they'd both regret.

SHE COULDN'T STOP THINKING about what he said. Or the way he'd felt, standing right behind her, his breath hot on her neck as he made her look at herself.

I've had you in my house for weeks and I haven't so much as touched you. And look at you, you're exactly my fucking type. Curvy in all the right places. Beautiful as hell.

He'd looked angry as he said it, and it had touched her. Because he was trying so damn hard to be a good guy.

Even if she didn't want him to.

She couldn't push him out of her mind. Not even when she was making herself an omelet and eating it in front of some inane TV show she barely watched. She had no idea what she was going to say to him when he got home.

Maybe she'd be in bed.

Yeah, maybe she would. And maybe in the morning he wouldn't mention it again. But it didn't stop his words from warming her. Knowing he felt this attraction as much as she did gave her a grim sense of satisfaction.

And at the same time it made her want things she couldn't have. Because she knew he was Matt's friend. He had a conscience and that was a good thing. She'd stop pushing him. She had to.

She cared about him too much to do anything else.

Scraping what was left of her dinner into the trash, she put her plate in the dishwasher and cleaned up the kitchen, shocked when she realized less than an hour had passed since he left.

In an attempt to stop thinking about that moment in front of the mirror, she grabbed her yoga mat and cued up some relaxing music on Gabe's stereo, determined to make herself relax.

It had been a weird day, but it was over now. She just needed to push it all away. Half an hour of meditation would help, it always did. And tomorrow she'd focus on her problems and work out what she was going to do with her life.

It had taken years for her to be able to meditate for thirty minutes without thoughts seeping back in. She concentrated on her breathing, on letting the oxygen into her chest, letting it expand before exhaling through her lips, counting the breaths, then doing it again.

She could feel the tenseness of her muscles, the tautness of her spine. One by one she relaxed them, keeping her breaths rhythmic and long, pushing the thoughts away every time they tried to invade her mind. By the time the thirty minutes was up, she felt like herself again. Calm, easy going. Able to face anything she had to. Letting out a final exhale, she opened her eyes, a smile pulling at her lips.

She had this.

Then she felt a prickle on her skin, itching at her neck. She put her hand to her throat, rubbing it softly, and turned to look at the living room door.

And saw Gabe leaning against it, his blue eyes trained on her, his dark hair a mess like he'd been pulling at it.

When her heart stopped exploding out of her chest she let her eyes meet his.

"Hi."

He pushed himself off the door. "Hi."

"I thought you'd be out for longer."

"It was dead in the Tavern. They all decided to go over to Marshall's Gap. So I came home."

"To Wild Sally's?"

"I'm guessing." He raised a brow.

"You could have gone. I would have come and picked you up if you'd gotten too drunk. I'd even let you ruin my shoes."

His lips twitched. "That's the best offer I've had all night."

"I very much doubt that."

He didn't say anything, just watched as she rolled up her mat and straightened her pony tail. She clipped the bungee around the mat to keep it secure, then looked up at him, her brows knitted.

"Are you okay?"

"No, I'm not. I'm sorry. I haven't stopped thinking about what I said to you. I should have kept my mouth shut."

"It's your house. You're allowed to say what you think in it." She pulled her lips together. The fact was, she'd liked hearing him say it. She just didn't like the way he kept fighting.

He nodded. "You want to watch some more Bourne?"

"Yeah, that sounds good." It really did. "But I need to take a shower first."

"Go for it. You stink."

She flashed him a smile and walked past him, her heart feeling so light she wondered if it was going to fly out of her chest. He'd come home to spend the rest of the evening with her instead of going to Marshall's Gap, and it made her feel good. And now they'd watch a movie together and this weirdness would disappear.

Which was a good thing. It was.

She walked to her bedroom, hearing him pop the cap of a beer, and stashed her yoga mat under the bed before heading to her bathroom. Folding her towel onto the rail, which was warm, thank you God, she pulled her clothes off and threw them into the hamper, then reached into the shower to turn the water on, because it always took a moment or two to warm up.

The shower head was angled upward, and she figured

the housekeeper must have done it when she'd cleaned earlier that day. Nicole reached in to adjust it, but she pulled it too far and ice cold spray washed over her face and body.

Shrieking, she reached for the handle and yanked it, her eyes widening as the damn thing came off into her hands. Freezing water was still shooting out of the shower head right onto her body, knocking the breath out of her as she attempted to put the handle back on, only to realize it had sheared off and there was no way to reconnect it.

"Shit." She pushed the spray head down so it wasn't soaking her so badly.

The bathroom door opened. "You okay? I heard screaming."

She turned to see Gabe in the doorway, his eyes widening as he saw her glistening body, and the shower handle in her hands.

"It fell off."

He grimaced, his eyes averted as though he was desperately trying not to look at her. "Can you get out? I'll take a look."

She climbed out of the cubicle and grabbed her towel, wrapping it around her body. Gabe reached in, water soaking his shirt and jeans as he leaned in and angled the shower head, trying to see how to connect the handle.

"Damn that's cold. Can you turn the water off? The shut off is in the kitchen, under the sink." He was leaning down, and water was pouring over his head, making his hair look almost black in the light of the bathroom.

Nicole clutched the towel around her and ran to the kitchen, her wet feet skidding on the tiled floor. Yanking open the cupboard beneath the sink, she grabbed the lever on the pipe, turning it clockwise until she heard a thud.

"It's off," she called out, heading back to her bedroom.

Gabe was still in the cubicle, but he'd taken his shirt off and thrown it into a pile of wet fabric on the floor. His back was to her, his muscles rippling as he turned the handle over to inspect the sheared metal. Water was dripping off his hair onto the floor.

He was beautiful. She couldn't help but stare at him, even though she knew it was wrong. His shoulders were broad and thick with muscle, his shoulder blades moving as he tried to refit the shower handle in vain. His body tapered down, in a long, defined line to his waistband, and the jeans he was wearing were soaked through.

Clinging to his behind.

Slowly, he turned around, his brows pulled together when he caught her gaze. But she couldn't pull it away. She felt frozen on the spot, blood racing through her veins, a little pulse fluttering between her legs.

What would it be like to have a man like this touch her? He was strong enough to pick her up off the ground and push her against the wall, and the thought of it made her cheeks flame.

Gabe swallowed, his eyes still capturing hers. Then they dipped, to her lips, to her bare shoulders, to the line of towel where it barely covered her breasts. The fluttering turned into a persistent throb, making her want to squirm in front of him.

"The water's off," she said softly.

"I noticed." His brows knitted, as though he was confused.

"You're wet."

The corner of his lip flickered. "I noticed that, too." He put the shower handle down. The waistband of his jeans was low on his hips, heavy with the weight of the wet fabric, but it was his torso that drew her eye, because she hadn't seen anything that beautiful in a long, long time.

His stomach was washboard flat, rippled with muscles all the way to his tight pectorals. His skin was wet and tan, his nipples tight and dark, and everything about him made her body heat up.

She let out a little noise, somewhere between a squeak and a growl. And that pulse between her legs quickened. Gabe's eyes raked down her body, then back to her face, with a quizzical expression on his own as he stepped out of the cubicle toward her.

A weird thought took hold of her mind. That if she didn't touch him soon she might die. She curled her fingers into a fist to stop herself from reaching for him.

Her teeth started to chatter, where the cooler air met her damp skin. Gabe took a step closer, blinking as he reached for her towel. For a moment she thought he was going to take it off, but instead he tightened it around her, tucking it in with deft fingers, leaving a trail of need across the swell of her breasts.

"You should put some clothes on." His voice was tight.

"So should you."

Her gaze flickered to his. The blue of his eyes had almost disappeared, the darkness of his pupils taking over.

"I'm wearing clothes."

"Not enough of them," she said softly.

He blinked, and she could see droplets clinging to his lashes. She reached up to brush them away, and he held himself as still as a statue, his breath catching in his throat.

"Nicole." His voice was rough.

"What?"

"You need to get dressed." His jaw tightened. "*Now.*"

"Or what?"

His mouth twisted, as though he was in pain. He parted his lips, then shook his head. "Or... I don't know. Nothing."

She was so tired of this push and pull. So tired of being the good girl. Fighting something that seemed so inevitable it was exhausting, and she wasn't sure she could do it anymore.

Wasn't sure her body would let her, even if she tried.

"Or what?" she said again, taking a step closer to him. She reached out and traced the curve of his shoulder, tracing her finger from the top of his arm to the dip where it met his neck. Gabe closed his eyes, his breathing soft, his lips trembling.

She pressed her thighs together, need pooling deep inside of her. Then she traced down to his chest, her finger circling his nipple. His eyes flew open at the same time he grabbed her wrist, yanking her toward him until her towel scratched against his bare skin. She lifted her head to look at him, and she could see so many emotions rushing through his eyes.

The same ones she felt.

Desire, need, confusion. And maybe a little bit of anger, too. He dropped his brow until it touched hers, the water from his hair dripping over her. He sighed, and the warmth of his breath suffused her. Then he ran his hand down her back, tracing the top of her towel, the dip of her spine, before he cupped his palm over her behind.

She'd never felt more feminine than she did right now, being in the arms of this strong, muscled man. Never felt more aware of the difference between them, or of the connection that made her body sing with need.

"This can't happen." He pulled her closer against him, and she could feel the hard ridge of him against her stomach.

"I know," she said softly.

"I made a promise. To take care of you."

"That's all you need to do. Take care of me." She looked up at him, and he shook his head.

"You're Matt's sister. I can't…"

"Nobody owns me, Gabe. Not Matt, not my family, not anybody. I'm mine, that's all. Just me." She ran her finger along his jaw, feeling the roughness of his beard growth. "We're adults. We're single. Nobody gets hurt here."

She pressed her thumb against his lips, her breath catching when she felt the soft, wet skin inside. He groaned and sucked at her softly. The sensation sent pleasure straight to her groin.

He dragged his tongue over the pad of her thumb, fluttering against her skin, and a strangled sigh escaped her lips. Then he pulled her hand away from him and leaned into her, pressing his lips against the dip in her throat, kissing her softly.

"We're playing with fire," he murmured against her skin.

"We are."

"I'm not good for you."

"Yes you are. So good."

He scraped his teeth on her neck, and she let out another sigh, arching her back with pleasure. He dipped his head further, kissing her shoulders, her chest, running his fingers along the fold of the towel where it covered her breasts.

They lingered on the seam, where he'd tucked it tightly in on itself. "If Matt finds out…"

"He doesn't need to know," she breathed. Need for him was heating her skin, making slickness pool between her legs. He dragged his hand down to her waist, cupping it, as he dipped to his knees and took her towel with him. "Nobody does."

"I'm not good at relationships," he told her. "I can't make you any promises…"

"I don't want promises," she told him, closing her eyes because he felt so damn good. "People only break them. I don't expect anything from you. Just touch me. Please."

Cool air rushed to her naked skin, and for a moment they were both silent, the only sound in the room was their breathing. His eyes drank her in, his gaze roaming from her face to her shoulders, narrowing as they took in the swell of her breasts. Then he continued his appraisal, taking in her stomach – almost flat, but still with a little curve – and the scant hair that covered the achiest part of her.

When he got to her thighs, she felt them clench. A spark of pleasure washed through her. "Do you know how long I've wanted to touch you like this?" he asked, his voice thick.

"Not as long as I've wanted you to touch me." She closed her eyes as he ran his hands up her calves, his thumbs brushing the back of her knees. He put a little pressure on her, enough for her to part her legs, then he let out an approving grunt.

"You're so damn beautiful." He pressed his lips to her leg. Nowhere near where she needed him. "When I first saw you, I thought you were a little gift just for me. It made me crazy that I couldn't have you because you're so my type." He kissed the inside of her knee, then the base of her thigh, his fingers digging into her skin in the most delicious way.

"You have a type?" she gasped as he dug his teeth into her skin, then sucked the aching pain away.

"Yeah, it's called trouble. And you're the most trouble I know." He'd reached the top of her thighs. She was so wet she knew he had to be able to see it.

"I'm a good girl."

"That's what I said. Exactly my type. And fucking trouble with a capital T. Do you know how many times I've touched myself, wondering what your skin feels like? Wondering what you taste like? Wondering if you'd scream my name as I made you come?"

"Now you don't have to wonder," she told him. "And I'd definitely scream your name."

A strangled groan escaped his lips. She twisted her fingers into his hair, pressing her pads against his scalp. "It's okay," she whispered.

"It's very far from okay, Nicole." His breath was there. Right where she needed him. And she realized he hadn't even kissed her. Was he going to make her orgasm before they'd even touched lips?

She'd never felt so dirty. Or so right.

He looked up, his eyes catching hers. "Tell me to stop."

"No."

He squeezed his eyes shut. "Do you know how good you smell? How much I want to lick you until you can't remember your name?" He pressed his mouth to the crease of her thigh, kissing her softly. "Tell me to stop, Nicole, before we both go crazy."

There was conflict in his eyes. He wanted to stop and he wanted to keep going. He wanted to make her come and he wanted her to disappear. There was a fever to his gaze that made her feel like she was so powerful. In complete control.

She could stop him with a word. But she didn't want to. She'd spent her whole life doing the right thing, and look where that had gotten her. And this wasn't wrong, it really wasn't. Sure, Matt might be pissed, but he'd get over it.

If he ever found out.

And this felt too good. In a way she'd never felt before.

Gabe wasn't taking, he was giving. There was so much power to him, in his muscles, in his demeanor. And yet he was giving it all to her.

And she was taking it. No promises. No way to break them. Just two people giving into the attraction between them.

"Gabe?"

He pulled his lips from her thigh, his breath catching as though he was waiting for the word.

For her to tell him to stop.

"Make me feel good," she whispered. "Make us both feel good."

CHAPTER 17

The words had barely escaped her lips before he was sliding his hands beneath her, picking her up so her breasts were pressed against his hard chest. She hooked her legs around his waist, feeling breathless as he walked forward until her back slammed against the cold tiled wall, his own breath short and harsh as his lips finally crashed into hers.

He'd never wanted anything as much as he wanted Nicole Rice in this moment. He wanted to touch her, to taste her, to feel her fluttering around him. He'd been fighting this feeling for so long he hadn't thought about what would happen when he finally lost the battle.

When, not if. Because this was as inevitable as breathing.

She was achingly beautiful, her body smooth and lithe beneath his touch. But there was a core of steel there, one that took as much as it gave, and it sent a shiver of excitement down his spine.

He leaned close, needing to kiss her again, the throb between his thighs a rhythm getting harder to ignore. She curled her hands into his hair, rubbing his scalp so deliciously he found himself moaning into her mouth, then she hooked her legs around his waist and he could feel her warm wetness against his stomach, where his jeans lay low on his hips.

He wasn't going to last long. Not after all these weeks of denial. Of watching her bend and stretch and use her body like it was a tool designed specifically to torture him.

Abstinence had never felt so damn painful.

"Kiss me again," she whispered, and he did exactly that, his tongue demanding entrance between her lips, a soft groan escaping as she yielded to him. She was soft in places he was hard, smooth where he was rough. She curved her body against his, and he could feel the tautness of her nipples against his skin.

He dipped his head to capture one, slicking his tongue across it before sucking it in, and it was her turn to cry out, her fingernails scraping his scalp as she pulled him closer. Then he kissed and sucked at her other breast, smiling to himself as her cries got louder, because he'd dreamt of this moment for way too long.

No, not dreamt. Fantasized. Imagined her calling his name as he touched himself to oblivion. And that fantasy had been good, but it was nothing compared to the reality of her, against him, her fingers teasing and soothing, her body warm and inviting and so damn needy.

Carrying her into her bedroom, he lay her on her mattress, her wet hair splaying out on the covers. He tugged his damp jeans off, leaving him only in his shorts, before joining her on the bed.

He kissed her stomach, then her hip, tracing the jut of it with his lips. Then he moved back, kneeling on the bed, his eyes dark as he took her in again.

Pale skin, dark nipples, thighs open wide enough that he could see her glistening. He leaned down and blew against her, and she gave a satisfying groan. Damn, he needed her. He pushed his hands against her thighs, spreading her out before him, and if he thought he was hard before, it was nothing compared to now. She was glistening before him, her hips moving in a rhythm that only she knew, and he slid his hands up to spread her legs further, before dipping his mouth to her core.

His cheeks brushed the warmth of her thighs as he pressed his mouth against her, and from the corner of his eyes he saw her fingers fisting the bedsheets. Then he licked her, soft at first, until she was begging him for more. Then harder, sucking her in, getting drunk on the taste of her.

He slid a finger over her, and she cried out, letting him in. He added another, moving inside of her as he continued to suck and lick at her clit. She was crying out, begging him for more, not to stop, telling him how much she needed him, and he gave a satisfied grunt, and curled his fingers against the place he knew would make her feel good.

She fluttered around him, her hands digging into his scalp, as she called out his name, telling him she was close.

He added a third finger, and she was so damn tight around him. She arched her back, getting even tighter, and he reached his other hand to touch her breast, his thumb and finger plucking her nipple until she practically lifted herself from the bed, her sweet body holding his fingers in a vice grip as she plateaued for long, pleasured moments before crashing down, her panting voice repeating his name.

She pulled at his face, and he moved over her, taking in her glassy eyes, her swollen lips, the hair mussed over her cheeks. He gently pushed it away and leaned in to kiss her, his mouth full of her taste. She kissed him back, pressing her body against his, letting the ebbing waves of pleasure wash over her.

He was aching to be inside of her, especially when she rocked her body against his. She kissed him again, her mouth warm and inviting, then she slid her hands down his back and tugged at his shorts.

"You have a condom?" he asked her.

She shook her head. "You?"

"In my room."

"Go get it," she whispered. "Please."

He'd never run so damn fast in his whole life. He was half afraid that by the time he got back she'd have come to her senses and know what a bad idea this was. But when he returned she was still laying on the bed, her cheeks blushed, her hair fanned out around her. Gabe ripped open the foil and slid the condom on, swallowing because even his own fingers felt too good right now.

He climbed over her, kissing her again because he could never get enough of her. Every cell of his body was tingling with desire. The tip of him found her almost immediately, and when he pressed against her she let out a soft sigh.

"You sure?" he asked her, their eyes meeting.

"Yes," she said softly. "Get inside of me now, Winter."

He didn't need telling twice. He took it slow, though, because he knew from his fingers that there wasn't a lot of room in there. She was so warm and so tight, like a velvet glove wrapped around him, and he had to still himself to stop from spilling into her right there and then.

He brushed the hair from her face and cupped her jaw with his palm. "You okay?" he asked her when his hips scraped hers.

She slid her hands down his back, her eyes dark and deep, then squeezed his ass until he began to move.

Her thighs wrapped around him, pulling him into her, as he rocked his hips, slowly picking up the rhythm. She felt so good, so tight, and she was so damn loud it made his blood heat up, as she dug her fingers into his ass and kissed him hard and wet.

"Gabe..."

"I know."

"So good."

"I know, Nic." He was on the edge, so close but not ready to fall. He concentrated on her lips, on kissing her jaw, on sliding his mouth to her perfectly pink nipples. When he dragged it between his lips, she let out another cry, her chest arching against him. He reached between them, finding the center of her pleasure, circling it with his thumb as he moved deeper inside of her.

Her cries were getting louder, and he wanted to memorize every one. Her thighs tightened around him, so he had to almost fight her to move, and she cupped his face as he kissed and sucked at her breasts. Then he felt her tighten, right as her breath caught in her throat, before it tumbled out of her lips in a long, plaintive cry.

He moved his head up, swallowing her pleasure with his kisses, tangling his tongue with hers until he felt the tremors die down. He was so close to falling with her, as she spasmed around him, bringing him to the edge until there was no way back.

"So good," he groaned. She was beautiful. She was staring up at him like he'd put the damn moon in the sky, her lips parted as he felt his whole body tense, pleasure coiling in his belly like a snake about to attack. It had never felt this good before. So intense, so real. He didn't want this moment to end.

She tightened around him again, letting out a cry. Had she been coming this whole time? The thought turned to black, as his spine straightened and he let out a deep groan, spilling inside of her, his mouth crashing against hers.

He dipped his head, his brow touching hers, their eyes connecting as pleasure suffused him.

He cupped her face tenderly, his kisses turning soft, her mouth curling beneath his. Emotions crashed down on him, filling him up until he could barely breathe. He stayed inside of her for a moment, savoring the connection, knowing it had to end.

And dreading that it would.

When he couldn't wait any longer, he pulled out, removing the condom, before twisting and tying it. Then he blinked as he looked at her. The light was shining on her face, making her skin look golden. Her hair was fanned out like a halo, framing her perfect beauty.

"I need to..." He gestured at the condom.

"But you're coming back?"

He blinked. Did she really think he was going to fuck her and leave her? "Yeah, I'm coming back."

Her smile was like the sun. "Good."

He shook his head, his own smile way too big for his face, and walked over to the bathroom, wincing when he saw the carnage in there.

Tomorrow he'd call a plumber. But tonight, was about her.

～

THERE WERE AT LEAST a million reasons why this was a bad idea. Gabe looked down at her as she slept, his brows pressed together. She was curled on her side, her hands pressed together like in prayer beneath her cheek, her lips softly parted with her regular breaths.

He'd fallen asleep, too, at some point, exhausted from their second round, even though this time she'd been the one to ride him, as he looked up at her, taking in every perfect curve of her body.

It wasn't just that he'd promised Matt he'd take care of her. Yes, Matt would be pissed, not that Gabe intended on telling him. But it was more than that. She was living in his house. If something went wrong – and it almost certainly would – he would have taken away the only safe haven she had right now.

And at some point she was going home to Washington D.C., and he was staying here.

He laid on his back, flinging his arm over his face. God knew he hated mess.

There were other things, too. She was just out of a long term relationship. And the breakup had been so bad that she'd skipped town. Sure, he didn't know all the details – he didn't want to know them – but he knew enough to understand that deep inside she was hurting.

He didn't want to add to that. She was a good person. She made him smile, made him laugh. For the first time in forever, this house felt like a home. He looked forward to coming back to it after a day at work, got excited when he pulled into the driveway. Loved smelling the aroma of whatever she was cooking that day, and seeing her soft smile when she noticed him walk into the kitchen.

Nicole muttered something, and he turned to look at her. Her eyes were still closed, her lips slightly moving. Was she a sleep talker? He blinked, leaning closer, but all he could hear were her soft breaths again.

He'd spent most of his adult years avoiding intimacy. It made him wary, afraid. Like it was a foreign language he'd never master. He'd watched his cousins fall in love fearlessly and been so happy for them, but he'd never wanted that for himself.

Never wanted to be that vulnerable to pain. Because he knew what pain was. Knew that he couldn't protect himself against it, let alone anybody else. He'd spent a lifetime building that wall to make sure there wasn't a chink of light there. Yet that wall had been damaged with every relationship he'd had.

And maybe that had been his intention all along.

"Gabe?" Nicole murmured. When he looked at her again, her eyes were open. She gave him a soft smile, and it made his chest feel strangely tight.

"You okay?" he asked her.

"Yeah. You're not leaving, are you?"

He shook his head. "Too cozy here." He pulled her into his arms, and pressed a kiss against her warm brow. "Go back to sleep, Batman. I got you."

CHAPTER 18

She kept looking at her phone, and that was a bad thing, because she was supposed to be in savasana, along with her class. It was almost one in the afternoon, and this was her last class this Sunday. And thank goodness, because every muscle inside of her ached like a bitch.

Gabe had woken her up at seven that morning, his hot, needy mouth moving against hers. She'd pulled him close and deepened the kiss, then they'd made love all over again, before he headed to the office for a shower, and she'd come here and used the gym bathrooms.

She knew he was working today – collating the data they'd gotten yesterday from all the practice runs, but she was still half-hoping he'd call her. Her screen remained annoyingly blank, though, and she had to give herself a good talking to.

He wasn't her boyfriend. He didn't owe her anything. They'd gone into this as consenting adults and she wasn't going to be clingy about it. She'd promised him that.

"Okay, slowly bring yourself back to consciousness," she

said, keeping her voice low so she didn't startle the class. They were a young crowd – and a few of them looked hungover from Saturday night fun.

She felt a little hungover herself. Not from alcohol, though, but from Gabe. Her body ached, and her brain felt mushy, like she couldn't quite follow her own thoughts.

Or maybe she didn't want to. Because last night had felt so good. The way he'd held her all night as she curled against his body. She wasn't usually a snuggly kind of sleeper, but somehow she'd been dead to the world in his arms. She'd felt protected and safe, and that was a strange thing to feel in the arms of a one night stand.

When class was over and she'd closed up the studio, she hefted her bag over her shoulder and walked up the stairs to reception. Alaska was at the desk, and she waved her over. Nicole formed a friendly *I didn't just do the deed three times with your cousin* smile on her lips.

"Hey. How did the test runs go yesterday?" Alaska asked her, leaning on the desk. "I wanted to come along but our receptionist called in last minute. Her husband and kids have stomach flu." She grimaced. "It doesn't sound pretty."

"It was good. The slope is amazing." Nicole put her bag on the floor. "I felt rusty though. I need to go skiing more."

"Hang around here for long enough and you will." Alaska grinned.

Nicole's phone started to beep. Excitement warmed her but then she saw the name on the screen.

Kara.

For a moment she thought about ignoring it, but Kara would keep trying until she answered. Nicole flashed a smile at Alaska and held her phone up. "Sorry, it's my sister. I should take it."

"Sure. I need to go make some calls from the office anyway." Alaska nodded. "I'll catch you later."

Grabbing her bag and putting it back over her shoulder, Nicole lifted a hand in goodbye then accepted the call.

"Hello?"

"Hey. Sorry I missed your call last week. I was on nights. How are you doing?"

"I'm good." She smiled because though they had very little in common, she did love her sister. With nine years between them, Kara had left for college before Nicole had made it out of elementary school, so their relationship never had the depth of the one Nicole had with Matt. "How are you?"

"Stressed. Trying to juggle work and some studying along with planning a wedding. And Mom keeps calling worried about Dad because he's over working again." Kara sighed. "Sorry, I'm offloading. I'm supposed to be asking if you're settling in okay."

"You can offload, it's fine." Nicole walked across the lobby, her sneakered feet slapping against the marble floor. "I'm sorry I'm not there to help with your wedding." Kara had asked her to be the maid of honor. She really should be taking some of the burden.

"I was hoping we could talk things through at Thanksgiving, but Mom says you're not coming."

Nicole swallowed. "Yeah, I don't think I can get away. I'm teaching yoga at a local hotel and there's nobody I can find to fill in and take my classes for those two days. Maybe you can email me? I can help with things from here"

"Is it because Luke will be there?"

Nicole let out a breath, pushing the lobby door open, cold air rushing over her skin. "That's not the only reason."

"I saw him the other day. He says you've blocked him on everything."

Nicole blinked. "You saw Luke?"

"I was at Mom's. He came over to pick up Dad's phone because he'd forgotten to take it. Don't you think you should speak to him? He looked like he hasn't been getting much sleep."

She bet he hadn't. "I'm not ready."

"Did something happen? Did he hurt you?"

Her chest contracted. "Nothing happened. We're just growing apart. Wanting different things."

"Oh." She could picture Kara blinking, trying to compute her words. "Mom's really hoping you two will sort things out."

Opening her car door, Nicole slid her bag onto the passenger seat, then followed it inside. She leaned her head back against the head rest and closed her eyes. She needed to change the subject and fast. "Tell me about your plans for the wedding. What colors did you settle on?"

WHEN SHE GOT BACK to the house, there was a big white van parked outside, with Raymond's Plumbing Services emblazoned across the side. Nicole pulled up beside it and climbed out, stepping lightly across the driveway to the front door.

Inside, she could hear voices coming from her bedroom. She put her bag on the floor and pushed the bedroom door open, blinking when she saw two guys in overalls in her bathroom, one of them kneeling down and looking at the exposed shower pipes, the other handing him tools as he called out for them like a surgeon. The tiles had been removed from the cubicle, exposing the interior of the wall.

Just outside the bathroom, standing by her dresser, was Gabe's older brother, North. He had a cell phone pressed against his cheek. "Yeah, got it. She's here now, actually." His eyes flickered to Nicole's and he gave her a smile. She smiled back.

"Okay. Just a sec." He pulled the phone from his ear and offered it to her. "It's Gabe. He wants to talk to you."

"Oh sure." She took the phone and gave North a confused smile. "Hello?"

"Hey. Sorry you just walked in on the plumbers. I was supposed to meet them at the house, but things had overrun here. I got North to let them in."

"That's fine. It's your house." She was aware of North's gaze. Could feel it warming her skin.

"You okay?" Gabe's voice was soft.

"Yeah, I'm fine. I just got back from the Inn."

"You feeling sore?"

"Not from yoga, no." She looked up. North's head was inclined, like he was trying to listen in.

"I'm not sore from yoga, either." She could hear the smile in Gabe's voice. "Anyway, they've looked at the shower and it's going to take longer to fix than I'd hoped. They have to replace the whole mechanism. Can you believe it's from Germany? It's going to take a week to get the parts in."

"Oh. Do we need to move out?"

"Nah. They're isolating the pipes to your bathroom then they'll turn on the rest of the water. My bathroom will be working, so we can share that for a while."

"Are you sure? I can move out if it's too much trouble."

"I'm certain, Nicole." His voice was firm. "It's a minor inconvenience, but hopefully you can live with it."

"I was more worried about inconveniencing you."

"Having a pretty woman use my shower every morning is no inconvenience. Seriously, it's all good. I just wanted to warn you, that's all. I'm sorry we can't get it repaired faster."

"I'm sorry I broke it in the first place." She ran the tip of her tongue over her lip. It was strange how good it felt to hear his voice.

"I'm not. I'm glad you did."

Her breath caught. "Yeah, so am I."

"You gonna be home tonight when I get there?" he asked her.

"That's the plan."

"I'll see you then." It sounded like a promise. One that made her feel more than warm inside.

"Okay." She couldn't help the smile that pulled at her lips. "I'll pass you back to North." She held the phone out and he took it, his eyes full of interest as he looked at her.

He put the phone back to his ear. "It's me. I'll settle up with the repair guys and you can owe me. If you drop in on your way home I'll give you all the details." Gabe must have replied, because there was silence from North.

"'Kay, bye." North hung up, and she looked around her bedroom, not sure what to do with herself with so many guys around.

"Can I get you guys something to drink?" she asked them. "Coffee, soda, something like that?"

"I'd love something cool," the guy kneeling in the shower called out.

The other guy looked up with a smile. "Can you make coffee without water? It's still switched off."

"I think there's some in the machine still."

"In that case, I'll have a coffee, please. With milk but no sugar."

"Sure." She glanced at North. "How about you?"

"I'll come help you."

He followed her to the kitchen, and grabbed a can of soda from the refrigerator, along with the milk carton. Nicole grabbed a coffee pod and slid it into the machine. "Did they say how long the water would be off for?" she asked him, putting a cup under the spout.

"Another hour or two." He leaned his long arms on the countertop. "If you need a shower or something, you're welcome to come to mine."

"It's okay. I can wait." She offered him a smile. "You run the Christmas Tree Farm, right?" She wanted him to like her. He was Gabe's brother, after all. And that meant something to her.

"That's right." He lifted a brow.

"I guess it's coming up to your busy time."

"Yeah. We're ramping up right now. We have a few private commissions before Thanksgiving, but it'll start getting crazy once that's over. We ship to retail outlets throughout the state, as well as selling trees in our own shop."

"It must be fun. Everybody loves Christmas."

He lifted a brow. "You should see the arguments people have trying to decide which tree to buy. It can get violent."

"Seriously?" She grinned, pressing the button on the machine. "People get that worked up over a tree?"

"You'd better believe it. I feel like a tree farmer and a relationship counselor all wrapped into one sometimes."

"Well you're obviously good at it." Gabe had told her that the farm was thriving. It was easy to see how proud he was of his big brother.

"Thank you." He watched as she poured milk into the coffee, then grabbed the soda and led her back into her bedroom. Taking the cup from her hand, he passed the drinks to the plumbers then brushed his palms clean on his jeans.

"I'm gonna head out, if you're okay to wait around until they've finished up," he said to her.

"That's fine." It was the least she could do. She'd broken the thing in the first place. "I can pay them, too."

North shook his head. "Gabe's asked me to pay, and he'll pay me back."

"But I'm the one who broke the shower. I should pay for the repair."

"Hey, I'm only doing what I'm told. Take the rest up with Gabe." North held his hands up good humoredly. "What's it gonna cost do you think?" he asked the plumbers.

"Three hundred for today, and then we'll invoice the rest once we've ordered the parts and have a delivery date."

North pulled his wallet from the back pocket of his jeans and peeled out a wad of twenties. "There you go."

The plumber took it from him and placed it in his bag. "Thanks."

"And you have my brother's details for the invoice?"

"Yep."

"Great." North turned to Nicole again. "You sure you're okay?"

"I'm good. Thank you for stepping in, I appreciate it."

"Any time." He tipped his head to the side. "You know, you should come to the farm sometime. We'll show you around."

"I'd like that." She grinned, because this whole damn family was so nice. "Thank you."

He said goodbye to the plumbers, and then she walked him to the door. Her own family could be hard to deal with, but Gabe's were a delight. And for now she'd take that.

"THREE HUNDRED," Gabe said, folding the bills into his brother's hand. "Thanks, man."

"Any time." North took the money and slid it into his wallet. "So, they think the parts should be in by next Friday if you pay for expedited shipping. They've booked themselves in for Monday and Tuesday, so it should be up and running before Thanksgiving."

"I still can't believe it will take so long." Gabe shook his head. "Thank God I have another bathroom."

"Gonna be weird sharing it with Nicole though." North glanced at him, his brows lifting. "All that hair in the drain and all the bottles of shampoo and conditioner and shower gel on the shelves."

"Nothing I didn't endure when I was competing. I had to share a lot of bathrooms then." Gabe shrugged, knowing his brother was trying to bait him.

"Yeah, with guys. Not with a beautiful woman."

"Is she beautiful?" Gabe asked, shaking his head. "I hadn't noticed."

North laughed. "Of course she is. And exactly your type. Athletic, sweet, and all that brown hair. The only downside I can see is that she throws up on your shoes."

"She did that *once*. And you better not have said anything about that to her. She's embarrassed enough about that."

North looked at him curiously. "You're very protective of her."

"Of course I am. I promised Matt I'd take care of her."

North coughed into his hand. "I don't think that's exactly what he meant by taking care of her."

"What exactly are you trying to say?"

"Whoa. No need to get angry. I'm just being a big brother. Looking out for you."

"If you hadn't noticed, I'm thirty-two. I'm getting pretty good at looking after myself. You don't need to worry about me. I'm offering a place to stay to a girl who needs it. End of story."

North looked at him carefully, then ran his finger along his jaw. "Shit."

"What now?" Gabe sighed.

"You like her."

"Of course I do. She's a friend."

"No, it's more than that. I was kind of kidding before, but Jesus, Gabe. She's your best friend's sister. If you're messing around with her you're an idiot. You and Matt have been tight since you were hardly adults. If you hurt her, you can wave goodbye to that friendship."

"I'm not hurting anybody," Gabe protested. "And what is this? You've never shown an interest in my love life before."

"That's because you've never had one that's been interesting enough to comment on." North shrugged.

"Maybe I liked it better that way." Gabe looked over his brother's shoulder at the floor to ceiling glass doors that spanned the back of the house. North's ranch was bigger than his, but the view of the snow topped mountains was equally as impressive.

"I just care." North's voice was soft. "It's just us, you know? Our parents were never up to shit. It's always been you, me, Kris, and the girls. We take care of each other. If one of us hurts, we all hurt."

Gabe swallowed, though his mouth was dry. He wasn't used to this kind of heart to heart from his brother. "I know you care, but we're all grown up now."

"Maybe I'm still beating myself up for when I wasn't

around to protect you." His eyes met Gabe's, and for a moment they said nothing.

Gabe finally blew out a mouthful of air. "That was a long time ago. You gotta stop blaming yourself for it."

North's lips twitched. "I will when you will."

"I'm serious. You were sick. What went down had nothing to do with you. Everybody's okay. It's over and done with." And they didn't talk about it. That was the agreement. Because some things were better left in the past. "Now I need to get home and see if my house has any water."

North nodded, his gaze soft. "Are we okay?"

"Yeah, we're okay. And I know you care, man. But I got this handled."

"I'm here if you need me."

"I know that." Gabe bumped his shoulder with his own. "And I'm thankful for it. Family is family."

"Exactly."

And though he didn't say it, Gabe knew what his brother was thinking. Nicole was Matt's family, and Matt was as protective of her as North was of them all.

CHAPTER 19

He'd been in the shower for a long, long time. Nicole glanced out of the kitchen where she was leaning on the counter, her Kindle in one hand, her eyes catching his bedroom door. From the moment he'd walked into the house an hour ago he'd been in a weird mood. Sure, he'd kissed her cheek and asked if she was okay, but he'd only half listened when she'd answered him. She wondered if he was distracted by a problem at work, or if he was regretting what had happened between them last night.

All she knew was that she hated not knowing. Putting her Kindle down on the counter, she took a deep breath and walked down the hallway to his bedroom. "Gabe?" she called softly, tapping on his door. There was no reply.

Pushing the door open a few inches, she could hear the rush of water coming from his bathroom. She'd only been in his room a handful of times. It was painted a deep, matte blue, with a gray rug covering the polished wooden floor. His bed was big, with a gray coverlet neatly pulled up to the pillows. The surfaces were scattered with photo frames of his family and friends. She swallowed hard and walked over to the closed door that led to his bathroom.

"Gabe? Everything okay?"

When he didn't answer, she pushed it open, not able to stand the tension anymore. "Gabe? It's me." A wall of steam hit her. "Just wanted to check that you're okay."

He looked around the glass door that covered the length of his double sized shower. "Just had a long day. You okay?" A frown played at his lips.

"Yeah," she said. "I'm just... I don't know. I thought I might have upset you. You seem a bit off."

He ran his hand over his wet hair. "I'm just thinking about something North said, that's all."

She swallowed. "Was it about me?"

"How'd you guess?"

"I don't know. I just got the feeling he knew something was going on. Between us, I mean."

"Yeah, I think he knows. I'm sorry." The shower was still running, steam rolling in the air. She ran her tongue over her bottom lip, considering his words.

"Can I get in?"

"The shower?" His voice was low.

"Yeah. Can I get in with you?" She wasn't sure what made her say it. She just knew that she needed to get close to him. To feel his skin against hers.

His eyes met hers. "Get in."

She pulled her sweater over her head, followed by her top and workout bra. Sliding her pants down her legs, she kicked off her panties and walked to the shower. He stepped back, letting her in, then as soon as she was there he put his arms around her and pulled her against him, pressing his lips to her brow. And for a moment they stood there like that, hot water cascading over them both in their sweet embrace.

"I'm sorry you had a bad day," she told him.

"It's better now," he murmured against her head.

Her lips curled. "Yeah, it is." Everything felt so much better when he was around. Why was that?

She felt him stir against her, the thickness of him pressing into her stomach. But instead of pressing harder against her, he dropped his head to her shoulder, his breath soft against her skin.

Water poured down on them as she brought her hands to his scalp, fingertips dragging against it, massaging him until he let out a satisfied groan.

"That feels good."

"It's supposed to." She moved her hands down, soothing the knotted muscles on his back. He slid his arms around her waist as though he couldn't bear to let her go.

Steam was rising all around them as she moved her hands to his shoulder blades, finding a knot there that made him tense until she'd soothed it away. "Nic..."

"It's okay," she whispered. "I've got you."

"I don't want to hurt you." His voice was a mumble against her shoulder.

"You're not hurting me. I'm the one making your muscles ache."

He exhaled heavily, his breath hot against her skin. "I mean your heart. I don't want to hurt your good, kind heart. It's only just healing."

"You're not hurting that either." She slid her hands down his sides. This man's body was so intensely strong it sent shivers down her spine. "I'm here because I want to be. The same reason you are." She pressed her lips to his temple. "Is that what North said?"

"Something like that."

She cupped his face, her eyes tender as they met his. "You haven't hurt me. You've taken care of me. And I don't mean just last night. You took me in, you made me smile, you've made my life better." She swallowed hard. "And last night was... it was so good, Gabe. And it was nobody's business but ours."

A half smile pulled at his lips. He rose up, his body dwarfing hers once more, sliding his hands around her waist and pulling her against him.

"It wasn't good, it was amazing."

She grinned. "I know."

"And it wasn't a onetime thing."

Her heart did a little lurch. "I was hoping it wouldn't be."

He pushed the wet hair back from her brow, dropping his head so his lips met hers. He kissed her hard, lifting her against him and turning so her back was against the tiles, his hard ridge pressing exactly where she needed it.

"Here?"

"Here. Just as soon as I get a condom."

"Don't take too long. I'm getting wet."

"So this one definitely has Matt Damon in it, right?" she asked him, as he put the big bowl of popcorn on the table and picked up the remote. It was almost nine o'clock, late to be starting a movie, but he seemed determined to make her watch it. Maybe he needed a rest after spending most of the evening between her thighs.

And it had been a good evening. Great even. The best.

They'd had more sex. Slow and gentle the second time, because they were both feeling achy and exhausted. He'd held her close as he made love to her, his lips capturing hers, and when she'd reached the plateau once more he'd grinned as though he'd won a gold medal.

"Yes, it has Matt Damon in it." He shook his head, grinning. "It's called *Jason Bourne*. Who do you think would be in it?"

"He wasn't in the last one," Nicole pointed out, grabbing a handful of popcorn. "And that was called *The Bourne Legacy*."

"*Legacy* being the operative word." Gabe sat down beside her, reaching across to steal a popcorn kernel from her hand.

"Hey, get your own."

"I just did." He winked and put it in his mouth. "*The Bourne Legacy* was a perfectly good movie without Matt Damon in it," he said when he swallowed the popcorn down.

"Good but not great. For it to be great, we need Damon abs."

"There you go, objectifying men again."

She lifted a brow. "I'm not objectifying. The guy obviously worked hard for those abs. He wants me to appreciate them, and I do. They put that in for the women, and the action in for the guys. Everybody knows that."

"So what do they put in romcoms for the guys?" he asked, shaking his head.

"Sex."

He wrinkled his nose. "Bullshit. Name me one romcom with good sex in it."

She cocked a brow. "*The Notebook*."

He gave her the side eye. "I haven't seen that one. Describe it."

"I'm not spoiling it for you. You can watch for yourself."

He grabbed the popcorn bowl and offered it to her. She took a handful and then he did, too. "How long is the sex scene?"

"I don't know. I didn't time it. What does it matter anyway? It's a good scene."

"Is it a good scene for women, or a good scene for men?" he asked suspiciously.

"Is there a difference? Good sex is good sex, right?"

He smirked, putting a handful of puffy corn in his mouth. "If you say so."

She tipped her head to the side. "What does that mean?"

"Just that what women like in a sex scene and what guys like aren't always the same."

"Are we back to talking about porn again?" she asked him. "Because I can call North to give you another lecture if you'd like."

Gabe laughed. "No, we're not. I'm just saying sometimes we want different things. You want all soft focus and love, we like to see the goods."

"The goods?" She shook her head. "You're a neanderthal."

"We're just visual beings. If we're watching a sex scene we want to see the bodies." He blinked then corrected himself. "*Her body.* Not his."

Nicole started to laugh. "I knew what you meant. I just think you should appreciate the emotions those scenes bring out. They're not about sex for us, they're about the connection. Even if there's no love there, there's tension."

"You're the one who's been talking about Matt Damon's abs." He lifted a brow.

Ugh. He had her there. She folded her arms over her chest. "That's it. You're not watching *The Notebook.* You don't deserve it."

Gabe reached for her hand, pulling it softly from beneath her arm. "But I want to watch it now. With you." His eyes caught hers, they were soft and warm. "I promise to be good." He pressed his lips to her wrist, and she felt a shiver snake down her spine. "Please?"

"It's your Netflix."

"Good point." He smiled. "We'll add it to our list. But I only want to watch it if you're with me."

Her heart did a little stutter. He wanted another night of watching movies with her. "Okay."

He grinned, leaning over to kiss her brow. "Good. Now let's get lost in Matt Damon's abs."

THEY'D FINISHED the popcorn and he'd put the bowl – empty save for the unpopped kernels – on the coffee table. When he sat back, he reached for Nicole, pulling her warm body into his, his legs on either side of her hips as she leaned against his chest and watched the movie.

He'd set up the huge television and surround sound speakers as soon as he'd moved into the house, but it was mostly for watching sports when he had the guys over. He'd never watched a movie with a date here until Nicole. Never held someone in his arms as she jumped with every volley of gunfire, never lowered his head into her hair just to smell how good her shampoo was.

And it was weird how normal it felt. How good. He'd spent a lifetime keeping his home and sex life separate and in a single day she'd knocked all his walls down. And he wouldn't have it any other way, because having her here in his arms felt perfect.

She was everything.

Nicole tipped her head to look up at him and when she caught his gaze she smiled softly. He smiled back, feeling a strange sensation in his chest.

"You okay?" she asked him. "You're not watching the movie."

"I've seen it before."

She pressed her lips against his jaw, and their softness made his chest even tighter. "You look like you're deep in thought. Are you still worried about what North said to you? Because you're not hurting me. You're helping me."

Maybe he was. That would explain the tightness across his ribcage. "He thinks I'm an idiot for threatening my friendship with your brother. That he'll never forgive me if he finds out about us."

"I thought we agreed he wouldn't find out?" She pulled her bottom lip between her teeth. "And anyway, this isn't a one sided thing. I'm a grown up. I make my own decisions. Matt couldn't only blame you for this."

"Yeah, we did agree." And that was a good thing, wasn't it? So why didn't the thought make him feel any better? One day soon this would end and she'd go back to her life in D.C., and he'd stay here and build the resort he'd been dreaming of. Their paths would rarely cross. Matt would never know what had happened between them. They'd be in the clear and everybody would be happy.

"Are you sure you're okay?" She stroked his jaw. "You look annoyed."

He kissed her cheek. "I'm fine. Just families, you know? They can hit every guilt button without even trying."

She lifted a brow. "Tell me about it. I had a call from my sister today."

He welcomed the change in subject. "What did she say?"

"She just sounded stressed. And worried about her

wedding next year. She was hoping to go over plans at Thanksgiving and I feel bad that I'm not going to be there to help her with it."

"Don't you want to go home for the holiday?" he asked her. "I know you miss your parents."

"They've invited Luke to dinner." She exhaled heavily. "So no, I don't want to go."

"Why'd they invite him?"

"He works for my dad. They always invite people who have nowhere else to go."

"Maybe if you told them what he did they wouldn't invite him anymore."

She shook her head. "I can't do that."

His jaw felt tight now. "You have to tell them at some point."

"And I will. When my dad's not so overwhelmed. Anyway, I'm not going, so that's that. I'm running some Black Friday Yoga Classes to help people work off the turkey. I can't be in two places at once."

"Would you go home if Luke wasn't there?" he asked her.

"I don't know. Maybe. You're right, I do miss my family."

"Why not invite them here for a weekend?"

She jerked her head up. "What?"

"Have them come here. That way they can't foist Luke on you. They can stay here if you like."

"You only have two bedrooms."

"Your parents can have the guest bedroom, and you and Kara can have mine. I'll stay at North's."

"You'd do that for me?" Her voice was thick.

"It's no big deal," he told her. "Unless they don't get the parts in for the bathroom, then it'll be a big deal." He shrugged. "But they've promised it should be ready by next week."

"It's a really big deal. And it'll stop Kara from panicking." She reached up to push the hair from his brow, looking at him as though he'd just offered to give her the world. And he liked it, this way she looked at him. Liked giving her things she didn't know she wanted or needed.

"Thank you," she whispered, pressing her lips to his. He cupped the back of her head, kissing her back, loving how perfectly she fit against him. Her breath was soft and warm against his lips, her hair tickling his face as it fell over them both in a thick, wavy curtain.

She slid her arms around his neck, and he moved his hands down, pressing into her back as they deepened the kiss. This was perfect. She was perfect.

Nothing else mattered.

CHAPTER 20

*S*he'd finished her last class of the day – a mother and baby class that had her all gooey and a little baby crazy until one of them filled their diaper and caused the room to stink so bad she had to open the windows at the top of the room. Savasana – the ending rest pose – was always interesting when there were babies involved. Some of them were calm and fell asleep against their mommy's stomachs. Others were restless and would cry out, and she'd show them an adjusted pose, where they lay on their sides, the mom spooning the baby, their slow breathing calming their child down.

Holly hung back at the end, cradling Candace against her chest. She'd been one of the sleepy babies, but she'd woken up at the end and her eyes were alert as Nicole walked over to them.

"Hey Candace." Nicole put her finger out and Candace captured it in her tiny hand. Nicole smiled and glanced up at Holly. "Her grasp is good. And her head control, too."

"She loves yoga," Holly said, kissing her daughter's head. "I do, too. I'm so glad you decided to run this class. Every mom I know is raving about it. And the dads that come too. Did you see Everley's friend Casey? He says it's his favorite part of the week."

Warmth rushed through her. "Don't tell the others, but it's my favorite class of the week. I get to cuddle babies for a whole hour and get paid for it." Nicole tickled Candace's cheek and was rewarded with a gummy smile.

"It sounds like a win-win to me." Holly shifted Candace in her arms. "I hear you're staying in town for Thanksgiving."

Nicole lifted a brow. "Word gets around fast, huh?"

"It does," Holly agreed. "So I was wondering if you'd like to join us for dinner. It's mostly family and a couple of friends. North will be there, and you know Everley and Dylan, of course. Everley's bringing a few friends, and Alaska will join us a bit later because she's working."

"What about Gabe?" Nicole asked. She tried to keep her expression neutral, because just saying his name made her feel all warm inside. They'd spent the last week in a state of bliss. Cooking together, watching movies and critiquing the sex scenes, taking long, long showers in his oversized shower.

And every night he'd insisted she sleep in his bed. Sure, it was because her room was full of tarps and tools, thanks to the work that was taking place in her bathroom, but it felt like more than that. Waking up in his arms and seeing the smile on his face made her body ache in all kinds of ways.

"Gabe said he'd come if you do." Holly shrugged. "I figure he doesn't want you alone on Thanksgiving. And nor do we. You're kind of family now, if we suffer you suffer."

"Eating turkey is hardly suffering," Nicole pointed out. She really liked Gabe's family. They were always so kind and welcoming.

"It would be if I was the one cooking. But luckily for you, Josh loves to take over in the kitchen." She shifted Candace in her arms. "So what do you say? Are you in? Or do I need to bribe you with baby cuddles?"

As though she could understand, Candace reached her arms out to Nicole, struggling in Holly's arms. "Is it okay if I take her for a minute?" Nicole asked.

"Be my guest. I need to put my coat on and grab my bag."

Candace gurgled happily as Nicole cradled her against her chest, moving her hips in a rhythm as Holly put her coat on, then grabbed Candace's. The baby struggled a little as Holly threaded her arms through the sleeves, but then she reached up and grabbed a handful of Nicole's ponytail, pulling at it as Holly fastened her buttons.

"I'll walk you up," Nicole suggested as Holly lifted her bag. It was huge, full of blankets and bottles and baby paraphernalia. Holly gave her a grateful smile and the two of them left the studio, the huge bag bobbing as they walked up the stairs to the lobby.

It was full of people. Alaska had told her that this was the week they decorate for the holidays, and a team of workers was everywhere. Some were on ladders, hanging ornaments on the tree donated by the Christmas Tree Farm, while others were constructing what looked like Nutcrackers, screwing together the legs with the bodies. When they were complete they'd be at least ten feet tall, but still dwarfed by the tree.

Alaska was behind the desk, and waved as they walked over. "Oh my God, look at Candace. Those leggings are to die for."

Candace was wearing a pair of yellow and grey striped leggings with a big lion's face on her bottom, along with a matching top that said "the lion might sleep but I don't." Nicole grinned and lifted Candace to show Alaska the front, but then her eyes caught the man Alaska was standing with.

Gabe.

He glanced at Candace then back at her face, a half smile pulling at the corner of his lip. Candace reached out for Gabe, who scooped her out of Nicole's arms.

"Hey." He kissed Nicole's cheek and she felt a shot of pleasure right to her toes.

"Hi yourself." She grinned as his biceps tensed. Candace looked tiny in his arms, her eyes fixed on his face. She looked fascinated by him.

Nicole knew how she felt.

She felt the warmth of Holly's stare as she looked from Nicole to Gabe and then back again. "Nicole said yes to Thanksgiving," she told Gabe. "You're coming too, right?"

"If it's okay with Nicole, it's okay with me," he murmured.

"Gabe just dropped in to ask me to pass you a message," Alaska said, leaning her elbows on the counter. "But he can give it to you himself now." There was a knowing smile on her lips. Did they all suspect there was something going on between them? If North knew, it was only a matter of time until the rest of them did.

They were a tight family. There weren't many secrets here. It wasn't that they were nosy or intrusive, but that they cared. They noticed things.

"Your bathroom is ready. I'm going home to inspect it now," Gabe told her. Candace was fussing against him, grabbing his shirt with her stubby fingers. "I thought I'd let you know."

He could have called. They both knew that. But she was glad he'd dropped in to see her. They had breakfast together every morning and dinner together every evening but she still missed him when they were working.

"No more using Gabe's shower," Alaska murmured.

"What a shame." Holly bit down a smile.

"Will you two shut up?" But Gabe was grinning.

Holly glanced at Alaska, her eyes sparkling. "Will we shut up?" she asked her cousin.

"No way," Alaska replied with a grin.

Candace started to whine, and Gabe shifted her, pressing his lips to her hair. When she cried out again, he rocked her gently, and Nicole tried not to watch too closely. It was hard though, because watching Gabe Winter rock a baby was better than any romance book she'd ever read.

It made her feel all tingly inside.

"I should go back and clean up the studio," she said, not really wanting to leave. "I left it open."

"And I should go home," Holly said, leaning forward to kiss her cheek. "This momma needs a shower after yoga, and Candace will need a bath before her daddy gets home." She glanced at Nicole again. "Do you have any allergies I should know about? For Thanksgiving?"

"No. I'll pretty much eat anything."

She ignored the way Gabe lifted a brow. *Dirty man.*

"Great. Okay then. Thank you for the class." Holly looked over at Alaska. "Call me when you're finished tonight."

"Will do," Alaska said. "I best go check on the decorators. I'll see you at Thanksgiving," she told Gabe, then patted Candace's cheek. "She looks good on you."

"Shut up," Gabe said good humoredly.

"Let me take her," Holly said, sliding Candace from his arms. "Oh God, she's drooled on you."

Nicole bit down a laugh at the big wet patch on his chest. "I guess you'll be needing a shower, too."

"Thanks." He winked at her. "Lucky that I'm heading home. You gonna be long?"

"About half an hour."

"I'll get dinner started. Steak okay for you?"

She nodded. "Steak sounds good."

He leaned forward and kissed her cheek again, and Holly and Alaska exchanged a glance.

Rolling his eyes at their scrutiny, he whispered in Nicole's ear, "See you soon."

CHAPTER 21

"Look at all these pumpkins," Nicole said, smiling at the beautiful fall decorations lining the steps to Holly and Josh's house. There were handprint turkeys stuck in the windows, the size of Candace's palm. "They've gone all out."

"Candace is a child prodigy. Making turkeys when she's still a baby," Gabe said to her, bumping her shoulder with his. A little frisson of excitement went through her. They'd spent the morning in bed – no work for either of them today – and it had been perfect. A little loving, a lot of spooning, and then Gabe had brought her a coffee and a croissant into his room, laughing when she worried about spilling crumbs on his comforter.

"We've spilled a lot worse, baby."

The door opened, and suddenly they were surrounded by people. Holly and Candace hugged her, followed by Everley who insisted on introducing her to everybody there. Everley's husband Dylan, and her friends Casey and David and their baby boy were in the living room, along with some of her other friends from the theater she ran, who hadn't been able to make it home for the holidays. Then there was Amber, North's friend, who co-owned the Christmas Tree Farm with him.

"Alaska will be here later, and Josh and North are in the kitchen," Holly said, when Everley had finished her introductions. "They're arguing over the amount of time it takes to cook a turkey." She rolled her eyes. "I remember when he used to get passionate about things other than stuffed birds."

"I remember when you were the stuffed bird," Everley teased. She'd taken Candace from Holly and was dancing her around.

"Shut up," Holly said with a grin, then took Nicole's hand. "Come say hi to the guys." Somebody pushed a glass of champagne into her other. She looked up to see Gabe smiling at her. She grinned back.

Sure enough, there were loud voices coming from the kitchen. "Guests coming in," Holly called out. "Watch your language."

Josh looked up as they entered the kitchen, a smile pulling at his lips when he saw Nicole there. The next moment she was enveloped in a bear hug that made her laugh.

"Tell North a turkey needs to be moist, not cremated," Josh whispered in her ear.

North kissed her cheek. "Tell *him* that his guests need to be fed, not poisoned. Salmonella is a serious thing."

Holly put her hands on her hips. "Can you two stop bickering for a moment? It's a damn turkey. If it's under-cooked you can roast it some more, and if it's overcooked we'll eat it anyway. It's Thanksgiving." She raised a brow at her cousin and her husband. "If you don't start working like a team, *I'll* do the cooking next year."

North and Josh looked at each other. "We'll get on it."

Holly laughed. "They hate my cooking," she told Nicole.

"That's because it's terrible." Josh kissed her cheek. "You're an amazing woman at so many things. But food isn't one of them."

"Can you cook?" North asked Nicole.

"Of course she can." Josh grinned at her. "She cooks for Gabe most days."

North stared at Nicole carefully for a moment, and she thought back to the conversation he'd had with Gabe. About them playing with fire and somebody getting hurt.

"He cooks for me, too," she told them. "He makes a mean steak and potatoes. And he's great at picking up takeout."

Josh and Holly looked at each other. Holly bit down on her lip like she was trying not to smile.

"Maybe you can stay and help," Josh said, his voice hopeful. "We need a mediator."

"Nope." Holly grabbed her hand. "Nicole's a guest. If you need some help ask Gabe." She side-eyed Nicole. "If he can cook steak, he can cook turkey."

Before they could ask again, she'd pulled Nicole out of the kitchen and closed the door. "Seriously, they're pains in my ass. North was over here first thing this morning because he was so afraid Josh was going to mess this up."

"Does Josh not cook very often?" Nicole asked, smiling.

"He cooks every day. North just finds it hard to let go. He's usually the one who cooks the turkey and he hates not being in charge."

"On the plus side, you have two hot guys in your kitchen making you the perfect meal," Nicole pointed out. Sure they were bickering, but she could see the affection there. This family had a whole lot of love going on. The easy going atmosphere felt like such a contrast to her own family.

For her parents, Thanksgiving was the one day they didn't work, but they still had their research constantly on their mind. Right now, they'd probably be having cocktails in the living room of their townhouse in Georgetown, trying to brainstorm a problem with one of her dad's experiments. In winter, the trees were bare enough to give a great view of the Potomac River as it gushed its way between Virginia and Washington D.C. The home was built in the 1870s, and every room had been painstakingly restored to its Victorian glory.

"You okay?" Gabe whispered in her ear.

Pulling herself away from thoughts of her family she nodded. "Did you know your brother and Josh are coming to blows in the kitchen?"

"I heard them." He lifted a brow. "Who knew two guys could get so angry about a bird?"

She laughed. "They take it very seriously."

"As long as it tastes good, and they keep pouring the champagne, they can argue as much as they like." He pushed a stray lock of hair from her face, his fingers lingering on her cheek. "You sure you don't mind being here? It's always goddamned mayhem."

As if on cue, Candace started to wail. About ten people rushed to pick her up from where she was laying on a blanket. In another corner, somebody had put the Macy's Thanksgiving Day Parade on the flat screen television, on mute, because Christmas music was blasting out of the stereo. David and Casey were arguing about how loud the volume should be, and whether it could damage their baby's hearing.

"I'm having a good time," she said softly, her eyes meeting his. "I love your family."

"Yeah, well they love you too," Gabe said, grabbing her hand. It sent a shot of warmth through her. "Even if they are a bunch of lunatics. Let's go grab some more champagne, I have a feeling we're going to need it."

THE TURKEY TURNED out to be the perfect combination of moist inside with a golden skin on the outside, glistening in the afternoon light as Josh and North carried it to the table. Then they'd argued over who should carve it, and everybody watched with amusement as they each carved one side, placing the meat onto plates and passing them around.

When the dinner was over, and they'd cleaned up, somebody put football on the television, and most of the guests huddled around, holding bottles of beers as the helmeted players charged into one another.

"Which one's Michael," North asked Gabe, leaning forward as the quarterback made a run for it.

"He's not on the field yet. Cam thinks he won't get game play until later in the year." Gabe took a mouthful of beer. "Says he's good, but cocky."

"Aren't they all?" North grinned.

"Who's Michael?" Nicole asked Gabe, sitting on the arm of the chair next to him, sipping at a mug of coffee. Her stomach was way too full for beer.

"He's our investor's kid." Gabe looked up at her. "Cam used to play for the Boston Bobcats. His stepson just got drafted. Mike's a safety, like Cam."

"I saw an article about him online the other day," Everley said, leaning on the back of the sofa. "He's crazy good looking."

"Cam thinks he needs the cockiness smoothed out of him." Gabe shrugged. "Not that he has much room to talk."

They jumped to their feet as the team made a touchdown. Gabe and North let out a whoop, and Josh laughed as some of the other guys did a little dance.

Then the doorbell rang, and Holly jumped up, sliding Candace into her husband's arms. "I bet that's Alaska." When she opened the front door, and Alaska walked in, it was like Nicole and Gabe's arrival all over again. Even the guys managed to pull themselves away from the game long enough to hug her and wish her a Happy Thanksgiving.

"I saved you some food," Holly said to her cousin. "Why don't we go into the kitchen and leave the others to the football?"

"Sounds good to me." Alaska beamed at her. "Thank you." She looked over at Nicole. "You're coming, too, right?"

Along with Holly, Everley, and Amber, she and Alaska walked into the kitchen. Holly busied herself with warming up food for her cousin, while Everley grabbed some glasses and filled them up with another bottle of champagne.

"Not too much for me," Nicole said, as the bubbles spilled over the glasses. "Remember the last time we were all together?"

"My head does," Holly said, grimacing. "I still haven't been able to drink a cocktail since."

"You're all lightweights. I was fresh as a daisy the next morning," Everley said, grinning.

"You were throwing up," Alaska said, shaking her head. "Dylan told me."

"He's such a sneak." Everley passed a glass to each of them.

"I've never been more happy to miss a girls' night out," Amber said, grinning at them. Nicole knew her less well than the others, but she seemed just as friendly. "Thank God I had a cold that night."

"Ah, but you weren't there to see Nicole throw up on Gabe. That was more than worth the hangover," Everley teased.

"I thought we weren't going to mention that again." Nicole blushed.

"But it's way too much fun seeing your cheeks go pink." Everley winked at her, then raised her champagne glass. "We should make a toast," she said.

"What to?" Alaska asked, smiling gratefully at Holly as she slid a plate full of food in front of her.

"To new beginnings," Everley said. "Isn't that the best part of Thanksgiving? Knowing that Christmas is around the corner, and things are going to go crazy?"

"Tell me about it," Alaska said. "We're fully booked until January at the Inn."

Amber nodded. "We're already working flat out at the farm. Tomorrow looks like it's going to be crazy busy."

"To new beginnings," they all said, holding their glasses up, then taking a sip. When she'd swallowed the champagne down, Nicole couldn't help but smile.

It felt like a new beginning for her, too, in so many ways. For the first time in forever she felt truly happy, and so much of that was thanks to the gorgeous, funny man watching football in the next room.

He made her feel good in ways she hadn't thought possible. And she liked that a lot.

"You know what I think is sweet?" Everley asked later in the evening, as she opened another bottle of champagne.

"What?" Holly asked. She'd come back from putting Candace to bed and was rinsing her bottle.

"The way Gabe keeps coming in to check on Nicole. Dylan and Josh haven't been in once."

"He's only been in twice," Nicole said, feeling that blush steal over her face again.

"Three times," Everley said, biting down a smile. "First he wanted water, then he wanted some snacks. The last time he didn't bother to make up an excuse."

"Why would he need an excuse?" Alaska asked.

"I have no idea." Everley lifted her brow. "It's just that neither of them seem to want us to know they're in some kind of relationship."

All four of the girls turned to look at Nicole. She tried not to laugh, but they were making it so obvious. "What?" she asked them.

"Are you in a relationship?" Alaska asked her.

"Define relationship." Nicole was playing for time. She didn't know how much she should tell them. Even if part of her was desperate to confide the way she felt about Gabe to them.

Every time he'd come into the kitchen he'd touched her. Not in a sexual way, but in a I-need-to-feel-your-skin-for-a-second-before-it-kills-me kind of way. She knew, because she felt the same.

It was near impossible not touching him, not kissing him. Not showing she cared because dammit, she did.

"You don't have to answer," Holly said softly. "It's none of our business."

"Well Gabe kind of is our business," Alaska mused, wrinkling her nose. "He's family, after all." She smiled at Nicole. "And you're our friend. We just want you to be happy. Both of you."

She was such a sweet person. Nicole hated lying to her.

"It's complicated," she admitted.

"Of course it is," Everley said, her eyes lighting up. "Aren't all the best relationships?"

"Yours definitely are," Alaska muttered. "Who else gets married to the same guy twice?"

Gabe had told Nicole about Everley and Dylan's relationship. The two of them had married young and split almost right away. Then last year they'd discovered their divorce hadn't gone through, and they'd reconnected and fallen in love all over again.

"You don't have to tell us anything," Holly said, shooting Everley a warning glance. "We just want you all to be happy, that's all."

"Gabe definitely looks happy every time he looks at you," Amber murmured to Nicole.

"He does," Alaska agreed. "I swear, I never thought I'd see the day. I've always worried about him. After everything that happened and all the blame he took. He never really was the same."

Nicole blinked. "What are you talking about?"

Alaska exchanged glances with Everley. "He hasn't told you?" she asked, her voice soft.

"I don't think so." Now she remembered them mentioning this before. Something about him and Alaska when they were kids. "Can you tell me?" she asked. Because whatever it was, it sounded like something she needed to know.

Alaska pulled her lip between her teeth. "You should probably ask Gabe. It's his story to tell."

"And yours," Everley pointed out.

"Yeah, but if Gabe hasn't told her, I'll feel like an ass

spilling the beans." Her soft eyes caught Nicole's. "You should ask him."

"Sure. It's no biggie." Nicole nodded. Alaska was right. He wouldn't like them gossiping about him. If he wanted her to know something, he'd tell her.

And if he didn't? Well that was his right. He didn't owe her anything. And as much as she loved spending time with his family, she wasn't one of them. She was a guest and there was no way she wanted to put them in an awkward position.

"There are way too many glum faces in here," Holly said, winking at Nicole, as though she knew it was time to change the subject. "How about we go annoy the guys? The football game must be nearly over by now."

CHAPTER 22

"Hey sleepyhead, we're back." Gabe touched Nicole's cheek softly. Dylan had offered them a ride home from Josh and Holly's house so they could both drink, and during the short time since they'd left, Nicole had managed to fall asleep against Gabe's shoulder. He'd go back to pick the truck up tomorrow.

"She looks out for the count," Dylan said, looking at them over his shoulder. "You need some help?"

"I got it." Gabe gently lifted her from his embrace and leaned her against the other side of the car. "Thanks for the ride, man."

"Any time." Dylan winked.

"It was good to see you both," Everley said. She sounded tired, too. It was no wonder, he'd seen the empty champagne bottles when he walked into the kitchen. So much for just a couple of drinks. His cousins were a bad influence.

Gabe climbed out of the truck and walked around to Nicole's side, pulling her door open and unfastening her seat belt. Her eyes fluttered open, and she stared at him glassily.

"We're home," he said. "Time to go to bed."

Sliding his arms around her waist, he helped her stand, then grabbed her purse. With a wave to his cousin and her husband, he closed the door, and helped a wobbly Nicole up the stairs.

"You okay there?" he asked when she stumbled on the last step. "I would have carried you, but I figured you wouldn't want Everley and Dylan to see that."

"Liar. You just didn't want to throw your back out," she teased.

"I could carry you no problem." He glanced at her body, taking in her achingly sweet curves. She was wearing a brown cashmere dress that would look demure on anybody else, but on her it made him want to trace every rise and dip of her. "I've carried you before." He slid the key into the lock.

"Mmhmm." A smile played at her lips as she leaned on the wall beside the door. She looked so damn adorable with hooded eyes and swollen lips. He pushed the door open and turned to her, but before she could say anything he scooped her up in his arms.

"Gabe!" She pushed his shoulder. "You'll hurt yourself. Seriously."

"If I want to carry my woman, I'll carry her."

"Is that what I am? Your woman?" She looked up at him, biting her lip. She liked it, maybe too much.

"Would you prefer girl?" He kicked the door closed behind him and dropped her purse on the floor, then walked easily down the hallway. She smelled like flowers in his arms, her skin all warm and soft. He felt a familiar stirring in his jeans.

"I like woman better," she murmured, pressing her face

into his neck. Her breath against his skin sent another shot of desire through him.

"I like *this* woman." He patted her behind. They'd reached her bedroom door, and he pushed his elbow down on the handle.

"Wait. Aren't we sleeping in your bed?" She looked up at him, her brows furrowed.

He swallowed. "I figured you needed a good night's sleep. You have a full day tomorrow."

"I'll sleep better in your bed."

It was crazy how happy those words made him. Truth was, he slept better when she was in his bed, too. "Okay, but no funny business." He kissed the tip of her nose. "I need my beauty sleep."

She tilted her head. "Don't you want to..."

"Of course I *want* to. But I also want you to sleep well. You're tired and a little drunk and I figure if I hold you it's enough."

"You're adorable." She nestled back into him as he carried her down to his room. "Seriously. No wonder you make all the women melt."

"All the women?" He quirked an eyebrow. "Who else do I melt?" He pushed his own door open, still holding her tight in his arms. He was reluctant to let go. The thought of her being with her family next weekend was messing with his head. Sure, he'd offered to have them stay, and North was happy for him to sleep at his place for two nights. But when he'd suggested it, he hadn't realized how much he liked holding her. Having her around to talk with.

It would be a long weekend without her.

"You know what women," Nicole murmured, as he laid her down on the bed. He leaned back and pulled her shoes off, placing them carefully on the floor. "All the ones you've had before."

"I didn't melt them." He slid his hands up her thighs, finding the tops of her stockings. Gently he rolled the first one down, trying to contain the desire forcing blood where he needed it the least. He hadn't lied, he wasn't going to have sex with her tonight, no matter how much his body wanted it. She'd be exhausted in the morning and she didn't need that. When he rolled the second stocking down, she let out a sigh, her thigh muscles tensing against his fingers.

And he got even harder.

"You're this perfect mixture of dirty and sweet. I never knew it was possible," Nicole said, her eyes closed as he turned her to the side to unzip her dress. It was weird how erotic it was, just undressing somebody like this.

"For the record, I'm not sweet." He slid his fingers down her spine, then turned her onto her back. He wasn't sure who he was trying to torture – her or himself.

"Yes you are." She lifted her arms so he could pull each sleeve off. "You're undressing me because I'm too tired to undress myself."

"I'm undressing you because I like this dress and I want to see you in it again." He pulled the bodice down, then shimmied it over her hips. She had to lift her ass for him to get the fabric down her legs and for a moment he wavered. That ass did things to him. Things that could make a guy lose his mind.

He gritted his teeth and looked away.

"You're sweet because you saved me when I drank too much at Marshall's Gap."

"I'm pretty sure you could have saved yourself." He stood and put her dress over the back of his bedroom chair, smoothing the fabric to ease out any creases. "You want me to get your pajamas?"

"I'll sleep naked."

Of course she would. "I'm gonna go freshen up. I'll bring your toothbrush and makeup wipes out."

"I'll come in with you." She sat up on the mattress, wearing only her bra and panties. Her skin looked luminescent in the soft glow of the bedroom light. Her breasts were close to spilling over the half cups of her bra, and her hips curved in a way that made his blood heat.

Climbing off the bed, she followed him into his bathroom, sitting on the corner of the tub while he squeezed toothpaste onto her brush. He passed it to her, then squeezed some on his own.

"You know how else you're sweet?" she asked, her voice half muffled by the brush.

"You're a chatty drunk," he said, trying not to grin.

"I'm not *that* drunk anymore. And you're avoiding my question."

He arched an eyebrow, looking at her in the mirror. Had he ever brushed his teeth in the same room as a woman before? He couldn't remember it if he had. And yet he had a feeling he'd remember this. Remember how she looked so damn good sitting there in her underwear, toothpaste foaming on her lips, her eyes still glassily drunk.

"Okay, how else am I sweet?"

"You bought me a ski suit so I could be part of your day."

"I bought you a ski suit because I had *Kill Bill* fantasies about you."

"Shut up. And you let me invite my family to stay and have even agreed to move out of your own house."

He rolled his eyes. "Okay, I got it. I'm sweet." He rinsed

his mouth and looked over his shoulder at her. "But only for you. No other women."

She pulled the brush from her mouth and stared up at him. "Why only for me?"

He put his brush back in the mug, then walked over to her. "You got some toothpaste on your face." He rubbed it off with his thumb.

"Are you changing the subject?" She frowned.

"You got me." He winked.

She stood and rinsed her own mouth, and it was his turn to watch her as she wiped off her makeup and covered her face with moisturizer. After tonight, she'd probably move it all back to her own bathroom.

The thought made him feel kind of mad.

"Can I ask you something else?" she said, throwing her makeup wipe in the trash.

"Okay?" A smile played at his lips.

"Everley and Alaska... well everybody really... they mentioned something that happened between you two."

"Between who?"

"You and Alaska. I asked what it was and they said I should ask you." She leaned on the counter. "So here I am, asking."

His gaze met hers. There was no guile there, just an innocent curiosity that made his stomach twist.

"It's nothing. Old news."

Her eyes pulled away. "It's okay if you don't want to tell me." She swallowed and forced a smile onto her lips. "Let's go to bed."

She turned and he caught her wrist. Blinking, she looked up at him again.

He could feel the thump of his heart against his chest.

"It's not as important as you think. Not as exciting, either. But if you want to know, I'll tell you."

She nodded silently, and he felt his stomach twist all over again.

"Shall we go to bed?" he asked. "I'll tell you there." And if she fell asleep mid-story, then that would be okay, too. Maybe it would be better. He hated talking about himself.

She walked over to her side – the fact she had a side was weird in itself – and lifted up the covers, then reached behind her back to unfasten her bra. He watched with a dry mouth as the silken fabric dropped to the floor, then she shimmied out of her panties, naked before him.

Everything about her was too much. Yet he wasn't sure he could ever get enough. The curve of her glorious breasts, the angle of her waist, the gorgeous swell of her ass that fit perfectly into his hands. She climbed onto the mattress as he pulled his own clothes off, aware of her watching gaze. He put the dark gray polo he was wearing on the chair over her dress, then pulled his jeans and socks off, leaving just his shorts and thick, jutting desire.

"It's automatic," he said thickly, as her eyes widened. "Ignore it." He pulled his shorts off, his hardness jutting proudly up. Then he climbed in beside her, reaching for her at the same time she rolled over to him.

Sliding his hands around her waist, he kissed her neck, then her jaw.

"Are you sure you don't want to..." she was breathless.

"I'm sure." His voice was thick. "It's good practice for next weekend. Anyway, you wanted to talk."

"I want to listen." She ran her fingers down his inner thigh, and it made him twitch. He grabbed her hand and put it against his chest.

She looked up, her expression soft. "Sorry."

"If I'm going to tell you it right, I need to think."

She nodded. "Okay."

He exhaled heavily, letting his desire ebb away. Her hand was still against his chest, and he wondered if she could feel how much his heart was racing.

"When I was eleven, Alaska disappeared," he said quickly, needing to get the words out.

"What?" Nicole's brow crumpled. "How? For how long?"

He inhaled through his nostrils. "About forty hours. She was only eight years old, so it was a pretty terrifying time. And everybody blamed me."

"They thought you were involved?" She sounded shocked.

"I don't know. Maybe." He lifted his hand to push his hair back from his brow. "We were camping when she disappeared. My brothers and I used to camp a lot, but this was the first time she was allowed to join us. Our grandma used to let us camp out behind the cabins during the summer months. At first, it was supposed to be North, Kris, and me, but then Everley insisted on joining us. And then Alaska begged until Grandma agreed she could camp when she was eight. So we chose the weekend after her birthday. Except Everley had to go to a dance competition for state, so that left the guys and Alaska."

"So what happened?"

"Kris got a better offer. A sleepover with a friend. And Grandma said we should cancel and try another time. But Alaska cried and begged until Grandma finally agreed. She gave North and me this huge lecture about responsibility. Then we set up camp and built a fire and started telling ghost stories to scare her. I guess we thought it was funny."

Nicole was stroking his back, her fingers soft and reassuring. "Why didn't North get the blame, too?"

"Because he got sick in the middle of the night and slept at the Inn. It was just me and Alaska out there. And when I woke up in the morning she was gone. At first I thought she'd gone inside to join North, but when I went to breakfast she wasn't there. The sheriff said if I'd raised the alarm earlier, we might have found her sooner."

"He said that to you?" Nicole looked horrified. "You were eleven years old."

"People like to have somebody to blame."

"So then what happened?" Her voice was soft as cashmere.

He swallowed hard. "I was questioned at the station. Had to go over what happened about a thousand times. Then Alaska's parents came in and started shouting at me."

"Oh Gabe." She ran her fingers through his hair. It felt so good. "They're assholes. So where was she?"

"Alaska?" He frowned. "We don't know."

"What do you mean? She came back. She must have told you where she was. Was she hurt?"

Gabe blinked. "She had this huge bruise on her head, but no other injuries. The doctor said..." his voice cracked. "That nobody had touched her. But she couldn't remember what happened. Still can't. The whole thing's a blank."

For a moment there was silence. He felt the heat of her gaze on his face. Then she cupped his cheek softly, her eyes full of anguish.

"That's crazy. But none of it is your fault. You were a kid, she was a kid." She scratched her fingers against his scalp.

"I was the oldest. It was my job to take care of her. And I failed."

She moved her hands down, cupping his cheeks. Her brow was pinched as she stared into his eyes. "You know that's bullshit, right? Whatever happened to her, you had nothing to do with it." She pressed her lips to his, moving them softly. It didn't feel sexual, it felt... emotional. *Real.* He couldn't remember feeling this close to somebody ever before. It felt like his skin was being pulled from his body. Uncomfortable and raw and fucking terrifying.

"It's old history," he told her. "It pulled our family apart. Pitched some of them against others. My dad and Everley's dad are still close, but her parents never really talked to me after that."

"Did your dad not stand up for you?" She frowned. "Surely he knew you were just a kid."

"My dad couldn't stand up for anybody. Not even himself." There was no bitterness in his voice. He'd long since accepted that as fact. "Alaska and Everley did though. And my grandma, and Holly." He ran his tongue over his bottom lip. "And North and Kris."

"You're so closely knit. It's beautiful to see."

"We've learned who to depend on. And who not to." He ran his hand over her face. Damn, she was beautiful. "So that's it. The sordid story of me and Alaska, and the night we went camping."

"I'm sorry you got so hurt. And I'm sorry for Alaska, too. It must be terrifying not knowing what happened."

"She's a strong woman. We're proud of her."

"You're all protective of her too," Nicole said. "I guess I understand why now."

"Guess we are. We feel lucky to have her, that she's okay." He nodded. "It could have been so much worse." He rolled onto his back, pulling her with him. "You got any more questions?"

"Are you okay now?"

The corner of his lip pulled up. "That's a weird question. But yes, I'm okay." He stroked her soft, silky hair. "And now we should both get to sleep. You're working tomorrow, and I have to spend the day with North at the farm."

She traced the lines on his stomach. "Thank you for telling me."

He nodded, his chest feeling full. "Thank you for listening."

Her smile was bright. "Any time."

CHAPTER 23

She wasn't in his bed when he woke up, which was weird because during the week since Thanksgiving they'd spent most of their time in it when they weren't at work. Gabe reached for his phone, frowning when he didn't find it on the table next to his bed. Then he realized it must still be in his jeans pocket, so he climbed out of the covers and walked naked across his carpeted floor, grabbing his phone and switching it on.

Seven a.m.

Pulling on his shorts and a t-shirt he grabbed from his drawer, he walked out of the bedroom, listening for Nicole. Things between them were so damn good, even better since their talk after they'd gotten home from Thanksgiving.

He'd told her his secrets and she hadn't judged. Just consoled.

She was everything he'd never knew he wanted. And every time he thought he'd finished falling for her, he'd find himself tumbling even deeper.

"Nic?" he called out.

"In the kitchen." Her voice sounded strange.

He walked in and saw her sitting at the breakfast bar. She was wearing his polo shirt and nothing else. But it was her face that drew his attention. She looked upset, her eyes red and her lips swollen.

"What's happened?" he asked, mentally going through the plans for today. She was supposed to be going to work while the cleaning service she'd hired got the house ready for her family's arrival.

"They're not coming." Her voice was thick.

"What?" He blinked, trying to work out what she was saying. "Who? The cleaners?"

She shook her head. "My family. My mom emailed me."

"But they're arriving tonight. It's all arranged." He still couldn't work out what was going on. He dragged his hand through his hair.

"I canceled the cleaning service. No need for them to come." She tried to smile, and it almost killed him. "I guess the good news is that you don't have to give up your bed if you don't want to."

"Fuck my bed." He pulled her into his arms, pressing her face against his chest. "Did they say why they aren't coming?"

"Apparently, Dad's made some kind of breakthrough in his research. But Mom's worried that he's not eating or taking care of himself, so she doesn't want to leave him. And Kara said she doesn't want to travel alone, so it's off."

"Seriously?" He shook his head. What kind of people let their daughter down at the last minute? He wanted to punch something. Or somebody. Preferably somebody related to Nicole. "But you'd arranged everything." She'd been so excited to show them the town. He'd listened, amused, as she'd told him she'd booked a horse drawn carriage ride, followed by dinner at the Inn for all four of them. He knew for a fact she'd wanted to show them the studio where she worked, and tomorrow she had some lessons she was going to invite them to – she'd even asked them to bring their own yoga gear.

She pulled away from him. This time her attempt at smiling worked. "It's fine. It really is. I never expected them to say yes in the first place. At least they emailed, I guess."

He kissed her brow. Her skin felt warm against his lips. "They're still assholes. So what do you want to do? Come back to bed?" He wanted to hold her until she felt better.

"I have classes today, remember?"

"Call them off. Stay home with me."

"I can't." Her eyes met his. "They're all fully booked. And anyway, it'll take my mind off things. Yoga always helps."

"I can take your mind off things."

Her laugh was genuine. It warmed his soul. "I bet you can. But I think I'm going to take a shower and head over to the studio. Do a little breathing and meditation. I just need to be alone for a little while. Get over myself."

"You don't need to get over anything." He reached out to cup her cheek. "Be mad. I am."

"Thank you for being mad for me." She put her hand over his, pressing his palm against her face. "I appreciate it."

"You sure I can't persuade you to stay home?"

She shook her head, but at least she was smiling again. He'd do anything to keep it there. Her goddamned family had a lot to answer for.

"I'm going to shower now," she murmured. It took him a moment to realize she was waiting for his reply.

"Good. Your family stinks."

～

SHE MANAGED to push down her disappointment for most of the morning. It helped that her classes were full, and that she had some new clients who needed extra attention to form the right poses. She'd already canceled her afternoon classes in preparation for her family to arrive.

But instead, she had an empty weekend ahead. If only she hadn't moved all of her things back into her room the other day, or spent a good two hours cleaning the bathroom after the repairs had been completed. Even though she'd canceled the cleaning service today, the house was still pretty spotless. Gabe had a housekeeper come in once a week, and he was amazingly neat. She guessed that came from sharing a house with two brothers growing up, or maybe from having to share hotel rooms with teammates.

Whatever it was, she liked it.

When her final class was over, she started to pack up the studio, cleaning the mats and blocks they'd used and stacking them neatly in their racks. She didn't hear the studio door open, so when she turned around and saw Gabe standing there, she jumped a few feet in the air.

He watched, amused, as she made a face and put her palm against her chest. "You scared me."

"I'm a scary kind of guy." He grinned at her. "You finished here?"

"Yeah." She nodded. "What are you doing here? Shouldn't you be working?"

"Change of plans." He held out a bag. "You need to take a shower. I brought you some clothes."

"You brought me clothes?" She blinked, confused. "I was going to shower at home."

"No time for that. We need to hit the road." His eyes caught hers, his gaze soft. "Traffic is busy. Everybody's going somewhere for the weekend."

Her gut did a strange little twist. "Why do we need to hit the road?"

"Because I'm taking you away for the weekend. You're free, I'm free, I figure we should have some fun."

Her throat tightened. "Where are we going?"

"To the Blue Ridge Spa Resort. It's a six hour drive so we need to leave now to get there before dinner. Then you have a full day of treatments booked for tomorrow."

"Treatments?"

"Yeah. I told them to book you in for everything. Might join you for the massage, though. We'll see how it goes."

"What will you do while I'm having treatments?"

His lip quirked. "Watch you."

She wasn't sure whether to laugh or cry. Was it normal to want to do both at once? "It'll get boring fast."

"I'll never get bored watching you. Now can we talk about this in the car?" He inclined his head at the door.

"Yeah." The tears won out. She felt them sting her eyes. When had anybody done something this nice for her? She couldn't remember if anyone ever had. "Oh!" She put her hand over her mouth. "I can't go. I have classes tomorrow."

"Alaska's taking care of that. She's calling each person and explaining. A few of them want to throw in to pay for your treatments."

"Oh my God." The tears started to spill over. "I don't believe this."

He dropped the bag and reached out for her, pulling her against his chest. "They love you, Nic. We all do. I just want to make you happy."

"I am happy."

"Then why are you crying?" He gently tipped her head to look at him, brushing the tears from her cheeks.

"They're happy tears."

He licked the pad of his thumb, and it made her body clench. "They taste the same as sad tears."

"How do you know what sad tears taste like?"

He shrugged. "Tasted my own."

She twisted her arms around him, rolling onto the balls of her feet to give her enough height, then pressed her lips against his jaw. "Thank you," she whispered.

"Tell me you're happy."

"I'm happy." She kissed the corner of his lips. They curled, and he let out a gratified sigh.

"Then I'm happy, too." He turned his head to press his mouth against hers, cupping her face with his palm to angle her right. "Now go shower."

"I know, I know." She laughed against his lips. "I stink."

"You don't yet. But you will later."

SHE LOVED WATCHING Gabe drive when he didn't know she was looking. There was an ease to him, a casual sexiness that sent her pulse racing. He had his left hand on the wheel, his right holding her thigh, as he cruised his truck over the mountain roads, rock music blasting from the stereo as he tapped his fingers against her jeans to the beat.

She'd had a little cry in the shower, feeling overwhelmed by the emotions of having everybody care so much. But she was determined that would be the last time she cried this weekend. He'd done this amazingly sweet thing for her, and she was going to show him how much she appreciated it. The music clicked over to a new track and Bruce Springsteen started singing about screen doors slamming and Mary's dress swaying.

"I love this one." Nicole grinned, sliding her hand over Gabe's. "I didn't know you're a Springsteen fan."

He squeezed her thigh. "What's not to like about Springsteen? He's the great American songwriter."

"Isn't that Bob Dylan?"

Gabe shrugged, smiling as he looked out of the windshield. He had a pair of aviators on, so she couldn't see his eyes. Her heart did a little skip because it was hard to believe that this man was here with her. Taking her away to make her happy. Sitting next to her in his gorgeous car, humming along to "Thunder Road", his thumb pressing into the soft skin of her inner thigh.

He was so going to get some tonight.

"Have you noticed how he always sings about Mary?" she asked. "Wasn't it Mary who he had to get a union job for when she got pregnant in "The River"?"

"I've no idea." Gabe chuckled. "I don't listen to the lyrics."

Her mouth dropped open. "What? But the lyrics are the best part. And you're lying, I can see you singing along."

"To the chorus," he said. "I know the chorus. But I've no idea what else he's singing."

"He's singing about trying to persuade Mary to come with him. He doesn't want to be lonely anymore," she told him. "He wants to leave his town of losers and hit the road with her."

Gabe tipped his head to the side. "Kind of like you and me."

She laughed. "I like that." She really did. Loved the idea that this open road ahead of them was their own Thunder Road. That they were leaving everything behind to be together. "I think Mary is his ideal woman. Like the manic pixie dream girl in movies."

"The manic pixie what now?" He shook his head, a smile playing at his lips. "You watch and listen to a lot of stuff. That brain of yours is a mine of information."

"I was a third child. I learned to entertain myself." She shrugged. "And I love a song with interesting lyrics. Doesn't matter if it's in a book, on the screen, or in music, a good story's a good story."

"So what's a manic pixie dream girl?" he asked her. She liked the way he sounded so interested.

"It's the ideal woman as written by guys in movies. The woman who's a little bit out there and only exists for the guy to become the man he should be. Like Natalie Portman in *Garden State*. Or Kirsten Dunst in *Elizabethtown*."

"I haven't seen either of those," Gabe mused. "We need to up our Netflix game." He glanced over at her. "Or aren't there enough naked guys in those movies for you?"

"Stop that." She tapped his hand with her fingers, and he grabbed it, squeezing her tight. "Maybe I'll make you watch them naked, then we'll both be happy."

"If you get naked, too, I'll be ecstatic."

She smiled to herself. "I'm not exactly a manic pixie dream girl. Too sturdy for that."

"Who wants a pixie? I like a woman." She had the impression he was looking at her behind his mirrored lenses. "Like you."

She pulled her lip between her teeth, because this man was so damn sweet when he wanted to be. She'd lost count of the ways. "Shut up and drive," she told him, but that didn't stop her heart from doing a little fist bump against her ribcage.

CHAPTER 24

It was dark by the time they reached the Blue Ridge Spa Resort, but the stillness of the night only added to the cool beauty of the sprawling buildings, lit with warm yellow lights, as Gabe drove toward the circle at the front of the reception building, and handed the valet his keys.

A bellhop ran out to grab the bags he'd packed from the trunk, and Gabe helped her climb down from the high passenger seat, his hands holding her waist steady for a heartbeat longer than needed.

Not that she minded. He'd been holding her for the whole journey, except for when he had to make a turn. It felt like there were no barriers between them anymore. He'd opened himself up to her last week, and she'd soothed his pain, and then he'd done the same for her today.

This morning, when she'd gotten that email, this weekend had felt like an empty hole in her life. Now it felt like everything.

"Mr. Winter, welcome." A man in a dark grey jacket walked out, shaking Gabe's hand. "I'm Larry, your concierge.

Your chalet is ready for you, would you like me to take you there now?"

"That would be great." Gabe nodded. "Thank you."

"Have you been to the resort before?" Larry asked, as he led them through reception, grabbing keys from the counter.

"I have," Gabe told him, taking Nicole's hand as they followed him back out into the dark night. There was a huge pool that snaked around the main resort building, steam rising off it, catching the lights that lined the exterior. "But it's Nicole's first time."

The footpaths had been cleared of snow, but the gardens and rooftops were clad with white. It looked like a winter wonderland. "When have you been here?" she asked, her heart dropping at the thought that it might have been with another woman.

"A couple of times with the team." He shrugged. "Can't remember if Matt came here or not."

Her heart suddenly felt lighter. "Okay." She smiled at him.

Larry glanced at her. "In that case, I'll explain the ethos of our resort for Mrs. Winter."

"It's Miss." Nicole widened her eyes at Gabe. He didn't seem perturbed at all. "Actually, just Nicole."

"I'm sorry, madam. Nicole." Larry nodded. "As you can see, we operate a Scandinavian style resort. This is our main outdoor bath, and we have an indoor one as well, inside the main resort building. But your chalet also has a private bath and hot tub, which are ready for you to use at any time. Our saunas and steam rooms are closed now, but they'll be open all day tomorrow. We have some designated to use the American way, and others you can use Scandinavian style."

"Scandinavian style? What's that?" she asked him.

"I think he means naked," Gabe whispered in her ear.

"All our guests use towels in the sauna and steam rooms." Larry cleared his throat. "But you can choose whether or not to have swimwear under."

"I like the idea of naked, just so you know." Gabe's words tickled her ear.

She tried really hard not to smile. "What are the benefits of the sauna?" she asked Larry, feeling sorry for the poor guy. The least she could do was sound interested.

He perked up. "They improve your overall wellness by reducing stress and releasing endorphins. As well as that, they're a great way to detoxify, because they encourage perspiration. We have a lot of athletes come use them, because they're extremely useful after intense physical exercise."

"Intense physical exercise you say?" Gabe murmured. She elbowed him in the waist and he chuckled.

"But most of our guests just say they feel good," Larry continued, ignoring Gabe, thank goodness. "And here we are. This is your chalet." He unlocked the door and ushered the bellhop over. He carried their suitcases through, and Larry ushered Gabe and Nicole inside. "We have you booked for dinner at eight, so feel free to use the pool or hot tub to relax before then."

He flicked a switch next to a pair of huge glass doors, and the exterior was flooded with light. Nicole stared out at their own personal hot tub and pool, overlooking the mountains. Nobody would see them in there. They could be butt naked if they wanted to.

And yeah, she wanted to.

"That's beautiful," she said, looking up at Gabe. He had an intense expression on his face, like he'd been staring at her for longer than she'd realized.

"You have a fully stocked mini bar, and of course a spa tub for relaxing in whenever you want. There's a television in your bathroom, too."

"Fancy." She grinned. She'd been to a lot of hotels in her time, but she'd never been anywhere with a television in the bathroom. Her mom would probably think it was completely tasteless.

But she loved it. Every part of it.

"Does the television have Netflix?" Gabe asked.

"Of course, Sir."

She looked up at him and grinned. He winked back.

"Is there anything else we can get for you?" Larry asked.

"Nope, I think we're all good here." Gabe shook his hand, and she could see the hint of a bill pass between them. She had no idea of the value though.

"Thank you, Sir," Larry murmured. "And if you need anything, just pick up the phone and call reception. We'd be delighted to help." He clicked his fingers and the bellhop followed him out, but not before Gabe slipped him a bill, too.

When the door was closed, she turned to look at Gabe, who was leaning against the wall, staring right at her.

"Naked saunas? Seriously?" She started to laugh.

"And Netflix in the bath. Don't forget that."

"You embarrassed that poor man. Did you see his cheeks go all pink when you started talking about intense physical exercise?"

Gabe grinned, pushing himself off the wall and walking toward her. "I was only telling him the truth. I have a lot of exercise planned for you. Really intense and really physical." He pulled her toward him, taking her mouth with his own. "You'll be needing that sauna, believe me."

She tried to think of a funny retort, but then he was

kissing her so hard that any thoughts she had flew right out of her brain, replaced by a need for him so overwhelming it made her tremble.

This man was going to be the death of her. And she was pretty sure she was falling for him, all the way.

DAMN, she was beautiful. He'd just got back from a workout in the gym – Nicole had refused to join him, telling him she'd hang out in the hot tub between treatments. She was laying in the bubbled water, her head back, holding her Kindle in one hand above her, using it to read and block out the winter sun at the same time. Steam rose up around her face, making her skin damp and glowy. Her lips were curled and her cheeks red, and he wondered if it was from the heat of the tub, or the part of the book she'd gotten to.

He wanted to take a photo of this moment, to store it in his memory banks for a time when they wouldn't be together. Because he knew without a doubt that time would come. She was only with him temporarily, while she got over her heartbreak. And yeah, maybe he was letting her use him to get over that pain, but that was okay. He wanted her to feel better.

Wanted her to always be smiling like this.

That was something he could give her. Along with the respite of having somewhere to stay while she figured out what she was going to do next. If he could give her more, he would. Give her a family that deserved her, a boyfriend that wouldn't cheat on her. But he was powerless to give her those things.

And it pissed him off.

He cleared his throat to let her know he was here –

remembering her startled response when he surprised her at the yoga studio. This time there was an electronic device involved, and there was no way he wanted her dropping that in the water.

She put the Kindle down on the table beside the tub and pushed her wet hair off her brow. A huge smile lit up her face. "Hey. How was the gym?"

"Good. How's the book?"

"Getting spicy." She raised a brow. "She's about to discover the alien has two... um... appendages."

"You're reading alien porn?"

"It's not porn, it's romance." She bit down a smile. "Really sexy alien romance. Who knew blue skin could be so hot?"

"I'm gonna get blue skin if I stand out here much longer." He was still wearing his shorts and a sports top. His shoes and socks were by the door. "Will that do?"

She lifted a brow. "Everything about you will do. Get in." She tapped the surface of the water, and it bubbled over her hand.

"I'm sweaty. Need to take a shower."

"There's one out here." She pointed at the outdoor shower – a simple steel pipe that led to a shower head. It was in between the hot tub and the pool.

"It's a cold shower, Nic. You ever seen a grown man cry?"

"No, but I'm kind of excited to watch." She turned so she was facing him, her arms folded over the edge of the tub, her chin resting on them. "Come on, you're man enough, aren't you?"

"I probably am now, but I won't be after. Unless you really do find blue skin hot, along with shrinking dicks and balls."

She pouted, and damn if he didn't want to kiss those lips

until they stung. "Come on. Do it for me." She tipped her head to the side and he was done for. If his brothers could see him now they'd laugh like crazy. He was a sap for this woman.

"If you insist." He stalked over to the shower and turned on the faucet, ice cold water running out of the sprinkler. Groaning – and resigned to his fate – he put his head under, letting out a loud oath as the water hit his head.

"I'm gonna need you naked for this," Nicole called out.

"I'm gonna need you naked, too," he grunted.

"Already done." She lifted herself up for him to see her bare chest, and his eyes were drawn to those rosy nipples.

Shaking his head, he pulled his top over his wet hair, then shucked off his shorts, and turned to look at her. Her eyes darted down his body, and he had to grit his teeth not to shiver in the cold. "If I end up at the ER, you can explain to my family," he told her.

"A big man like you?" Her eyes dipped down. "You don't have to worry about hypothermia. Now get in. The faster you get clean, the faster you can get in here with me." Her voice was throaty as hell. He felt himself begin to stir.

And then he stepped under the shower and any thought of stirring disappeared. It took all the strength he had not to scream like a baby. He knew about cold – he'd grown up in the snow, based a whole career around it – but this was something else.

"Oh my God! I didn't really think you'd do it." Her eyes were wide with alarm.

His teeth were chattering. "Do you not know this about guys? You dare us, we'll do it. Every time."

"Get out of there before you freeze to death," she told him. "You must be clean by now. Come warm up before you really do end up in the ER."

Because he was a macho ass, he took his time, running his hands through his freezing, wet hair and shaking it. And then he saw her sneaking a look at him, and maybe he took a little bit longer, because he liked the way her lips parted.

"Gabe!"

"It's not so bad when you get used to it." Lies, all lies.

"I want you in here with me. Come on." She was pouting again. The things he could do with those lips.

Turning the shower off, he had to grit his teeth to stop them from clattering against each other. Then he slowly sauntered over to the hot tub, stopping right in front of her. She swallowed hard, lifting her head to gaze up at him, her chest rising and falling in a quick rhythm.

"It's your turn," he said, shaking his head at her, cold water flying from his hair. She shrieked and shrunk back, but he lunged for her, half pulling her out of the tub and pressing her oh-so-warm body against his.

"Gabe! You're freezing."

"And you're toasty." He rubbed his face against hers and she grimaced. "Maybe you need a cold shower."

"Hell no. I'm not going anywhere near that thing." Her breath caught. "Am I?" Her eyes met his, and he could see so many emotions in there that it made his muscles tighten. There was laughter, and a little bit of fear, and passion as well, but most of all he saw trust. As though she'd go wherever he took her, because she knew he'd take care of her.

It made him feel ten feet tall.

"No, you're not. I like you warm and soft."

She kissed his jaw. "I like you cold and hard."

He dipped his head, his lips capturing hers, and though he was cold as hell, her mouth was everything. Heated and enticing and everything he never knew he wanted.

"Take me inside, big man," she said against his lips. "Show me what a bad girl I am for teasing you."

She didn't need to ask twice. He lifted her clean out of the tub and she hooked her legs around his waist as he took her inside, both of them dripping on the marble floor. Being careful not to slip, he carried her to the bedroom, then into the bathroom with the huge spa bath and the oversized rain shower. Without letting her go, he switched it on, then walked them both underneath the blissfully warm water.

"We have a thing about showers," she said, kissing him again, her soft tongue sliding against his.

"I have a thing about you," he muttered. And it was true, he did.

And then he showed her exactly how powerful that thing was.

CHAPTER 25

"I got another email from my mom," Nicole told him the next morning. They were getting their couples massage, laying on black leather tables side by side. She was on her front and so was he, their faces turned so they could watch each other.

"Don't tell me they've changed their mind. My muscles feel like jelly. I don't think I can drive us back to Winterville right now." The masseur was pushing hard against his back and he groaned. "Shit."

"It's a knot," the masseur said, pushing down harder until Gabe groaned again. "We'll get it out."

Nicole watched as the masseur slowly eased Gabe's pain. "They haven't changed their mind." She was getting distracted by the thick bands of muscles on his back and arm. Like her, he was covered in a white towel from his waist to his thighs, but the rest of him was visible, and way too delectable. "Mom was asking if I'll still come to Dad's award ceremony in a couple of weeks. They need to give numbers for the table."

Gabe's eyes flickered, but he said nothing.

"I'm not sure if I'll go."

"Do you want to go?"

She blinked. "Honestly? I don't know. I guess it would be nice for my dad. But Luke will be there, of course, so I'd have to deal with that." She sounded braver than she thought she would. But she felt braver, too. This weekend with Gabe had made her look differently at herself.

She was a good person, worthy of their attention. She loved them, but they frustrated the hell out of her. She'd spent a lifetime fighting for her moment in the sun with them. Maybe it was time to accept the way things were.

You couldn't choose your family, but you could accept them. Learn how to live with them without letting them affect you. And that was her plan.

"If you want to go, I can talk to Alaska. See if we can find a stand in for you. She'll need to get someone when you move back to D.C. full time, anyway."

Nicole caught his eye. For a moment she said nothing. Then she nodded. "I guess she will." It was crazy how much she wanted him to tell her not to go. To stay with him. But he wasn't going to. They were having fun together, but this wasn't a long term thing for him.

"If I went you could come with me," she said, and her eyes widened, because where did that thought come from? A blush stole up her cheeks, and she couldn't look at him. If only the massage table would swallow her up whole.

"I don't think that's a good idea." His voice was gentle, but it still pierced her.

She nodded, trying to will the embarrassment away.

He reached out to tip her head up, so he could look into her eyes. "You haven't seen them for a while. It'd be weird walking in with me at your side. Are you ready to explain that?"

She sighed. "I guess not."

"I could drive you though."

Her brows knitted. "To D.C.?"

"Yeah. I have a few friends there I could catch up with. If you need a friendly face nearby for a bit of courage."

"We're just going to leave the room for a moment," the one masseur said. "If you two could turn around and cover yourselves up again, that would be great. Call us in when you're ready."

They left and the two of them rolled over, and for a moment she was facing him, wearing only panties and nothing else. She felt exposed, yet completely protected. It was a strange combination.

"You don't need to be my knight in shining armor, Gabe."

"I know. But I want to be there. I want to be with you."

Her heart clenched. "If I go, I'd want you to be there, too. Let me think about it and I'll decide this week. Is that okay?"

"Fine by me." He inclined his head at her towel. "We should probably lie down and cover ourselves up before they get an eyeful of the best breasts I've ever seen."

She smiled, but really she wanted to let out a whoop and do a fist bump. Because he wanted to go with her to D.C. And whether she went or not, that felt good.

It wasn't a declaration of love. He was being the friend he was. Good, kind, and always caring.

She'd take that. And wish that it was more.

~

THE ROOM WAS COMPLETELY DARK, save for the glow of the moon filtering through the gauze curtains that covered the windows. Gabe was on his side, his head propped on his hand, watching her sleep.

She looked so young when she was dreaming. Too young for him, he knew that. Yet he wasn't willing to give her up. It was crazy how much she'd turned his life upside down in a few weeks. He'd been a confirmed bachelor, used to playing the field and not getting attached. Yet all it had taken was this beautiful, kind, funny woman to move into his house and change everything he thought he knew for fact.

Like he'd never fall in love.

And yeah, he was falling for Nicole. He wasn't sure when exactly it had happened. Was it when they made love for the first time? When she brought him a sandwich to say sorry for vomiting on his shoes? Or maybe during those late night sofa discussions while they watched yet another Bourne movie, and she'd tease him mercilessly about being caught watching porn by his brother.

All he knew was he'd do anything for her. Anything to stop her from getting hurt by those she loved. He loved her smile, loved the way she was so soft and gentle, yet in private so damn dirty.

He had no idea what to do with that thought.

He stroked her hair, and she murmured. For a moment he considered waking her up and making love to her again. When he was inside her, her lips soft against his, everything felt right. Perfect, even.

She was his addiction and he wasn't sure he could ever give her up.

Nicole let out a little sigh, and he laid his head down on

the pillow, willing himself to sleep. He reached for her, pulling her soft, warm body against his and let out a contented sigh. They'd do this again. Go away and be with each other. He would take her somewhere warm next time, somewhere she could wear a bikini on the beach and he could carry her into the water and make her squeal when he threw her into the spray.

The shrill sound of a phone cut through his thoughts. He reached for the room phone, knocking it off the cradle, then frowned when the screeching continued, and he saw Nicole's phone lighting up and vibrating on the table on her side of the bed.

Her eyelids flew open, and her face looked confused as she dragged herself out of whatever dream she'd been having.

"What's happening?" she asked, still blinking to acclimatize herself.

"It's your phone."

"Shit." She reached for it, her fingers stumbling twice before they got purchase on the case. "It's my mom," she whispered, then answered it, her expression full of fear only a middle-of-the-night phone call could create.

"Hello?" A pause. "Kara?" There was another pause, then she sat straight up in the bed, a horrified expression on her face. "When? Is he okay?"

Another long piece of silence, punctuated only by the muffled voice on the other end of the line. Nicole's breaths were short, her chest catching. Gabe sat up and ran his hand through his hair, reaching out to touch her shoulder because he had no idea what else to do.

"I'll be there. Just tell him to hang on, okay?" She inhaled raggedly. "Yeah, I know. I'll get there as fast as I can."

When she ended the call, she turned to look at him, and he could see the tears pooling in her eyes.

"What is it?" he asked. "What happened?"

"It's my dad. He had a heart attack." She lifted her hand to her lips and let out a sob. "He's at Jefferson Memorial Hospital. I need to get there."

A wave of horror washed over him. They were at least eight hours away from D.C. "Of course you do. Let me see if there are any flights." He grabbed the room phone and pressed one for reception, then quickly asked them for the next flights. Nicole watched him with shiny eyes, her chest hitching as he talked quickly into the mouthpiece.

"There's nothing until tomorrow morning," Gabe told her, and she sobbed again. This was all his fault. He was the one who'd insisted on taking her away this weekend. If they'd been in Winterville it was only a four hour drive. But eight hours? Anything could happen.

He glanced at his watch. It was one in the morning. If they left now they could be there before the first flight even took off from Asheville. "I'll drive," he said. "We can be there by morning."

Her eyes were full of tears. "I can't ask you to do that."

"You're not asking. I'm telling you we're driving. We can pack, check out, and be on the road in ten minutes. Tell your sister we'll be there by morning. And to keep in touch if there are any changes."

She clambered over the mattress to where he was standing and threw her arms around his waist. "Thank you," she mumbled into his chest. He stroked her hair, feeling the silkiness of her tresses between his fingers.

"It's going to be okay," he murmured, pressing his lips to her brow. It had to be. Because if anything happened to her dad and she wasn't there to be with him, he wasn't sure she'd forgive him.

Wasn't sure he'd forgive himself, either.

She said nothing, just breathed brokenly against his chest. "It's going to be okay," he repeated, his voice firmer. "Now go get dressed and I'll throw our clothes in our bags."

$\mathcal{N}$icole slept fitfully as he merged onto the 181, following the same route they'd used to drive down here, except this time he'd been diverting east once they reached Front Royal. She'd been awake for the first part of the trip, alternatively talking to her sister for updates, then telling him what was going on.

Her dad had been rushed to the hospital in an ambulance after waking up with intense chest pain. He was currently in the ER, where they were trying to stabilize his heart rhythm, and right now she didn't know much more than that.

He could tell how anxious she was by the way she kept twisting her fingers together and glancing at the clock on his dash. From what she'd told him, her dad had a minor heart attack a few months earlier, and this was what they'd all feared.

By three in the morning he'd managed to persuade her to get some sleep. He'd pulled off the road for a few minutes and bought himself a coffee from the nearest drive-thru, needing a caffeine injection to keep himself awake and aware. And then he'd turned on the stereo to an all-night talk channel – figuring having voices talking softly in the background wouldn't hurt.

If he was going to get her to D.C. as quickly as possible, he wanted to make sure they arrived there in one piece. So coffee and talk it was.

Every now and then he'd look over to check she was still asleep. Only twice did he see her eyes open, as she stared glassily out of the window. She didn't want to talk, and that was okay. He wasn't sure what to say anyway.

He could tell her that her dad was going to be okay like he did earlier, but the truth was, none of them knew that for a fact. He could hope, he could pray, but he couldn't make it happen for her.

It made him feel impotent and he hated that.

The sun hadn't even begun to rise when they passed Front Royal, and he saw the mountain road that would eventually lead to Winterville. Instead of taking it, he followed the road through Cedar Creek Park, then took the ramp to the I66.

The roads were empty, due to the time of day and the fact it was a Sunday. It made it harder to concentrate and not drift off in thought. But he gritted his teeth and tightened his grip on the steering wheel, stopping once more for an Americano before making the final push for D.C.

They reached the metro area just before eight, passing Arlington Cemetery and crossing the Potomac River on the Roosevelt Bridge. There were more cars now, people heading to weekend work and to early church services, and he had to slow his speed to the twenty-five MPH as he worked his way through the city grid system, heading north past Dupont Circle.

They'd almost reached the hospital when Nicole

stirred again. She sat up straight, rubbing her eyes then blinking at the brightness of the winter sun. "Are we here?"

"About five minutes away."

She grabbed her phone and checked her messages. "No change."

"Hopefully you'll learn more when we get there."

The large, white building of the Jefferson Memorial Hospital was ahead, set among landscaped gardens with evergreen trees and perfectly tended lawns. He followed the directions to the parking lot – thankfully half empty due to it being early on a Sunday, and pulled into a space.

As he killed the engine, Nicole sent a message to her sister and climbed out of the car, and he followed, leaving their luggage in the trunk. She was walking fast, but he could walk faster, and within moments they were at the big glass doors at the entrance to reception.

"Kara says it's a maze in there. She's going to meet me in a minute."

"That's good." He reached for her hand then pulled back. She had enough to worry about. She didn't need her sister seeing him touching her, too.

Nicole gave her name to the clerk at reception, and she printed her out a badge, sliding it into a plastic case. "And you, are you family, too?" the clerk asked him.

"Ah, no."

She gave a sympathetic smile. "Only family at the moment, I'm afraid."

He opened his mouth to tell her it was fine, but then somebody called out Nicole's name. He looked up to see a woman approaching, and realized it had to be her sister. They had the same color hair, and those melted chocolate eyes, though their body shapes were completely different.

Where Nicole was strong and curved, her sister was tiny and willowy.

And she wasn't alone.

There were two men with her, and he recognized neither of them. It wasn't until he felt Nicole stiffen beside him that he started to suspect who at least one of them was.

Before he could ask her the question, Nicole was in her sister's arms. "It took you so long, Mom keeps asking where you are."

"Brad White, Kara's fiancé." One of the men held his hand out to Gabe.

He shook it. "Gabe Winter. I'm a…"

"You remember, Matt's friend." Nicole pulled away from her sister's embrace. "Gabe, this is Kara."

"Thank you for bringing her." Kara gave him a curt nod, then looked back at Nicole. "Brad and Luke are going to get coffee. Would you like one?"

"How's Dad?" Nicole asked, her voice wavering.

"We're waiting to see his doctor. Mom's with him now. They said he's stable but they won't tell us anything else." Kara grimaced. "I overheard them saying something about his heart beats being erratic, but hopefully mom will have more news soon. Come up with me and we can find out."

Nicole turned to look at Gabe, her eyes uncertain. "Go," he told her. "I'll be fine."

"What will you do? Drive home?" Her brows were knitted.

Damn, he wanted to hold her, smooth those frown lines away. Make her feel safe and loved, the way he knew he could. "I'm too tired to drive. I'll probably find a hotel, get some rest."

Nicole opened her mouth to say something, then closed it again. He felt the warmth of her ex boyfriend's stare.

"That sounds like a good idea," Luke said. "Get some sleep then go home." He looked at Nicole. "I'll get you some coffee and a pastry, sweetheart. You look beat."

Nicole opened her mouth to say something, then closed it again. Her eyes met Gabe's but he couldn't read her expression at all.

It felt like he'd lost part of her already. That it was being swallowed up by her family and that parasite who'd cheated on her. And yeah, he was feeling pretty fucking jealous that this guy could call her sweetheart, and he couldn't.

But there was no way he was going to make a scene in front of her family. Her day was difficult enough as it was. He'd go sleep then he'd call her and find out how her dad was. It was the only thing he could do right now.

"Unless you want me to stay here?" he asked Nicole, ignoring the stares he was getting from her ex and her sister. "I can sit in one of these chairs in case you need me."

Nicole's expression softened. For a moment, they stared at each other, neither one of them saying anything at all. Then she ran her tongue along her dry bottom lip and shook her head. "You need sleep," she whispered. "I'll be fine."

"I'll keep my phone on. Let me know what's happening, okay?"

"You know what?" Luke said. "Brad, you go get the coffees. I'm going to stay with Nicole."

"Are you allowed up there?" Nicole frowned. "I thought they said family only?"

Kara laughed. "Luke's family. Dad would want him there."

"I guess..."

Then Luke put his arm around her, and Gabe had to

squeeze his jaw tight not to say anything. Yes, he was jealous as hell, and yes, there was no way he could show it.

He was doing this for Nicole. That's all that mattered.

"Thank you for bringing her to us," Luke said, his eyes narrowing. "She's with family now. We'll take it from here."

"Let me know when you hear some news," he told Nicole, his voice gruff.

"Of course." There was such a sad look in her eyes that it took everything he had not to walk over there and hug her. "Thank you," she said softly.

"Any time."

THEY WERE ALLOWED to go in and see her father one by one. When it was Nicole's turn, she stepped into his private room quietly, taking the seat next to his bed and holding his hand. "Daddy?"

He turned his head, and she couldn't believe how ashen his face looked. "Nicole." His voice was hoarse, like he'd been shouting for days. "How long have you been here?"

"I just got here. You gave us all a scare." She squeezed his hand, and he nodded. "How are you feeling?"

"Like I've been cage fighting."

She smiled. If he was joking, that was a good sign. "Have you seen the doctor yet?"

"I don't know. So many people keep introducing themselves and coming in, I'm losing track of who I've seen."

"Hopefully somebody will come talk to you soon and let you know how you're doing." She glanced down at their joined hands. His was cold and clammy. "Are you in any pain?"

"Not at the moment." He grimaced. "But last night was bad. So bad. I never want to go through that again."

She swallowed hard. "You won't have to. The doctors will make sure of that."

Her dad let out a long breath. "I've missed you, sweetheart."

"I've missed you, too."

"I don't know why you left, but I hope you're back for good. Your mom says Luke is here. Are you two…"

She pulled her lip between her teeth. "Don't worry about me, just concentrate on getting well, okay?"

He nodded. "Okay." His eyes started to droop. She watched as his head tipped back and he let out a long, sleepy breath. His hand loosened in hers, but she kept hold of it until a nurse came in, and smiled gently at her.

"I have to check some vitals," she said. "It may be easier if you step out for a few moments."

"Of course." Nicole nodded. She gently released her dad's hand, then leaned forward to kiss his slack cheek. "I'll be back soon, Daddy."

When she stepped outside the room, she closed her eyes for a moment, and let out a long breath, a wave of exhaustion washing over her. Was it only a few hours ago that she and Gabe were at the spa? It felt like another life right now.

"How did he look?"

She opened her eyes to see Luke a few feet away from her. "Tired."

Luke nodded. "You look tired, too."

"I am. It was a long trip."

"How have you been?" His jaw was tight. "I've tried to call you a few times."

"I blocked you." She didn't smile at him. She couldn't.

But she didn't have the energy to hate him, either. "Why are you here, Luke?"

"Because I care about your father. And you." His gaze was soft. "I know how much you love him. I wanted to be here for you."

"And what about your girlfriend?"

"That's over. It has been for a while. That's what I called to tell you. I messed up, Nic. I know that."

She squeezed her eyes shut again. There was a throbbing in her temple that made her wince. She didn't want to think about this. She didn't want to think about anything. Truth be told, she wanted to see Gabe, to talk to him, to feel his arms wrapped around her, to feel safe again.

"I can't talk about this now," she told Luke, as he pushed open the door to the waiting room. "It's too much."

"Of course." His voice was soft. "We'll talk later."

No, that wasn't what she meant. But her family was staring up at her, Kara and Brad eating pastries, her mom sipping a coffee.

"Matt called," Kara said, glancing from Nicole to Luke. "He's getting on a plane now. Should be here tonight."

"That's good." Nicole's smile was genuine. "Have you heard from the doctor yet?"

"He's coming to talk to us after rounds." Her mom sounded tired. Nicole took the seat next to her, and slid her palm into hers. Her mom didn't resist, just squeezed back. "Daddy looked so sick, didn't he?" she said to Nicole.

"He's very tired," Nicole said. "But he's in the right place. He's young and he's got a lot of fight in him."

"I don't think I can go through something like this again." Her mom tipped her head back against the wall. "He was in so much pain, it was terrible. And the ambulance took so long. I was so scared we were going to lose him."

"He's still here, Mom," Nicole whispered.

"I know." She nodded.

It was almost eleven by the time the doctor finally met with them, taking them to a quiet room so they could talk in private. "Are you all family?" he asked as he watched them file in.

"These are my daughters," her mom said, pointing to Nicole and Kara. "Brad is Kara's fiancé. And Luke is Nicole's partner."

Nicole frowned. "*Mom.*"

Her mom patted her shoulder. "It's fine. They can come in, can't they, doctor?"

"Of course." He gave them a reassuring smile. The room smelled of antiseptic and coffee, and Nicole's stomach did a little twist. She needed to talk to her mom and Luke, because this was crazy.

But not here, not now.

The doctor folded his hands in front of him, resting his elbows on the table as he looked straight at her mom. "Mrs. Rice, we've confirmed your husband has suffered from a myocardial infarction - a heart attack. Quite a major one, I'm afraid. We've given him a number of different medications to stabilize him. Statins, which are blood thinners, will attempt to prevent another blockage to his heart. And he's been on oxygen therapy, of course. Plus we've been treating him for the pain that he experienced in his chest and arms last night."

Her mom nodded, her face looking white.

"Today we've been running tests on your husband, and I'm afraid he has a number of blocked arteries. We were hoping to carry out a percutaneous coronary intervention – that's a non-surgical procedure that you may know better as angioplasty. But unfortunately, the blockage is too severe, so I'm recommending surgery."

"What kind of surgery?" Her mom's voice was thin.

"It's called a coronary artery bypass graft. We'll need to graft three new arteries into your husband's chest during an open heart surgery."

"Is it bypass surgery?" Brad asked.

"That's correct." The doctor nodded. "In Mr. Rice's case, it's a triple bypass."

Nicole's stomach twisted.

"How long will it take?" Kara asked.

"The surgery itself can take from three to eight hours. In my experience, a triple bypass surgery will take around five to six hours. Your husband would then be moved into an ICU bed for monitoring for around twenty-four hours. Once we're happy with him, he'll be released home, usually within a week."

"And if he doesn't have the surgery there's every chance he'll have another heart attack" Kara murmured, always the doctor. Brad was stroking her hair.

"Yes, ma'am. Your father's coronary arteries are blocked. There would be a very high likelihood of another myocardial infarction."

"A deadly one?" Nicole asked.

"Very possible, yes."

"When are you planning to do the surgery?" Kara looked at the doctor.

Luke was trying to grab Nicole's hand. She placed it under her legs to avoid his touch.

"We'd like to do it as soon as possible, hopefully this afternoon. There are a few more things we need to do to get your father ready, but by four this afternoon I should be scrubbing up."

There was silence for a moment. Nicole looked at her mom, who had her face in her hands. She was usually so unflappable.

"I'd like to go talk to your husband now," the doctor told her mom. "Maybe you can accompany me?"

"Yes, of course." She nodded, but there were tears in her eyes.

"And can I recommend that afterward, you all go home and get some rest? I know you've been here since last night, and your husband will need your strength. His recovery will take weeks."

"That sounds like a good idea," Brad said softly.

Nicole slumped back in her seat. She'd need to call Alaska. And she had to talk to Gabe. It didn't look like she was going back to Winterville any time soon.

CHAPTER 27

"Could you please stop following me?" Nicole whipped around to see Luke bearing down on her. He'd been her shadow for the past few hours. The only place she'd managed to hide from him was in the ladies' room, and delightful though that was – now she knew why insurance premiums were so high – there was only so long she could hide out in a bathroom stall.

And anyway, apparently he'd worked out her ruse, because he'd been waiting for her right outside.

"I just want to talk to you."

She stopped walking and turned to stare him down. "Now isn't the time. My dad's about to go into surgery, my mom's losing it, and Kara is... well... Kara. Please just let me freak out in peace."

"When is the time?" Luke asked. "Because I've been trying to talk to you for weeks. You're twenty-five years old, Nicole, you can't keep avoiding me like I mean nothing."

"You had sex with another woman in our bed. I'm entitled to do what I want."

He raked his fingers through his dark blonde hair, and it

landed perfectly back in place. All at once an image of Gabe, furious as hell, his hair falling everywhere, burst into her mind.

Dark hair. Warm eyes. She missed them. And he was one of the reasons she'd wanted to be alone. To send him a message to update him. She hadn't wanted to call – the guy needed his sleep – but she needed some connection to him.

Because even after a few hours here in D.C. with her family she was starting to feel like Winterville had never happened. That she was still this Nicole. And she didn't like it one bit.

"It was a mistake." He reached for her shoulder. "Let me explain."

"Sure. Explain how a penis magically enters a vagina by mistake."

He winced. "Do you have to be so vulgar?"

Against her better judgement, she started to laugh. Because this was so messed up. This man, her father's assistant, she'd thought he was everything. She'd thought she wasn't good enough for him. Somehow, he'd convinced her that he'd have to mold her into being the girlfriend she needed to be. And the worst part was that she'd let him. Let him make her feel less of a person, the same way she'd let her family make her feel that same way.

But she wasn't less. She was exactly who she was meant to be. And if it wasn't good enough for him or her family, wasn't that *their* problem?

"It's over, Luke. It probably shouldn't have ever begun."

"You're upset. I get that. But at some point we need to talk this through. You still have things at my place. That shows me you're not over me."

"You need to go."

He blinked. "But..."

"I'm serious. I'll arrange for my things to get picked up, but it's over, Luke. I don't want to hear any explanations or excuses because I don't care. I really don't. And yes, I should have been grown up enough to tell you that before, but you hurt me, and I didn't know how to handle that. And maybe I needed this time away, I don't know. All I know is that I'll never be the person you want me to be. And I don't want to. So feel free to have sex with your assistant or whoever it is that rocks your boat, because I don't care anymore."

"Is there somebody else?" He narrowed his eyes.

"Why does there always have to be someone else? Why can't it be that I'm a strong, independent woman who knows her own worth?"

He smirked as though he knew her better than she knew herself.

He was wrong.

GABE SLEPT for six hours straight. His whole body felt groggy as he looked around the room, working out where the hell he was, and more importantly why the hell he was in some nondescript room that looked – and smelled – scarily like the ones he used to stay in during boarding competitions.

And then he remembered. Nicole's dad. The hospital. Sitting up, he grabbed his phone, frowning when he saw he had a message from her. He should have stayed awake, dammit. Or been with her.

Yeah, and made a great impression on her family by falling asleep in the waiting room.

Not to mention her asshole of an ex. Just thinking about him being anywhere near her made Gabe's blood boil. He felt like an ass being here in a hotel room, powerless to do anything to help.

What are you going to do? Perform heart surgery?

Weird how the sarcastic voice in his head sounded exactly like his brother. He could even picture North's lifted brow. And no, he wasn't intending on cutting anybody open, now or ever, but he could at least be there for her.

Sure. Try explaining *that* to her family.

Shaking his head, he pulled up her message and typed out a fast reply.

Just woke up. Sorry I'm not there. Any more news on your dad? – G

Three little dots appeared on the screen. A moment later her reply landed.

He's about to go into surgery. Mom and Kara are going to head home for some rest. I guess I'll do the same. – N

You want to come here? – G

Probably best not to. – N

He tried not to let that hurt. She was right, they didn't need to raise any questions right now. But it didn't stop him from gritting his teeth and wondering exactly where she would be resting.

I'M OUTSIDE NOW. **Can I call you? – N**

HE DIDN'T WAIT to type out a reply, instead he hit the phone icon. A moment later, it connected.

"Hey." Her voice was low. He could hear the sound of talking and car engines in the background.

"You sound tired. You holding up okay?" Damn, he wanted to hold her right now.

"I'll be better when Dad's out of surgery. It's going to be a long few hours. Mom's almost beside herself and Kara isn't much better. Hopefully if they get some rest they'll calm down." She exhaled heavily. "How about you, you feeling any more awake?"

"I'm fine. You don't need to worry about me."

"But I do worry. You're exhausted because of me."

"And you're exhausted, too. You sure you don't want to come here? The room's paid for through tomorrow."

"Are you not staying there tonight?" Her voice lifted.

"I think I should probably go home." He paused. "Unless you want me to stay?"

He wanted her to say yes. But he knew everything had changed. Had known it the moment her phone rang in the hotel room. They'd been living in some kind of bubble for the past few weeks, and reality had popped it.

He hated that.

"It's okay," she said softly. "You need to get back to work." She paused for a moment. "And I need to call Alaska. I don't think I'll be running any classes for a while."

That was so typical of Nicole, worrying about everybody else.

"I've already spoken to her and let her know it's a possibility," he reassured her. "I'll chat with her when I'm back, see if there's a solution. She sends you her love, they all do."

Her breath sounded ragged. "Everything is so upside down. I don't know what to do."

His heart clenched for her. "Nic?"

"Yes?"

"He's going to be okay."

"I know. It's not just... it doesn't matter." She paused again before asking, "When will you leave?"

"I don't know. I was thinking I'd stay until I hear that your dad's out of surgery and then head home. I'll need to get some sleep before work tomorrow."

"You don't have to stay until you hear from me. I can message you while you're on the road."

"I'm staying, Nicole." There was a firmness to his voice.

"Thank you," she said softly. "Can I ask you a favor?"

"Of course."

"Will you come see me before you leave? Just so I can say goodbye? I don't know when I'll get back to Winterville."

"Just say where and when and I'll be there."

"Did Luke talk to you?" her mom asked later that day. They'd all had some sleep and were drinking coffee in the kitchen. Kara had decided to come home with them – though Brad was back at their apartment.

"He did." Nicole took another sip, praying for the caffeine to work. She really hoped Gabe didn't feel as shitty as she did – otherwise his drive back to Winterville was going to be a mess.

"And?" Her mom lifted her chin. "Did you make up with him?"

Nicole frowned. "No. And we're not going to."

"Oh Nicole." Her mom let out a long sigh. "You two were perfect for each other."

She shook her head. "We weren't. It wasn't working out."

Kara frowned. "He seems so happy to see you. Maybe you can give him another chance."

She could see they didn't understand, but this wasn't the time or place to tell them about what he'd done.

"I really thought you'd found a good place in life," her mom said, shaking her head. "That I wouldn't have to worry about you anymore."

"You don't have to worry about me." Her voice felt thick.

"Of course I do. You've always been the one I worry about. Kara always sailed through life. Matt, too. Even if he isn't doing what your father and I would have wanted, at least he has a passion. He's successful. But you…"

"I have passion."

"For yoga?" Her mom lifted a brow. "That's not even a sport."

"But it's what makes me happy."

Her mom blinked. "It does?"

"Yes, it does. I wasn't happy with Luke. We were so incompatible, that's why he always kept trying to change me. But these past couple of months in Winterville, they've shown me what I can be if I try hard. That I can run my own life, that I can have my own business. People love my classes, Mom. And I love running them."

There was silence for a moment. Her mom's eyes met hers.

"What?" Nicole asked her.

"I just don't understand how you can be so… different to than rest of us."

"There's nothing wrong with that," Nicole told her. "I just want different things than you. But like you, I want to be happy, but to do that I can't keep trying to make myself be somebody I'm not. It's taken me twenty-five years, but I know who I am now. And I like her. I hope you will, too, but if you don't, then I'll live with that."

"I want you to be happy, too," her mom said, her eyes cloudy.

"Then let me live my life the way I want to."

Pressing her lips together, her mom nodded. Then her phone started to buzz, and she lunged for her purse, swallowing hard when she found her phone.

"It's your brother," she told them, then swiped the screen, putting it on speaker as she talked into the mouthpiece. "Matt, it's Mom."

"I know. I'm the one calling you."

Nicole tried not to laugh.

"Where are you?" her mom asked.

"I just landed. Waiting for my luggage. Any news on dad?"

"We're waiting for the hospital to call," Kara said.

"How long will it be?" Matt's voice sounded crackly.

"He went into surgery about four hours ago," their mom told him. "We should hear something soon."

"I'll head straight to the hospital then. Should be there in about forty minutes. Or should I come to your place first?"

Her mom cleared her throat. "Go to the hospital. We'll meet you there."

"Sounds good. They're starting up the luggage belt, so I should be out of here soon. Love you guys."

"Love you too," they chorused. Her mom ended the call and let out a long breath.

"Okay," she said, her eyes soft as she looked at Nicole. "Let's go see how your dad is doing."

$\mathcal{A}$s soon as they got to the hospital, her mom was taken to the recovery room, where her dad had been wheeled to moments earlier. The nurse who came to get her didn't have too much information, but she seemed to think the surgery went well, and that he would be moved to ICU just as soon as he was discharged from post-op.

She warned them that he'd remain sedated for at least twenty-four hours, while his oxygen tube was in. After that they'd remove the tube and bring him slowly around, and once he was stable he'd be moved to the cardiac ward, where he'd stay until discharge in a week's time.

"We'll come get you when he's settled in the ICU," the nurse told her and Kara. Brad had made it, too, and was sitting with her sister, holding her hand. "We restrict visitors to two at a time. There are a lot of machines and we need to be able to access him at all times."

"We understand." Nicole nodded.

Kara had promised their mom that she'd keep every-body updated on their dad's recovery, so she spent the next twenty minutes making calls and sending messages. While she was busy, Nicole quickly tapped out a message to Gabe.

HE'S OUT OF SURGERY. **All went well. Mom's with him but we'll probably be able to see him in an hour or so. – N**

THAT'S GREAT NEWS. **I've just checked out of the hotel. Can I drive over and see you now? – G**

YES PLEASE. **I'll meet you in the parking lot. Message when you get here. – N**

SHE'D SENT the last message right when Matt walked in, pulling a suitcase behind him. He was wearing a pair of jeans and a navy blue hoodie, his hair a mess from long hours on a transatlantic flight. Nicole jumped up and hugged the hell out of him, and he slipped his arms around her, hugging her back.

"Any more news?" he asked.

"You know as much as we do. Mom's with him now. The nurse says it could take an hour to get moved to ICU and settled. He'll be asleep when we visit him, but it'll be good to see him."

Matt nodded. "It will." He had dark shadows under his eyes.

"You look tired. Let me get you some coffee," she suggested gently. "And maybe something to eat?"

Kara looked up from where she was still on the phone, talking to yet another of her dad's contacts. She nodded at

Matt and pointed at the phone, rolling her eyes. Matt winked at her and mimed drinking coffee.

She smiled gratefully.

He mouthed, 'want one?'

"Latte please," Kara said, covering the mouthpiece. Brad stood and shook Matt's hand. "I'll go with you. If that's okay with you, babe?"

Kara covered the mouthpiece. "All good. I have a few more people to call."

"Want me to make some calls, take the slack from you?" Nicole asked her. Her sister shook her head.

"It's all good. I got it."

Matt parked his suitcase next to Kara and the three of them walked to the hospital café, Matt shooting out questions and Nicole and Brad answering them as best they could.

"Luke was here?" Matt grimaced. "*Why*?"

"He's dad's right hand man. And mom seems to think he's family." Nicole sighed.

"Well, he's not. And I'll tell him that when I see him."

Brad muffled a laugh.

Nicole patted her brother's arm, thankful he was back, even if he was as overprotective as usual. "You don't need to fight my battles. I've already told him that. He's not here, is he?"

There was a long line for coffee – it was almost shift change, and the staff were getting their caffeine fix before their night's work began. They'd made it halfway to the counter when Nicole's phone started to vibrate. Gabe's name lit up the screen and she quickly angled it away from her brother so he couldn't see and accepted the call.

"Hey," she said, keeping her voice as neutral as she could.

"You okay?"

"Yes, all good here." Did she just squeak? Please God no.

"Is Matt there?"

"That's right." Why was her heart beating so fast?

"Okay. Don't panic. I'm in the parking lot. Come down and say goodbye, it won't take long."

"That sounds great. I'll come get it now."

Gabe coughed as though she'd said something funny. "I wasn't offering you sex." His voice softened. "I'll see you in a minute."

"Okay, bye." She quickly ended the call. "I just need to go do something," she told Matt and Brad. Thankfully, they'd gotten into a conversation about the various transatlantic airlines, and the best ones in their personal opinions. "I'll meet you back in the waiting room."

"You want me to pick you up a coffee?" Matt asked.

"Sure." She nodded. "An Americano, please."

He winked. "I'll get you a pastry, too."

God, it felt good to have him here. She gave him a smile then rushed out of the café.

Not bothering to take the elevator, she ran down the two flights of steps, then pushed her way through the revolving door into the night time air, thankful she was still wearing her coat because it was cold outside.

Following the path to the parking lot, she felt her heart racing all over again, but for an entirely different reason. Was it really only a few hours since she last saw Gabe? It felt like a lifetime.

And there he was, leaning against his truck, wearing a gray Henley and a thick padded coat. As soon as he caught sight of her he smiled, and it sent a warmth rushing through her.

She ran toward him, her heart beating wildly, and he

held his hands out for her, pulling her in until her body met his hard planes. He cupped her face with his palms, scanning her with his gaze until, seemingly satisfied she was okay, he pressed his lips against hers.

And damn if it didn't make everything feel okay again. He was here and he was perfect and, dear Lord, she loved this man. Loved the way he took care of her. Loved that he'd waited to see her because she couldn't bear for him to go back to Winterville without having seen a glimpse of that handsome, lovely face.

When she was brave enough she'd tell him.

"You okay?" he asked.

"I am now."

A grin pulled at his lips and he leaned down to kiss her again. "Any more news on your dad?"

"He's out of surgery but that's all we know. I'll keep you updated."

"I'll have my phone on Bluetooth for the drive home. Call me any time, okay?"

"You might regret offering that."

He winked. "Never." Then he lifted her head until her lips were in line with his, brushing his mouth softly over them, sending shivers down her spine.

She hooked her arms around his neck, needing him closer. She wasn't sure he'd ever get close enough. He slid his hands down her back, pushing them inside her padded jacket, inside her top, and she felt the cool hardness of them against her spine.

She sighed against his mouth, because he felt so, so good. She brushed her fingertips against the nape of his neck and he groaned, the low, deep resonance sending shots of delight through her body. He lowered his head to kiss her jaw, her chin, the soft skin of her throat, and it was her turn to sigh.

"Jesus, Nic." He pushed her against his car, caging her with his hands, and looked at her intently, his brow touching hers. She could see him fighting for breath, the same way she was. And when he pushed himself against her, she could feel his excitement, the same way she could feel hers, making her thighs feel achy and tight.

He smiled at her, and she started to smile, too. Sure, nothing was right in that hospital, but out here? It was perfect. And she'd take this stolen moment and keep it in her memories.

But then she saw Luke walking toward them and all her breath rushed out of her lungs, her eyes widening as her gaze met her ex-boyfriend's.

FOR A SECOND, Gabe thought he'd done something wrong. She'd gone from being soft and sinuous in his hands to stiff as a board, her eyes wide and panicky as she tried to pull out of his grasp.

It was only when he tried to catch her gaze that he realized she was staring over his shoulder. He turned to follow her line of sight and saw her ex storming toward them, his jaw tight as he closed the gap between his car and Gabe's.

"So there's nobody else, huh?" Luke said, letting out a mirthless laugh. "So you're a liar as well as a cheat."

Nicole was trembling. Gabe touched her face, but she winced so he didn't do it again. Instead he stepped back, and she ducked under his arm, pulling her jacket down to cover the slither of skin he'd exposed.

Gabe turned to look at Luke, but he was staring right at Nicole, his mouth twisted with anger.

"I'm not cheating." She let out a ragged breath.

"So what do you call humping another guy in the parking lot? Does your mom know about this?"

"Watch your damn language," Gabe said, his voice low. He wanted to reach for her again, but she seemed so far away.

"Or what? You gonna hit me? I should be the one hitting you. Did you know she's *my* girlfriend?" The man was about five-foot-eight. He looked like he'd fall down if Gabe so much as blew on him.

"Last thing I heard, you had another girlfriend."

Nicole's face was as white as a ghost.

"That was a mistake. Nicole knows that. And now we're going to try again."

Gabe frowned. "Is that right?"

She shook her head. "No…"

Luke let out a grunt. "It's okay. I don't want her now, anyway. Seeing her all over another guy is enough to put me off." He raised a brow at her. "Does your family know about this?"

Nicole swallowed hard. "You can't tell them. Not here. Not now."

Luke shook his head. "I'm going into the hospital. And then I'm finding your mom, because this is bullshit." His brought his icy eyes to Gabe's. "Did she tell you she never split up with me? Just ran away and wouldn't take my calls. So as far as I'm concerned, we're still together. And you just put your hands, and God knows what else, on her."

Gabe's voice was tight. "Go inside, little man. Before I show you exactly what these hands can do."

Luke went to walk away, but it was as though some

thought caught his brain. Because the next moment he turned and started barreling toward Gabe, his surprisingly hard head slamming into Gabe's stomach, sending both of them flying.

Gabe hit the concrete with a hard thud, the wind knocked out of him so hard he couldn't catch a breath. He could vaguely hear screaming, and for a moment he thought it was his own voice, until he realized Nicole was shouting at Luke, pulling him off of Gabe.

"What the hell's going on?" a fourth voice called out. Gabe blinked, trying to stand as Matt ran toward them, his long, thick hair lifting in the wind. "Gabe?" He frowned. "What are you doing here?"

"Trying to fuck your sister," Luke said. "What else?"

Matt blinked. "What?"

"Get out of here," Nicole shouted at Luke. "Why did you come anyway?"

"Kara called. Said your dad was out of surgery. I thought you might need some comfort." Luke shook his head. "Looks like I got beaten to it."

"Can somebody tell me what the hell's going on here?" Matt asked.

Nicole wouldn't look at Gabe, no matter how much he tried to catch her gaze. He wanted to tell her it was okay. To hold her like he'd done before. To stroke her soft hair and press his lips against hers.

"Nic?" Matt said softly. "What's going on? I came out to find you. Your coffee's getting cold."

"Nothing's happening." She let out a thin breath. "We should go inside."

"Gabe?" Matt asked, turning to him. "Are you and Nic together?"

Finally, she looked at him. She gave a little shake of her head.

"Yeah," he told Matt. "We are."

Matt slammed his hand against Gabe's car. "You promised me, goddamn it."

"We're just friends," Nicole said. "He's been taking care of me."

"Sure looks like it," Luke goaded. "I wish all my friends treated me like that. Well the female ones, anyway."

"They do." Nicole rolled her eyes at him. "Now get the hell out of here."

"Not going anywhere."

"You should both go," Matt said, his eyes still on Gabe. "I want to talk to my *friend*. Man to man."

"No." Nicole's voice was firmer now. "I'm staying. Whatever you have to say to him, you can say to me."

Matt squeezed his eyes shut for a moment, rubbing his brow with his fingertips. "Will you please just go in? It's cold and Dad's inside and Mom needs us. And Luke, go home. Before I knock you out for what you did to my sister."

"Matt, please..." Nicole reached for him. "Let me explain, okay?" Her teeth started to chatter. "It's not what you think."

Luke started to chuckle and she turned to look at him. Gabe couldn't see the expression on her face, but it had to be pure fury, because Luke put his hands up as though in self-defense and took a step back. "Okay, I'll go." He took another step back. "Goddamned crazy family. I'm better off out of it."

Nicole let out a long, deep sigh as her ex walked back to his car and climbed in deliberately slow, his eyes on them through the window as he started up the engine. Then he cruised out of the lot, three pairs of eyes following him until his car was a pinprick of lights in the night.

"Okay. Now can we talk like adults?" Nicole asked, her voice wobbling. "Because this is stupid. It's cold and it's dark and we're standing outside of a hospital. And I for one would like to go upstairs and find out how Dad's doing." She put her hand over her mouth to cover up a sob.

Gabe winced, because she was right. "Go inside and find out," he told her. He was already beating himself up for this whole situation. He shouldn't have come. Should have driven straight home and left her with her family. He knew Matt would be here, that he would take care of her.

But now he'd made everything worse. He'd outed them at a time when she really didn't need to be dealing with this crap. And he'd made her cry – because those really were tears rolling down her cheeks.

He had to make it right. It was a special kind of torture to watch her cry and not be able to kiss the pain away. "Nic," his voice was soft. "Go inside, please. Let me talk with Matt." He needed to make this right. For her.

He'd known as soon as they walked into the hospital lobby early this morning that he was going to lose her. Sure, it had taken until now for him to realize what that tugging in his stomach had been. It had been loss. Sadness.

The knowledge that the woman he'd fallen for wasn't supposed to be with him.

She was with her family, where she should be. And he didn't belong there. He was Gabe Winter, the guy you went to for a good time, not for a lifetime.

The man who let people down when they needed him the most.

The way he'd let Alaska down that night when they were both kids. And now he was doing it again.

"Gabe?"

"Yeah?" He looked over at Nicole.

"Don't leave without saying goodbye."

He attempted a smile. "I won't."

"I'm going to wait for you in the lobby."

"Okay."

She touched Matt's arm. "I wanted this," she told him. "It took two of us."

Matt nodded but said nothing as Nicole turned and walked over to the path, following it to the hospital building before disappearing inside.

"I'm sorry." Gabe's eyes flickered to Matt's.

"I trusted you. You promised to take care of her."

"I know." There was a tightness in his throat.

"You're an asshole, you know that?"

Gabe swallowed. "Yeah, I know."

"Have you two had sex?"

He wasn't going to lie. "Yes."

Matt's jaw tightened. "She's my sister. Of all the people you could have messed with, you chose her. I sent her to you because you were the only one I could rely on." Matt's voice cracked, and it killed him. "You know what's going to happen? Luke's gonna tell our mom, and everybody's going to go crazy about it, and poor Nic, she's gonna be messed up all over again. And they'll all blame her because everybody always blames her. And all because you couldn't keep your dick in your pants."

Matt's words felt worse than a punch. He'd have preferred a fist to the face over listening to the truth. Because this was the truth. He'd made a promise and he'd broken it.

Failed to protect the person he was supposed to. *Again.*

And it wasn't him that would pay the price. He could

probably walk into that lobby and demand that Nicole tell them all they were in a relationship and she'd agree to it. And then she'd cause a massive mess in the center of the family that already treated her like shit.

For him.

"They shouldn't blame her. It's not her fault."

"Damn right it's not." Matt's jaw was tight. "All those times I called you, called her. Were you two already fucking?"

"Please don't call it fucking."

"What do you want me to call it? Lovemaking? Were you making love to my sister and lying to me?"

"Matt..."

"You know what? Just go. Get out of here. I'll go clear up your messes the way I always do. You know how many girls used to beg me to pass on messages to you? How many freaking hearts you broke over the years? How many times I had to smooth things over because you're my friend and that's what friends do?"

"I don't..." Gabe's voice cracked.

"And now I'm going to do it all over again. But not for you. Not this time. I'll do it for Nicole because I was stupid enough to send her into the arms of the one man she should have avoided."

Gabe exhaled heavily. "I'm sorry."

"You need to go. *Now*."

He nodded. Matt was right. This was such a damn mess. What seemed so easy back home was so complicated here. Yet there was a pain in his chest he wasn't sure would ever go away. He loved her.

And if he loved her, he'd want her life to be easy. He'd want her to smile, to laugh, to have her family surrounding her. He knew how much she was desperate for that. So many times she'd watch him and his cousins, a wistful smile on her lips, because his family seemed so easy compared with hers.

He couldn't take this from her. Couldn't make her fight for him. And then there was his deepest fear, that maybe she wouldn't fight for him, even if she knew how he felt. Because he was Gabe, the goodtime guy, the one that made people laugh and have fun but never settled down.

"I'll go tell her goodbye."

Matt stared at him, unsmiling. "Don't hurt her any more than you already have."

He wasn't sure that was possible. But he'd try anyway.

CHAPTER 29

As soon as he walked into the lobby she *knew*. It was in the slope of his shoulders, the sadness in his eyes, the way he stopped walking and took a long, aching breath before looking around the chairs until his eyes met hers.

She stood and walked over, keeping her lips pressed together. Whatever he and Matt had talked about, it had changed everything.

"I'm leaving," he told her.

"Okay." It was getting hard to breathe.

"And I'm sorry. For this. For everything. For making your life more difficult than it has to be. For messing things up with your family."

Her chest hitched. He wasn't going to fight for her. And she wanted him to, so desperately. Wanted to be the one worth fighting for, the one worth winning.

But she wasn't going to be that. Not this time.

She'd spent a lifetime wanting to be important to somebody. To find that connection that made her feel like she was at home. And for a moment she'd thought she had it with Gabe. She really had.

But he clearly didn't feel the same.

She exhaled softly. "You didn't mess anything up. Thank you for giving me a home when I needed it."

"Any time, Nic. I mean it. Any time you need something, you just call, okay?"

She nodded, but she already knew she wouldn't. Not just because it would hurt to hear his voice, but because if she needed something, she'd figure it out for herself.

"Gabe?"

His brows knitted. "Yeah?"

"I didn't cheat on Luke. We were over when I came to Winterville." She had no idea why telling him this felt so important, but it did.

He swallowed. "I know. But it doesn't matter. We agreed no promises, right? No promises, nothing to break, nobody gets hurt."

Yeah, they'd said it, but still she hurt. She had no right to feel this way, she knew that. He told her he couldn't commit. Thank god she had enough pride left not to beg.

He wasn't going to fight for her. Luke had never fought for her – even his little tantrum in the parking lot was about him, not her. About his ego, his annoyance, his need to win, even if it meant nothing.

She'd spent a lifetime wanting to matter, but maybe the only person she needed to matter to was herself.

"I should go up to the waiting room," she said, before he could see her cry. "My dad…"

The next moment he was wrapping his arms around her, pressing her face against his shoulder, and the smell of him wrapped around her. She closed her eyes and clenched her teeth, because she wasn't going to let the tears escape. He'd been a ray of light in her life and she'd be thankful for that.

"Please tell Alaska I'll call her," she mumbled into his shoulder.

"Of course." His voice was thick.

"And I'll arrange to have my things picked up from your place. Maybe you could pack them up or something."

"They can stay as long as they'd like. That room's yours whenever you need it."

She pulled back and looked at him. "I think that's a bad idea."

He visibly tensed. "Okay." Stepping back, he ran his hand through his hair. "Take care of yourself. Don't let them..." He sighed. "I don't know. Hurt you."

"I won't."

"Nic?" Matt said, walking into the lobby. Had he been waiting outside all this time? "Kara just called. Mom's back in the waiting room, she wants to give us an update."

"Okay." She nodded at him. "I'll be right up."

"I'll head to the elevator. Hold it for you."

"Thank you." She looked back at Gabe. "I should go."

He winced. "Yeah, you should."

Without thinking, she hugged him again, taking one last breath of him, wishing she could keep this feeling of him inside of her forever. No, he wasn't going to fight for her, but he'd still given her so much. Made her stronger. Showed her that happiness didn't always depend on being what people wanted you to be.

And she'd take that. It was a special gift, and she'd always thank him for that. "Drive carefully."

"I will." He stroked her hair and for a moment she wanted to run away with him. But instead she pulled back and gave him a soft smile before walking over to where Matt was waiting.

A moment later the elevator pinged, and she followed Matt inside. The last thing she saw as the doors closed was Gabe Winter walking out of the hospital – and her life – forever.

IN THE EARLY hours of the morning he pulled up outside his ranch house, pressing the button to kill the engine before climbing out and walking wearily to the front door. He'd gone over the speed limit most of the way home and was surprised he hadn't gotten a ticket. Maybe God was taking it easy on him tonight, knowing what a fuck up he was.

He couldn't be bothered to bring his luggage in – was too tired for that. He'd do it tomorrow, either before or after work. And wasn't that a miserable thought, not only that he had to work, but that when it was over he'd come home to an empty house. One devoid of her sweet smile and warm food and cuddles in front of the television.

He could smell her fragrance as soon as he walked into the house. Sweet notes of fruit and flowers that made his throat tight with the memory of her. It would fade soon enough – he'd call his housekeeper and ask her to come early this week – but right now it felt like it was everywhere.

Walking straight to his bedroom, he stripped off his clothes and headed right into the shower, turning it so hot that it scalded his skin. But he liked it, the almost-pain, the wincing, the gasps. They reminded him that he wasn't dead. Yet.

He kept his eyes closed, because he didn't want to see the wall where he'd kissed her like crazy, or the tiles where he'd stood and she'd held him the night that he'd had that argument with North. He'd fucked up. He should never have let himself touch her.

Because now he knew what it felt like to love.

And what it felt like to hurt so bad you wanted to peel your skin off to alleviate the pain. And yes, he could tell himself he'd done the right thing for her, but for him, it was excruciating.

In a few days he'd feel better. He'd dealt with pain before. Broken bones and torn ligaments healed, and so would an aching heart. He'd just push through until it mended, keep himself busy with work, with his family, with Christmas.

Or maybe she'll call, the little voice in his head said. *She'll call and tell you she needs you.*

And if she did? He'd be there like a bat out of hell. That would be all it took for him to go running to her. Because he was weak and he'd do anything for her.

Even give her up.

He shook his head, and the spray bounced off the glass door. Sighing, he turned off the shower and dried his over-heated skin with a soft towel. Then he brushed his teeth and went to bed – not bothering to dress, resolutely moving himself to the middle when he realized he'd been laying on 'his' side for five minutes.

The first night without her. This would be the hardest. After this it would get easier. And as he closed his eyes, he tried to push away the thought of her, but somehow she still managed to linger in his dreams.

～

"I don't want this ruining your friendship," Nicole told Matt. It was the middle of the night and they were at their parents' house. Their mom had stayed at the hospital – the nurses had found her a comfortable chair and wrapped her in a blanket – and Kara and Brad had dropped them off on their way back to their apartment.

"He broke my trust. He made a promise and didn't keep it." Matt looked at her carefully over the rim of his mug. She'd made them both hot chocolate in the hope it would help them sleep. Kara had drawn up a schedule for tomorrow, making sure their dad would have somebody sitting with him at all times. Nicole was first up – Matt would drive her there in their mom's car, and pick their mom up at the same time. It was only when they were talking about logistics that she'd realized her car was still in Winterville, along with her clothes and the suitcase she'd left in Gabe's Mercedes.

But she'd worry about that tomorrow.

"There were two of us involved," she said carefully. She didn't want her brother to think badly of Gabe. Because she didn't. She just missed him. "If anybody's to blame, it's me. I kept pushing him." She blushed, remembering how she'd goaded him at the bar in Marshall's Gap. "He's a good man, Matt. And you've been friends for years."

"That's why I'm mad at him. He was supposed to take care of you."

"I didn't need anybody to take care of me. I just needed somewhere to run. Somewhere to think about my life. And he provided that. I found..." she let out a long breath. "I found myself." Wasn't that an amazing thing? And even though the ache in her heart intensified at the thought, nothing could take that away. She'd discovered who she really was when she wasn't trying to make everybody like her.

She wasn't clever like her family. But she was *somebody*. Someone who deserved kindness and love, even when it was only from herself. Somebody she wanted to stand up for.

Matt eyed her carefully.

"What?"

"I feel like we're talking about two different people, that's all. I'm not saying he's not a good guy, or a fun guy, but he's not that deep."

She blinked, because maybe they *were* talking about two different people. Maybe the Gabe she saw wasn't the one everybody else did. Maybe even he made sure of that.

Or maybe she'd been seeing things that weren't there. Assumed he felt the same way about her that she did about him. She startled, because that was so obviously the case. Yes, he'd cared about her. He liked taking care of her, but that's what he did for everybody. Or those he was close to, anyway.

He took care of Alaska, of Everley, and Holly. Look at how he'd stayed with them that night at the bar until he knew they were safe. He did the same thing for her. Tried to protect her from Kyle. Damn, he even tried to protect her from himself.

She was stupid. She'd assumed that protection was the same as love. That he cared deeply for her because he took care of her. But people took care of animals, of children, of those in pain. That was a human instinct. And maybe for Gabe it was also a little bit of a salvation complex, too, making up for the mistakes he felt he'd made with Alaska.

"We should hit the hay," Matt said softly. "We need to be up in a few hours."

"Yeah, we should." She nodded and took his mug, sliding it into the dishwasher with her own. They walked up the stairs together, then Matt hugged her before she walked into the room that once was hers, and he continued along the hallway to the one that had been his.

"You okay?" he asked, turning back to check on her.

"Yeah." She nodded. Or at least, she would be when her own heart stopped hurting so much.

CHAPTER 30

"Winterville Inn, Alaska speaking."

"It's Nicole." She let out a long breath. It was the following afternoon and she'd spent the morning sitting with her dad. He was still in the ICU and intubated, but they were talking about taking the tube out later that afternoon. Kara had arrived at lunchtime to take over, and their mom would be there in the evening in case their dad woke up. Matt had offered to take the overnight, claiming he was still working on French time, so now she was killing time trying to sort out her life.

"How's your dad?" Alaska asked her. "I'm so sorry he's sick. You must be out of your mind."

"He's still unconscious, but we're hoping that they'll bring him around later. As soon as he's off the machines." Nicole cleared her throat. "I'm sorry I left so suddenly. I hate letting you down."

"Oh pfft. That doesn't matter. I've found someone who can cover classes this week. She's not as good as you, of course, but it's a start. Until you come back."

"The thing is, I'm not sure when I'll be back. Or if I'm coming back." Nicole pulled her lip between her teeth.

"What? Is it because of your dad? I thought he'd be okay in a few weeks?"

Maybe she hadn't talked to Gabe. And Nicole didn't want to talk for him. They were his family, after all, and they'd always be on his side. And if that didn't make her stomach twist just a little, then nothing would.

"I'm just trying to work out a few things. In the meantime, I need to arrange to have my things packed up and my car shipped back."

"You're not coming to pick up your car?" Alaska's voice rose. "What's going on? Did you and Gabe fight?"

"No." It was stupid, but that was the truth. There was no fighting involved. At least not between them. But that didn't mean she didn't hurt from the inside out. "The plan was always for me to come back. With dad so sick, it seems like the time is now."

"I guess..." Alaska sighed. "I wish you could stay here though. And not just because I've finally mastered the downward facing dog. You were fun to have around. And Gabe was fun to have around when you were around, too."

"Gabe's always fun."

"Yeah, I suppose he is." Alaska paused. "Do you want me to help get your car and your things sent to you?"

"Oh no. I can do that." And she needed somewhere to ship them *to*. Because that place wasn't going to be her parents' house. Sure, she was happy to stay for a week or two – at most to help her mom when her dad was discharged – but this wasn't her home.

She didn't have one. That was something she had to remedy and fast. Along with getting a job to help pay for that home. She exhaled, because that all seemed like a lot to deal with right now.

But she would deal with it soon, because she was fighting for herself. And she didn't intend to stop.

THREE DAYS. That's how long it had been. Seventy-two hours, and he'd felt every single one of them, even if only briefly when he woke to find her not lying next to him and reality came crashing back through.

Matt had called last night, and he'd apologized again, but there was a wall between them that wasn't there before, and it hurt.

But that was nothing compared to this aching voice in his chest every time he thought of *her*. The only thing that stopped him from picking up the phone and calling to hear her voice was the knowledge that this was the right thing for her.

She hadn't wanted him. That was the simple truth. Yeah, he could fool himself that he'd done the right thing by letting her go, but the truth was had she uttered only one word and he would have stayed and fought every single one of them. He'd even laid it open for her, told her to call him if she needed anything.

And of course, by anything he'd meant himself. But she hadn't called. Not for three days. It killed him.

He was still thinking about it as he walked into the office. "Any messages?" he asked his assistant and she shook her head. Of course there weren't any messages, just like there were no calls.

He wasn't needed. She'd moved on from him. Maybe he was proud of her for that.

"Hey man." Josh looked up from his desk. "We have a meeting with the bankers at three. And the website design is up, can you take a look at it? Lots to change, but I'd like to get your input."

"Sure." Gabe nodded.

"Oh, and Kyle Walker's coming in at ten. Wants to talk through the next round of clearances. Said you tasked him with more eco-friendly removal and he wants to brainstorm his ideas."

Gabe grimaced. The last thing he wanted was to talk to any of the Walker brothers. Especially Kyle. "Can you deal with it?"

"No can do. I have a video conference at ten. I said you'd meet him out by the finished run." Josh lifted a brow. "I figured putting you two in an enclosed space is a bad idea. Especially with the mood you've been in."

"I'm not in a mood."

"Sure. And I'm not the most sleep deprived father in Winterville." Josh turned back to his laptop, and Gabe felt grateful to him because at least he wasn't pushing him. That's why he'd been avoiding the rest of his family. They all wanted to know what happened with him and Nicole and he wasn't ready to talk about it with them. So far he'd successfully avoided calls from Alaska and Everley and batted off Josh's half-hearted attempt at inviting him to dinner – at Holly's request, no doubt.

And North was working doubles at the Christmas Tree Farm. Now that Thanksgiving was over, his business was cranking into overdrive, and he was working from eight til eight fulfilling orders. He was due to help out in the shop this weekend –a favor he'd made weeks ago – and he could only hope that North wouldn't use it as an opportunity for a lecture.

Because he really didn't need one of those right now. He knew he'd messed up, he had to look himself in the mirror every day. And he didn't like what he saw.

"I'm going to head out now, take a walk around the site," Gabe said, glad he hadn't taken off his jacket. "I'll take a look at the website later, before our meeting with the bankers."

"Cool." Josh nodded. "And so you know, I've been told I have to do this."

"Do what?"

"Ask you if you're okay." Josh looked almost pained saying it.

He nodded, unsmiling. "I'm okay."

"Because I have to give Holly a report every evening. It would really make my life easier if you called her directly."

"I will." Gabe caught his eye. "When I'm ready to talk."

Josh sighed. "Man, I hope it's soon. I'm like the meat between a moody Winter sandwich. I never signed up for this."

"Hey, I stood up for you when North got all twisted over you and Holly. And I caught you asleep in the conference room the other week and didn't say a word." Gabe lifted a brow. "You owe me."

Josh studied him for a moment, then nodded. "You know it's just a matter of time, right? The girls will be lighting torches and stomping to your place at midnight if you don't talk to them soon."

"It's been three days." Gabe held three fingers up. "Count them."

"I know. But we live in a small town, and your cousins talk. *A lot*. They care for you, man. We all do."

It was Gabe's turn to sigh. "I know. But I'm not a talker. And I really don't want to talk about this."

"Fair enough. I don't either." Josh bit down a smile.

"Now, are you getting out of here or what? I have work to do."

"I'm going." Gabe lifted a hand and changed into the snow boots they had lined up by the glass doors overlooking the site. His coat was thick enough to withstand the cold winter air, but his sneakers weren't. As soon as he stepped outside he felt the ice cold wind slap at his cheeks, then whistle around the office building as he trudged toward the slopes.

The site was coming along. It would be another eight months until the first phase of construction was done, then they'd be waiting for the snow all over again for their first season to commence. Despite the bad weather, the resort buildings were going up, and huge trucks and diggers were working on the road and parking lots they'd need. In the spring, the lifts would be constructed, and he was hoping they'd be able to use them during the summer for mountain bikers. Next winter, they'd begin to welcome guests while construction continued.

It would take years for it all to be finished, but with the projections Josh had made they could at least start earning money to offset the investment by next summer.

He was trying hard not to think about the future. Right now, he wanted to get through today and then tomorrow, because then he'd have made it five days without her.

Two more days after that it would be a week.

If he could make it a week, maybe he'd be okay.

An hour later, he saw Kyle's truck parked in the makeshift lot, and walked over to the meeting point Josh had given him. Kyle was already there, looking at the mountain with a pencil in his hand, his eyes narrowed as though he was deep in thought.

"Walker."

Kyle looked up. "Winter."

"You wanted to run some things by me?"

Kyle lifted a brow. "You asked me how we can make the tree clearance more eco-friendly. I have some ideas. Some of them might be expensive, some of them are no brainers. But I wanted to talk them through with you to know which ones to pursue."

"Shoot."

He was only half listening as Kyle talked about sustainable forestry and biodiversity and planned replantation. He really tried to concentrate, managing to ask a few questions about converting wood into pellets that could feed the energy needs of the resort and possibly be sold to factories and plants that used sustainable fuels. But he kept getting distracted by his thoughts – and by a little spot of land that they weren't building on.

It was about the size of a gymnasium, and easily accessed by the road. It had enough space to build a parking lot on it, too. And all he could think about was that it would be the perfect area for a yoga studio for Nicole.

"So you want me to go ahead and send you that information?" Kyle asked.

Gabe blinked. "Yeah, sure, send it over."

Kyle nodded then was silent. Gabe could feel the heat of his stare. He sighed loudly.

"What?"

"Is it true she's gone?"

Oh Jesus, not him too. "Yeah, she's gone." He didn't have the energy to pretend he didn't know who Kyle was talking about. Anyway, the sooner everybody knew, the better.

"And you didn't ask her to stay?"

"What the hell is this?" Gabe frowned. "Are we besties now? You want to do my hair and I'll do your makeup?"

Kyle narrowed his eyes. "Just trying to figure out why you'd let somebody like that walk away. If she was mine, I'd chase her down and beg her to come back."

"Yeah, well she's not yours. Not mine, either." And since when was their relationship a well-known thing? Small fucking towns. This place was driving him nuts.

"Coulda fooled me. With the way she looked at you she was definitely yours."

"What are you talking about?" Gabe frowned.

The corner of Kyle's lip twitched. "Doesn't matter." He shrugged and slid his pencil behind his ear. "I should get going. Need to check on a site in the valley."

"Wait," Gabe said, moving so he was standing in Kyle's way. "What did you mean by that? How did she look at me?"

"Like the sun fucking rose and set wherever you were standing, man. Like you were her day and her night and everything in between." Kyle stared right at him. "If a girl looked at me like that, there's no way I'd let her go. I definitely wouldn't be standing here talking to somebody I don't even like about fucking wood pellets and eco sustainability. I'd be too busy chasing her down until she looked at me like that again, for the rest of our goddamn lives. And now I'm leaving, because I don't like you and I want to drive in my truck and enjoy your misery for a while. See ya later, Winter." He shot Gabe a sour smile and trudged back through the snow.

Gabe shook his head, then looked at the footprints Kyle left in the snow. Had that really just happened? Maybe he was hallucinating, or maybe Kyle was full of shit.

He really hoped Kyle wasn't full of shit.

Lifting his beanie from his head, he raked his fingers through his hair. He needed to get back to the office, look at the website, and talk to the bankers.

And not think about how the sun could rise and set wherever he was. Because that way lay madness.

CHAPTER 31

"Are you sure you're ready for this?" Matt gave her a skeptical glance as they sat in their mom's car outside a brownstone apartment block in the center of D.C.

"I'm sure." Nicole nodded. "I need to get my things." She'd called Luke and arranged to meet him. He'd been surprisingly sanguine about the whole thing. She wouldn't be surprised if he'd already moved on – again.

And the truth was, she wanted to do this. Wanted to put the final end to their relationship. She should have done this months ago, but now was fine.

"At least let me come up with you. I can carry stuff down."

She bumped her shoulder with his. "I don't think that's a good idea. And anyway there's not that much stuff. Two trips down probably." And they were in a no parking zone. He needed to stay with the car in case he got spotted.

"Okay, but if he starts being an ass, you call me."

"Will do." She climbed out of the car and stared up at the tall building. Luke's apartment – the apartment they'd once shared – was on the top floor – of course. It had a 180 degree view of Washington, and Luke always claimed he could see the Capitol Building if he angled his head just right. She'd never tried, because really, who cared?

He answered as soon as she pressed the buzzer, and a minute later when she walked out of the elevator he was waiting in the doorway of his apartment. He was in his work clothes, his tie still perfectly knotted. "Come in." He nodded at her.

"Thank you for meeting me," she said, walking into the spacious living area. "This shouldn't take long."

"I packed up everything I could find into boxes. They're in the spare room."

She blinked, surprised.

He shrugged. "I wasn't sure you'd want to go into the bedroom after..." He cleared his throat. "Yeah."

The boxes were cardboard – big enough that she could only carry one at a time. After the third trip, and her third check in with Matt, she went back up one final time.

"Luke?"

"Yeah?"

"Do you know if my evening dress is in one of the boxes?"

His brow puckered. "What evening dress?"

"The red one. I wore it to the college summer gala."

"Ah, no. I don't remember seeing it. Was it in my closet?"

"Yeah, in one of those zip up bags. I had it cleaned after the event." And didn't that seem a lifetime ago?

"In that case, it's probably still in there. I have a few things in those bags myself. You want me to get it?" he asked her, tipping his head toward the room.

"No, it's fine. I'll get it." She walked over to the room, what once had been their room together, and pushed the door open, steeling herself for her reaction. The last time she'd walked in here her life had changed forever. She'd cried and ran and felt like her heart was breaking.

But this time there was nothing. Not that awful heart crunching pain. Not the panic about what she would do next. She wasn't even impressed by the fact he'd made his own bed today.

She didn't care. Not about him and not about what he did to her.

For kicks, she tried to picture Gabe in the bed with another woman, looking up in surprise because she'd interrupted him mid flow.

And that's when she felt the slam of pain against her ribcage. The thought of him with somebody else was too much.

The stupid thing was, she knew it would happen. He'd find somebody else. Of course he would. Maybe they'd watch Netflix together, another action movie, or a romcom.

They might decide a rewatch of Bourne was in order.

Tears pricked at her eyes. The thought of him watching *their* movies with somebody else felt like more of a betrayal than anything physical ever could. Would it be wrong for her to message him and ask him to promise never to do that?

Yes, yes it would. And also, she was losing it.

Taking a deep breath, she walked over to the closet, sliding the far left door open to reveal neatly hanging suits and bags. She could tell which one was her dress right away – the black bag with the dry cleaner logo was longer than the ones containing his suits. She unhooked it from the rail and folded it carefully over her arm, then walked out of his bedroom, closing the door behind her.

Luke was waiting in the living room, scrolling through

his phone. When he saw her walk in, he lifted his brows. "Sorry, didn't know it was there."

"It's fine." She nodded. "So this is the last thing. I'm done."

He looked at her for a moment, then exhaled heavily. "I'm sorry."

She shook her head. "It's history." And his apology meant exactly nothing to her. She couldn't even find it in herself to be angry at him for what he did. Though she still wasn't quite over his performance at the hospital. "But you should work on yourself because what you did was awful. Next time you want out of a relationship, tell the poor woman before you jump into the next."

He grimaced. "I know. I will." He had the grace to look embarrassed. "What will you do now?" he asked her.

"I'll stay with mom and dad until he's recovered. She's going to need help taking care of him."

"Making him rest up, you mean?" He lifted a brow.

"Yeah. Exactly."

"He's already sent me a message about an experiment we're running. Should I block him?"

Nicole shook her head. "No. Just don't encourage him."

"Sure." His eyes flickered up. "What will you do after he's better?"

"I'm not sure yet. I want to start my own yoga studio, but it's going to need some capital. I may have to find some side work to build up my bank balance first."

"In D.C.?"

"I don't think so. I want to go somewhere smaller. Where the cost of living is lower." Somewhere that every-body knew your business, even when it drove you crazy. Where people knew your coffee order and started making it before you even walked into their café. Somewhere she could find friendship, and family, and maybe one day – love.

Somewhere almost exactly like Winterville.

Luke nodded. "Good luck."

"Thank you."

She was reaching for his front door when he called out again.

"Nicole?"

"Yes?"

"Why was the dress so important?"

She looked at the garment bag folded over her forearm. "I need it for next week. I'm going to accept Dad's award for him."

Six days. That's how long Gabe had made it. Tomorrow would be seven and that made a week.

"And if I can make a week I can make a month," he muttered to himself. If he said it enough times it had to come true, right?

He got home from work at eight, parking, and climbing the steps, rolling his head to loosen the kinks in his neck from sitting for too long at a computer screen. He wasn't built for inertia, he was a mover. A runner, a skier, a doer. But this week he couldn't find the energy to do any of that.

He unlocked the door and was greeted by the depressing sound of silence. He hadn't gotten used to that yet, just like he hadn't gotten used to the smell of her shampoo disappearing with each day. He'd told the housekeeper not to change his sheets this week because – pathetically – he'd decided he didn't want to wash away the last remnants of her after all. Maybe next week, when he'd be a little more over her. Nobody had to know – it was between him and the housekeeper.

When he walked into the kitchen and saw a brunette sitting at the breakfast bar with her back to him he about lost his mind. For one aching moment he wondered if it was her, but this woman was too petite, her hair the wrong shade.

And he was related to her.

"Alaska." He sighed. "How'd you get in here?"

"North lent me a key."

He blinked. Of course North did. "Where's your car?"

"I walked from North's. I figured if you saw my car outside you wouldn't come in." She jumped off the stool and faced him, her eyes soft. "He was right, you look like crap."

"Thanks." He grabbed a glass from the cupboard. "Want a drink?"

"What you got?"

"Water."

"Then no." She grinned and he filled his glass from the refrigerator. "I guess at least you're not drinking too much. That's something to be grateful for."

He took a long, slow sip from his glass, and wondered how she'd react if he hoisted her over his shoulder and carried her back to North's. Knowing Alaska, she'd probably laugh her head off. And the fact was, he didn't want to hurt her. She was special to him.

"So did you get elected or something?" he asked. "Are you the official Winter cousin spokesperson?"

She lifted her brows. "Something like that. But if you haven't noticed, we've all been trying to get a hold of you for days. We're worried about you."

"You don't need to be."

She reached for his hand and squeezed it. He looked

down at her tiny fingers wrapped around his skin. Was this the first time somebody had touched him in a week? It felt strange and yet... nice.

"Can we sit down?" she asked him. "I've been on my feet all day. My toes feel like they're going to fall off."

"Sure." He nodded, and they walked into his living room. Alaska slumped on the sofa and he took one of the easy chairs. How many times had they sat like this? He couldn't even begin to count, yet she looked wrong, sitting where Nicole always sat.

Surely this would feel better soon?

"So what happened?" Alaska asked him, her voice soft. "You were so happy. I saw it with my own eyes, when you came to pick her up from the Inn."

"Her dad got sick."

"I know that. She told me."

He blinked. "You've talked to her?"

"Yes of course I have." She gave him a 'duh' look.

"How is she?" His chest clenched.

"Why don't you call and ask her yourself?"

Gabe sighed. "Because I promised I wouldn't."

"What?" She frowned. "Why would you say something like that? And why would her dad getting sick have anything to do with you two ending things? It feels like something is missing in this whole conversation."

"Do we really have to do this now?" He hated talking about this stuff. He wanted to sleep or box or do anything that didn't involve using his brain right now.

"Think of me as a boil," Alaska said, her expression serious. "Either you lance me now, or I keep getting more annoying until I'm everywhere you look and you can't go out because this is all too painful."

Dear God. "That is a very apt description."

She grinned. "So get rid of me. It's simple. Tell me what happened and I'll go."

He rubbed his eyes with the heels of his hands. "Is it really that easy?"

She looked right at him. "Try me."

"Okay. Her dad got sick and her family closed ranks. We were saying goodbye and her ex and her brother spotted us and went crazy. I realized that she needed them more than she needed me, so I left. End of story."

"Whoa there." Alaska put up her hand. "I say when it's the end of the story. There's still a lot of pus in here, buddy."

He shot her a pleading look. "You told me this would be simple."

"The procedure just got complicated. The patient isn't divulging everything. What makes you think she needs them more than she needs you?"

"They're her family. I know how much she wants their love."

"And?" Alaska blinked.

"And what?"

She gave a loud sigh. "What does their love have to do with your relationship?"

"Matt got pissed at me. Told me I'm not good enough for her. And he's right. I promised to look after her and I let him down."

Alaska's eyes met his. "Let me get this straight. You gave her a home, let her vomit on your shoes, made sure she had family to spend Thanksgiving with, then when her *own* family let her down you whisked her off to a beautiful spa, but none of that is looking after her?"

"Wouldn't anybody do that?"

"No, Gabe. Most people wouldn't. But you did, because you're a good guy and you're in love with her."

"You can tell that?" He didn't bother to deny it.

"Of course I can, silly." She rolled her eyes. "It's in the way you look at her. Like she's the center of your universe. Remember all those times on Thanksgiving when you kept coming into the kitchen to check on her? You had this googly eye thing going on that none of us have ever seen before. And I'm so pissed with you, because you're letting her go without a fight. She's the best thing that's ever happened to you, damn it, and you're just sitting here feeling sorry for yourself."

"I told her to call me if she needed me."

"That's it?" Alaska's jaw tightened. "You're an idiot."

"What the hell did you expect me to do? She didn't ask me to stay, she didn't tell me she loved me. She just said okay and told me she needed to go see her dad."

Alaska squared her shoulders. "I take it back. You're not an idiot. You're a damn imbecile. She was worried about her dad, she thought you didn't love her. Any self-respecting woman would have walked away. But you..." She shook her head, her eyes narrowing. "You should have fought for her. And you didn't because you gave up fighting for anything years ago."

"What do you mean?"

"I meant what I said. When was the last time you really fought for something you loved? When was the last time you put yourself out there not knowing if you'd get it or not, but knew you had to try?"

"Every time I entered a snowboarding competition." His voice was low. She was pissing him off now.

"Bullshit." She looked as surprised as he was at her oath. "Sure you don't like losing, but if you didn't get those trophies did it hit you deep inside? Did it hit the wound you still have from when I disappeared? You liked snowboarding because you were good at it. But it didn't hurt you or love you or disappoint you. But that's not fighting, Gabe, that's coasting." She swallowed hard. "When did you last fight for somebody? Even yourself?"

His chest felt like it had a vice around it. He could see the sadness in his cousin's eyes and it was killing him. "I..."

"You don't know. But I do. It was when we were kids. When you tried to stand up for yourself in a dingy office in the sheriff's station and nobody helped you. And I hate that for you, Gabe." She put her hand on her heart, her voice cracking. "I hate that what happened to us still affects you so much. I hate that when things go wrong you're still that scared little kid who's being blamed for something he didn't do with no adults protecting him, telling him it'll be okay."

"Alaska..." He wasn't going to cry. He wasn't. But his eyes were stinging anyway.

Her lip trembled. "You stopped fighting, Gabe. And now you've lost something so damn precious. I have no idea whether to hug you or slap you because this is never going to feel better until you start fighting for yourself again." Tears spilled down her face. And damn it, he couldn't stand to watch it anymore. He was out of his chair and at her feet, hugging her tight, because he'd made her cry.

"You wear this armor that you think nobody can see." Her voice was muffled against his chest. "This easy going Gabe, the good time guy. The one that nothing can ruffle. And you think it'll protect you from all the pain that comes from loving somebody." She lifted her head, her eyes shining up at him. "How's that going for you?"

He frowned. "Pretty fucking shitty."

She laughed, even though she was crying. "You need to start fighting again. And I don't mean using that damn punching bag in your office."

An image of Nicole stomping into there, wearing just her pajamas, ready to fight an intruder to protect his house flashed into his brain. That's when he crumpled. She'd been willing to fight for him even when they were acquaintances. Willing to stand up to some imaginary assailant because it was the right thing to do.

And he'd been wallowing for six days. Telling himself he'd be fine eventually, instead of pulling his head out of his ass, realizing that he'd never be fine until he knew for sure that she didn't want him. Until he started fighting himself and all his wrong instincts, because he was his own worst enemy.

She was beautiful. She was everything, and he needed to be the man she deserved. The only way to do that was to take the fight to her.

Alaska was watching him carefully, the tears drying on her cheeks. When his eyes met hers, a slow smile pulled at her lips.

"Are you going to do it?"

"Yes." His voice was resolute. He was going to fight for the best thing he'd ever had. "I need to make a call."

"Of course you do."

"Not to her. Not yet."

"Oh Gabe…"

He lifted his hand, then used the other to pull his phone from his pocket, pulling up the one person he knew could help get this all in motion.

And when it connected he smiled for the first time in a week.

"Matt, it's me. Don't hang up. I need to tell you I'm so in love with your sister it hurts. And I need your help to get her back."

CHAPTER 32

"You look beautiful." Her dad smiled at her from his bed. He'd been discharged from the hospital two days ago. The doctors were happy with his progress, but had read him the riot act that he still had a long way to go before he was recovered. Thankfully, he was listening to them, and was resting in his bedroom for most of the day.

He held his hands out, and she took them, carefully sitting down on the edge of his bed.

"Thank you." She'd gone all out for this, and it felt good. Her hair had been done at her mom's favorite salon, and they'd arranged for a make-up artist to come to the house. She wanted to make him proud, but more importantly, she wanted to make herself proud. She was going to go up to that podium and accept his award and represent this family.

"I'm the one who should be thanking you. You didn't have to do this. They were willing to give me the award without anybody representing me, you know?"

"I know. But I want to do it. It's a celebration of your achievements, one of us should be there to accept it."

She and Matt had discussed which of them should be the one to represent him. Kara had already bowed out – she hated public speaking. Matt would have done it in a heartbeat, she knew that, yet he'd sensed her need to prove herself.

Another reason why he was the perfect big brother.

"Your mom appreciates everything you're doing for us, too," her dad told her. "She'd be exhausted without you here."

"I'm happy to do it." It was the truth. She needed to do this. To show them she was a member of this family in her own right. And then, when she was ready, she'd push out on her own.

She had a whole life to live, and yes, she still ached knowing that Gabe wouldn't be part of it, but that didn't mean she wasn't a little excited. She wanted to achieve things, but most of all she wanted to find happiness. It had to be out there for her.

"Your mom told me about Luke," he said, his voice low. "I'm so sorry. I'd fire him, but..." He pointed at his chest. "It may take a while before I can take the helm again."

"You don't need to fire him. He's a good scientist." She wrinkled her nose. "But a terrible boyfriend."

"I wish you'd told me when it happened. I could have done something then."

"You were so busy with your project. I'm glad I didn't. Plus, it all worked out fine." She thought about how sick he'd been, and how it could have been worse.

He nodded, then ran his hand over his chin. "She told me you got involved with somebody else while you were away."

Of course she did. Even when you weren't in a small town, secrets weren't safe. "I did, but that's over now."

"You don't sound too happy about that," he said, his voice light.

"He's a good guy."

"Just not good enough for you."

She pressed her lips together. "Something like that."

"You'll find him, you know," he told her. "When you least expect it he'll be there. The right man for you. You're a beautiful, kind, funny girl, and in my opinion you'd be a catch for anybody."

She didn't want to cry. It would ruin her makeup. But it didn't stop her throat from feeling all thick and tight. "Thank you, Daddy."

"And when you decide where you're going, your mom and I would like to come visit you. Be there for you. The way we haven't been."

She nodded, saying nothing.

"Don't be too hard on her," he whispered. "She loves you, too, you know? Did I ever tell you my mom didn't like her?"

Nicole blinked. "No. I never knew that."

"They didn't like that she didn't go to an Ivy League college. But look at her now, she's out earning me by the power of ten." He smiled.

She tried to imagine her grandma hating her mom, but it was almost impossible. "What happened?"

"We eloped. And when we got back I told them that either they accept my wife or I cut them out of my life. The next month we had a vow renewal of sorts and they were both sitting at the front of the church."

"That's so romantic."

"I know that you always feel like you're not the same as the rest of us. But you have to know that a lot of your mom's actions come from fear. She doesn't want you to go through the things she did. She worries that you'll be rejected and hurt, and she doesn't want that." He patted her hand. "That's why she was so happy when you started dating Luke. She knows his parents and they love you. She thought you'd found happiness and she wanted you to keep it."

Nicole knew some of this from her recent late night conversations with her mother, but her dad was giving it a whole new dimension. And though they'd never see completely eye to eye, at least she had some understanding of her parents now.

"The thing is," she told him, "you can't fight my battles for me. They're mine to win or lose."

Her dad nodded. "I never doubted that. Not for a moment. Of all my children, you're the fighter."

"You really think that?"

"Yes. I don't mean you're combative or confrontational. But you never give up. I admire that about you. In another life, I'd try to recruit you to the firm."

"I'd hate that."

He chuckled. "I know."

"Nic? The car's here." Matt was standing in the doorway, wearing a tux. He hadn't fastened the bowtie – no doubt she'd have to do it in the car for him.

"That's my cue." She leaned forward to kiss her dad's cheek. "Be good for Mom."

"Wouldn't dream of doing anything else. Now go make me proud."

"That's the plan."

She stood and smoothed the red silk of her dress. She'd always loved this one. It had a plunging neckline with an integral bra that managed to keep her contained, and a flowing skirt with a long slit that revealed her thighs if she was so inclined.

Beautiful but sexy. A dangerous combination. She felt a little twinge, wishing Gabe could see her now. He was used to her in yoga pants with her hair in a bun and no makeup on. Maybe someone would post a picture on social media, and he'd come across it.

Who was she kidding? The man wasn't even on social media.

They were almost at the front door when Matt patted his pocket. "Shit, I've forgotten my phone. Get in the car and I'll be there in a minute."

She rolled her eyes. "If you make us late, I'll kill you."

"We won't be late."

Mumbling under her breath, she pulled open the front door and gasped as the winter air hit her. They'd had a dusting of snow here in yesterday, but nothing like they saw in Winterville. Picking up her skirt she walked down the steps of her parents' townhouse to the waiting limo. The driver jumped out and opened the door, and she was about to slip inside when she saw him.

Gabe Winter.

Dressed in a tuxedo, with his tie expertly fastened. His dark hair had been cut, his face freshly shaved, and she could smell the smooth, pine aroma of his cologne.

Her body immediately tensed

"What are you doing here?" she asked, confused.

"I heard you were going out fighting. I wanted to be your wing man."

She shivered, because it was damn cold out here. "What?"

"Get in." He held his hand out to her. She slid her palm against his and let him help her into the warm backseat. When she was sitting next to him, she let out a ragged breath. "Matt will be here any minute."

He shook his head. "Matt's getting another car. I paid for it."

She blinked. "He knows you're here?"

"Your whole family does. Even Kara. Who, by the way, is more talkative than you led me to believe."

"Why have you been talking to my whole family?"

"Because I wanted to apologize for what happened at the hospital. And to make sure they knew my intentions, before I started to fight for you."

"That's remarkably old fashioned," she said lightly.

"Warcraft one oh one. Pick off the easy targets first, then clear the field for the battle that matters."

"And I'm the battle?" she asked him.

"No," he said softly. "You're the prize. I'm the battle. And the battler." He lifted her hand to his lips. "I'm in love with you, Nicole. I should have told you that weeks ago. I never should have left the hospital. Damn, I never should have left without telling you that. I'll regret walking away from you until my dying day."

She swallowed hard. "Why did you walk away?"

"Because I convinced myself that it was better for you. But really, I was afraid. Afraid of fighting for something I might not win. Afraid of being vulnerable and getting hurt. So instead of fighting I ran away. I was a coward, but I'm not that man anymore."

"Who are you?" she whispered.

"The man who's so damn in love with you he doesn't know how to express it. The one who wants to fight for you, but knows you're more than capable of fighting for yourself. I want to be the Mickey to your Rocky. I want to be riding that bike and shouting encouragement at you while you run the hardest you ever have."

"I have no idea what you're talking about. But it sounds kind of lovely."

"You haven't watched *Rocky*?"

She shook her head.

"Damn. We need to do something about that."

The driver started up the engine and the screen between him and the rest of the car came down. "We need to leave now if we're going to make it on time," he told them.

Gabe looked at her and she nodded. "Let's go." The screen went up again and she turned to Gabe. "Tell me more about Mickey."

"It's something I want you to see. Adrienne's kind of the star of the movie, but Mickey's great, too. And Rocky... you... are amazing. And you look so damn beautiful tonight I'm going to be jealous of every man that watches you as you accept your dad's award. You're Rocky, you're Batman. You're every damn character that's saved the world, not because you have a superpower but because you have a heart that's so big you can't do anything but save it."

"You need to stop talking now. My makeup is going to be ruined." She wiped a tear.

His gaze dipped to her lips, then resolutely back up. Was he thinking about kissing her? Because now that's all she could think about. His lips on hers, his hands in her hair, her clambering all over him in the car as it drove through the busy streets of D.C.

"I love you." He looked her right in the eye. "I love you so much that I'll fight anybody for you. Even myself. And if you can find a way to forgive me, I'll prove that to you every day. I'll fight for you, I'll fight with you, just say the word and I'll be there."

"I don't need you to fight."

"I know. That's what makes you so damn beautiful. You

don't need me." He exhaled softly, then kissed her palm. "But I'm really hoping you want me."

She pressed her lips together, then stopped because she really didn't want to ruin her makeup. "I *do* want you."

He smiled against her hand. "Thank God."

"But if you ever shut down on me again, I'll come down on you like a ton of Rockys."

He chuckled. "That's fair."

"We're almost at the venue," the driver said through the loud speaker. She assumed he was worried they were in some kind of compromising position. But Gabe hadn't even kissed her, and she wasn't sure how happy she was about that.

Your makeup, remember your makeup.

She ran her tongue over her bottom lip, then glanced at him. His eyes were heavy lidded, and he was staring right at her mouth.

Did he feel it, too? And now she was confused. Was she supposed to fight for herself and kiss him because that's what she really needed right now? Or should she let him be Rocky, and wait for him to kiss her?

Before she could follow that thought any further, the driver brought the limo to a stop, then pulled the screen between them down once more.

"Miss Rice, Mr. Winter? We're here."

Okay. It was time to face the music.

SHE WAS NERVOUS. He could tell by the way her hands were gripping the podium, but nobody in the audience seemed to notice. He was watching her from the table nearest the stage, as she glanced down at her notes then spoke to the waiting crowd. Matt was sitting on the other side of her empty seat, looking as proud as Gabe felt.

"My dad would have loved to be here today," she was saying. "Those of you who know him will understand that. He's never one to miss a party, especially one that's all about him." Laughter filled the air, and she visibly relaxed.

Damn, she was beautiful. How could he have thought he could live without her? No, that wasn't right. How could he have let her go without a fight? That was better. There were no guarantees except what he'd do to make her his.

And the answer to that was everything.

He'd spent the last week talking to Matt, and then to her family, arranging to be here with her tonight. He'd booked the limos, gotten his tux cleaned, and told Josh he'd be away for a few nights. He'd worried about leaving North in a bind with the farm, but North had waved him away.

And now he was here, watching the woman he loved stand up in front of a crowd and metaphorically kick its ass. She made another joke, this one a little riskier because it was about her dad's heart attack, and the crowd only laughed harder.

"Finally, I'd like to thank all of you who've asked about my dad, whether here or by phone or with all the messages he's received. He's asked me to reply on his behalf, so he wrote down exactly what he wanted me to say, to make sure I got it right."

She pulled a folded piece of paper out of her purse and slowly opened it, keeping the audience on tenterhooks. "Oh that's nice," she said, smiling at the words. Then she looked out at them all.

"He says, 'you're all assholes and you owe me a drink.' Thank you, and good night." She lifted his award and grinned, then held her dress up with her free hand, walking off the stage, and down the steps at the side. The crowd erupted, clapping loudly, many of them standing, and Gabe joined them, jumping to his feet and grinning at her.

Her eyes immediately caught his, and he could see every emotion passing through them. Joy, elation, relief.

And love.

When she reached the table she put the award in front of Matt. "I'm sorry," she said.

"For what?" Matt frowned.

Instead of answering him, she turned to Gabe, swiping a piece of dust from the lapel of his jacket. Then she curled her fingers around it and pulled him toward her, and damn if it didn't send a shot of blood straight where he needed it least.

"Either you're going to kiss me, or I'm going to kiss you," she muttered, "because this tension is killing me."

She'd barely finished talking before his lips were on hers, moving softly as he cupped the back of her neck. She let out a little sigh, warm and gentle on his mouth, then curled her hands around his neck and pushed her beautiful body against his.

He held her firmly, kissing her like she was the only air he needed. Releasing her head, he ran his hands down her arms, then pressed them against her back. Her tongue fluttered against his, and it only made him harder. This woman, this fighter. She was everything.

And he'd do whatever it took to make her his.

"*You're* sorry? I'm the one who's sorry," Matt muttered. "Sorry I had to see that."

They pulled apart and she was laughing, and Gabe was laughing, too, because damn he wanted to make Matt even sorrier right now.

"Shall we go?" she asked Gabe. "I think I'm partied out right now."

"Yeah, we'll go." He glanced at Matt. "Sorry."

Matt held his hands up. "Sure you are. Whatever."

"Tell me you have a hotel room," she said breathlessly.

From the corner of his eye he saw Matt press his hands against his ears.

Gabe leaned in to whisper. "I do. And by the way, Batman, you were amazing. The audience was entranced. But not as entranced as me." He ran his hand over her hair.

"I'm Batman again? I thought I was Rocky." She frowned. "I'm getting confused now."

"You're all and none of those things. You're Nicole Rice. The most beautiful woman in this room. My own super-hero." He grinned.

"I do have a few magic powers." She lifted a brow. "Want me to demonstrate them?"

"Dear God, will you just get a room?" Matt looked like he was about to throw up.

Gabe winked at her. "It's okay. I already have."

EPILOGUE

hristmas Morning

IT HADN'T BEEN her idea to go skiing on Christmas morning. If she had her way they'd still be in bed, under his covers, their limbs tangled together to keep each other warm. But Gabe had insisted, and she'd rolled her eyes when he'd found the *Kill Bill* style ski suit he'd bought her, but because it was Christmas and he was as eager as a puppy dog, she'd dutifully put it on and gotten into his truck so he could drive them to the trail.

They were cross country skiing – so she didn't have to worry about too many downhills, but he was still a nightmare to keep up with. Every now and again he'd stop and wait for her to catch up, but damn the man had stamina.

Tell her something she didn't know.

She'd come back with him after the gala for a few days, not willing to be parted from him again. Kara had promised to help their mom take care of their dad, and Matt had insisted that he needed them to be at least a state away from wherever he was. She assumed he was joking, but he still looked a little green every time Gabe kissed her.

Which was often and a lot, thank goodness.

She'd video called her dad every night since she returned to Winterville to check in on him – and with her mom who was definitely not Florence Nightingale. She and Gabe would visit them after Christmas, where she'd be able to introduce them properly. And in the New Year, now that her dad was on the mend, she'd move to Winterville for good.

And she was so excited for that.

The stand in teacher Alaska found had agreed to continue taking some classes going forward. That would free Nicole up to concentrate on her private clients, as well as on the classes she loved the most – including the mother and baby ones.

"We're nearly there," Gabe told her when she'd caught up with him once more.

"Nearly where? I didn't know we were going anywhere. Isn't this a stupid Christmas morning attempt at exercise?"

She followed him out of the tree line, and her breath caught because the view in front of her was beautiful. They were at the top of a hill, facing a ridge of snowy white mountains. Though it was freezing, the sky was a brilliant blue, the sun a hazy yellow as it cast a glow across the mountaintops. She inhaled slowly, feeling so blessed to be here with the man she loved, awed by the nature that surrounded them every day.

"You see over there?" Gabe pointed to their left. "Just around that mountain is where the resort buildings will be. I should have brought binoculars, you can see the ski run we went down from here."

"There?"

"Yeah. And you know what's also there?"

She looked up at him. He was grinning at her and it made her heart feel full. "What?"

"A little piece of land that belongs to you."

She blinked. "What?"

"It's not huge. But it's big enough to build a studio on. And it has great road access. Plus a captive audience. Turns out that a lot of couples only have one skier. And I need to find a way to keep them both happy when they visit."

"But that's too much."

"No, it's not enough. Not nearly. You gave me my life back, I give you a piece of land to build a studio on. I figure it's hardly a down payment on what I owe you." He pulled her close, pressing his lips against her cheek. "I love you so much. Having you here with me, by my side, it's everything I never knew I wanted. There's also something else I want to give you."

"No more gifts." She laughed. "You've already given me enough."

But then he dropped to one knee and she wasn't laughing anymore. "This is quick. I know it's fast, but I've seen enough movies to know that when you get the girl, you have to do whatever it takes to keep her." Gabe smiled up at her, and she felt a wave of warmth wash over her, despite the cold air. "Short of imprisonment, of course, because that's a felony." He pulled a box out of his pocket and opened it, the beautiful sapphire encased in diamonds catching the sun's light. "Nicole Rice, will you do me the honor of forever being the Robin to your Batman. The Mickey to your Rocky, the Noah to your Allie."

She started to laugh, because they'd watched *The Notebook* the second night she'd come back with him. And he'd agreed that the sex was hot, then showed her exactly how hot it was. And now she was all flustered and he was saying something and she had no idea what it was.

"Yes!" she said, holding out her hand. "The answer's yes."

His warm eyes met hers as he slid the beautiful sapphire and diamond ring on her finger, and she held it up to admire it. Then he was pulling her down to him, kissing her, murmuring soft words against her lips.

And when they pulled back for breath, he smoothed the hair back from her face and kissed her brow.

"Merry Christmas, darling."

She grinned. "Yes, it is."

~

LATER THE FOLLOWING YEAR...

IT WAS THE PERFECT WEDDING. Alaska watched as Gabe leaned down to kiss his new bride, and everybody burst into applause. Beside her, Everley wiped a tear from her eye, and Holly loudly blew her nose. He was the first of their boy cousins to get married, and it was emotional.

She'd been so happy when Nicole and Gabe had decided to have their wedding at the Winterville Inn. She wouldn't have blamed them if Nicole had insisted on getting married in Washington D.C. – that's where her family was, after all. But instead she'd invited them here, and Alaska had made sure their stay was perfect in every way. And she'd shed a little tear as Nicole's dad walked her down the aisle, now fully recovered from his heart surgery.

"I need to go check on things," she whispered to Holly, who nodded.

"You need help?"

"No, I've got this."

Nicole had decided not to have a big wedding party. Having been a maid of honor to her sister, she said that she wouldn't subject anybody else to that role. She just wanted them all to have a good time without worrying about her.

But they'd still arranged a kick ass bachelorette weekend in Vegas, and the four of them had all sat together to plan the décor and music and menu. It was like having a fourth girl cousin – they all loved her so much. She was perfect for Gabe and that made them all very happy.

She was almost at the Inn when she saw it laying on the ground. A little white stuffed toy – a rabbit with ears that were almost falling off. She bent to pick it up, and her heart slammed against her ribcage because a memory flashed into her mind.

She used to have a rabbit like this.

But she hadn't seen it for years. Not since she was eight years old. How could she have forgotten that? What was its name?

Mr. Bunny. She almost laughed because that was the most unoriginal name ever. But the laugh died on her lips when she realized she hadn't seen him since *that day.*

The one she couldn't remember. The one that Gabe couldn't forget. She felt dizzy and disoriented as she picked the bunny up. She'd take it inside to the counter and hopefully somebody would get it back to the owner.

Once she'd put it in the lost property box, she hurried to the kitchen. "The ceremony is over. We need waiters outside with champagne. And dinner's in an hour."

Everybody sprang into action. The wait staffed filled the

glasses that were already laid out on silver trays, and the chef called his crew together, while he shouted instructions. It was beautiful to see. She loved this kitchen almost as much as she loved working in the Inn itself.

"You okay?" Carl the chef, asked her as he walked past.

"Yeah, I'm fine. Why?"

"You were just looking a little white when you walked in."

She forced a smile onto her face. "It was nothing. Just found a lost object. That's all."

"I was wondering if that guy found you."

She frowned. "What guy?"

Carl shrugged. "Ria dealt with him. Said he was a huge man. Dark hair and a beard. And had the bluest eyes she'd ever seen. Came into reception and asked if the Winters still owned the place. When she said you were at a wedding he left right away."

Alaska frowned. "Did he give a name?"

"Don't think so."

"Strange."

"That's what Ria said. He'll probably come back when you're less busy, right?"

"Probably." Alaska smiled at him. "Okay, I need to get back out there. I'll make sure everybody's seated in forty-five. Any problems, call me."

"Got it, chief." He tapped his brow.

Following the wait staff as they carried trays of champagne out to the lawned area, she joined her cousins and sister, and smiled at the bride and groom as they mingled with their guests.

"Everything okay?" Everley asked. Alaska smiled and nodded, deciding not to tell her about the strange man, or the flashback she'd had.

Instead, she fixed her gaze on Gabe and the way he stared at his bride. The two of them were so beautiful to watch it was like staring into the sun.

"Everything is perfect," she murmured. And it was.

How could it not be on a day like this?

THE END

DEAR READER

Thank you so much for reading Gabe and Nicole's story. If you enjoyed it and you get a chance, I'd be so grateful if you can leave a review. And don't forget to keep an eye out for MEMORIES OF MISTLETOE, Mason and Alaska's story.

I can't wait to share more stories with you.

Yours,

Carrie xx

ALSO BY CARRIE ELKS

THE WINTERVILLE SERIES

A gorgeously wintery small town romance series, featuring six cousins who fight to save the sound their grandmother built.

Welcome to Winterville

Hearts In Winter

Leave Me Breathless

Memories of Mistletoe

ANGEL SANDS SERIES

A heartwarming small town beach series, full of best friends, hot guys and happily-ever-afters.

Let Me Burn

She's Like the Wind

Sweet Little Lies

Just A Kiss

Baby I'm Yours

Pieces Of Us

Chasing The Sun

Heart And Soul

Lost In Him (releases May 2022)

THE HEARTBREAK BROTHERS SERIES

A gorgeous small town series about four brothers and the women who capture their hearts.

Take Me Home

Still The One

A Better Man

Somebody Like You

When We Touch

THE SHAKESPEARE SISTERS SERIES

An epic series about four strong yet vulnerable sisters, and the alpha men who steal their hearts.

Summer's Lease

A Winter's Tale

Absent in the Spring

By Virtue Fall

THE LOVE IN LONDON SERIES

Three books about strong and sassy women finding love in the big city.

Coming Down

Broken Chords

Canada Square

STANDALONE

Fix You

An epic romance that spans the decades. Breathtaking and angsty and all the things in between.

ABOUT THE AUTHOR

Carrie Elks writes contemporary romance with a sizzling edge. Her first book, *Fix You*, has been translated into eight languages and made a surprise appearance on *Big Brother* in Brazil. Luckily for her, it wasn't voted out.

Carrie lives with her husband, two lovely children and a larger-than-life black pug called Plato. When she isn't writing or reading, she can be found baking, drinking an occasional (!) glass of wine, or chatting on social media.

You can find Carrie in all these places
www.carrieelks.com
carrie.elks@mail.com